W9-CVA-205

A TURN OF
TRAITORS

SOUTHGATE PUBLIC LIBRARY

Palma Harcourt

A TURN OF
TRAITORS

CHARLES SCRIBNER'S SONS
New York

Copyright © Palma Harcourt 1981

Library of Congress Cataloging in Publication Data
Harcourt, Palma.
    A turn of traitors.
    I. Title.
PR6058.A62T8   1982   823'.914   81-9336
ISBN 0-684-17346-8   AACR2

Copyright under the Berne Convention.

All rights reserved. No part of this book
may be reproduced in any form without the
permission of Charles Scribner's Sons.

1 3 5 7 9 11 13 15 17 19 F/C 20 18 16 14 12 10 8 6 4 2

Printed in the United States of America.

SOUTHGATE PUBLIC LIBRARY
14680 DIX - TOLEDO ROAD
SOUTHGATE, MICH. 48195

For Kathleen and Helier

ONE

'He calls himself Richard Lavery, but – '

'You don't believe he's entitled to the name?'

'God knows! He may have a legal right to it. The – original one could have been changed by deed-poll. The point is that whatever he calls himself or whoever he's supposed to be, I'd swear – '

'You'd swear, Maurice? On oath?' The interruption was cutting.

Charles Bigrel put down the alabaster egg he had been fondling and pushed back his chair. He stood. He managed a thin smile. Maurice Jackson was an old friend, but with an in-tray piled high and a full day's calendar that included an appointment at the FCO in fifty minutes, Bigrel could feel his patience cracking. And yet, if by some God-given chance Maurice was right . . . His hand shook as he removed the Who's Who from its shelf and took it to his desk. He began to riffle through the pages.

'I've already done that, Charles.' Now it was Jackson's turn to be impatient. Usually a happy, relaxed man, today he was taut as a bow-string. 'The brigadier's entry mentions "one son", but what bloody help is that?'

Bigrel ignored him. He had found what he wanted. His eyes skimmed down the lines. 'LAVERY, Brig. John Richard, CBE 1960; DSO 1945; late RE, retired; b 3 Sept. 1914; s of Richard and Alice Lavery; m 1950 Veronica Mary White; one s.' The rest was a brief résumé of the brigadier's career, his address in Kent and his London club which, predictably, was the Army and Navy. It was, as Jackson had implied, not particularly helpful.

Bigrel shut the book carefully. 'You haven't answered my question yet, Maurice. Could you swear to it that this young man is not the son of John and Veronica Lavery as he's said to be – as he may even believe he is?'

7

'No. Of course I couldn't. Though when I met him – when Emma introduced him – at that moment I had no doubt whatever. Christ! I thought I was seeing a ghost. It was a most appalling shock.' Jackson slowly shook his head, remembering. 'Helen and I aren't possessive parents, as you know, Charles, and Emma's twenty-six. She's gone her own way for years. Normally we wouldn't dream of interfering. We knew she and Richard were living together – have been for the last eighteen months – but we'd never met him. Then last week she rang up and said they'd decided to get married and she was bringing him home for the weekend. Of course we were delighted. Helen still is – I hope.' Jackson sighed. 'Helen's not a fool. She realized my reactions to Richard weren't what – what they ought to be. I had to plead indigestion. I didn't dare tell her what I feared.'

'I should think not!' Bigrel glanced at his watch. In eight minutes he would have to leave, but, first he had to reassure Maurice; he couldn't have him going off at half-cock over this business. 'Maurice, I'm sorry, but as of this minute I'm all but due at the FCO. Will you leave it with me and I'll make some discreet enquiries? That's what you want, isn't it?'

'Yes. I thought – But if you're trying to fob me off, Charles – '

'I'm not. I promise you.' Bigrel pressed the button on the underside of his desk and almost at once Lorna Day, his Personal Assistant, appeared at the door. 'It may take a few days, Maurice, but I'll telephone you at the Ministry the moment I get any hard information. Meanwhile, don't hint at your suspicions to anyone, not even to Helen. Please. And try not to worry too much. It's probably just one of those extraordinary resemblances that nature produces occasionally. Otherwise I'm sure we should have known.' He gave Jackson what he hoped was an encouraging smile and offered his hand.

Jackson didn't return the smile. His face was bleak. He loved his younger daughter and the two boys, but his darling Emma was something special. So how could he not worry, when he was scared to death she was heading for a marriage that could only bring her grief? He told himself to stay calm, not to harry Charles.

8

He said: 'All right. Thanks, Charles. I'll wait to hear from you, then. But – but, remember, there isn't much time. They're planning to marry almost at once.'

'Yes. I appreciate that. I won't dally. Goodbye, Maurice.'

Bigrel's manner was kind but dismissive, and Jackson reluctantly let Lorna Day usher him from the office. Bigrel was already making for his private bathroom. He called after Lorna.

'I want David Grant at once, and make sure my car's ready, please.' There was no trace in his voice of his rising excitement.

David Grant arrived as Bigrel emerged from the bathroom. He was in his mid-thirties, and a somewhat nondescript-looking man except for heavy horn-rimmed spectacles. He had worked directly for Charles Bigrel ever since he had joined the SIS twelve years ago, and by now he knew that the more po-faced his director appeared, the more likely he was to be plotting something devious. And at the moment Bigrel appeared very po-faced indeed.

He said: 'David, I want everything you can get on one Richard Lavery. He's thirty. Educated Stowe and Christ Church, Oxford. Junior partner of White, White, Kingston and Lavery, solicitors. And I want it yesterday. Start with his beginnings and go on from there.'

'Anything particular we're after, sir?'

'Some little discrepancy between fact and fiction, perhaps. I don't want to prompt you. This could be big, David.'

'Does that mean Category Z, then, sir?'

'Definitely not. Keep it strictly legal. And whatever you do, be discreet!'

Grant raised an eyebrow at the warning which they both knew was totally unnecessary, but he said nothing. Charles Bigrel was not in the habit of underlining the obvious.

'Report to me this evening. I'll be home by eight thirty.'

'Yes, sir.'

Grant waited for Bigrel to leave the office before he perched himself on the corner of Lorna Day's desk. He seemed in no hurry to start his enquiries. He sat there swinging his legs while Lorna, pretending she was alone, continued with her work.

'Come on, love. Give.'

Lorna looked up and laughed. She was a plain woman in her mid-forties, excessively thin, with the dead white skin that often goes with red hair. Rumour had it that she was in love with Charles Bigrel, but if so it was a lost cause. Grant felt rather sorry for her.

He said: 'Why all this excitement over Richard Lavery? Has he run off with the secret funds?'

'Nothing like that, David.' Lorna relented. 'He's going to marry Emma Jackson, daughter of Maurice Jackson, Director of Scientific Intelligence at the Ministry of Defence. And before the great event takes place Mr Jackson, who happens to be a personal friend of Mr Bigrel, has asked us to vet young Lavery in depth, to make sure he's a suitable husband for his beloved daughter.'

Grant gave her a long, appraising look. 'Lorna, you disappoint me. I always thought you such a good liar, but if you expect me to swallow that – '

'It's the truth. Why should I bother to tell you fibs? Mr Jackson would hate to have a son-in-law whose ancestry isn't – impeccable.'

'Okay.' Grant slid off the desk. 'I suppose I must take your word for it, love. But I wasn't hired as a private eye. I'm meant to be in the Secret Intelligence Service.' He didn't add that the boss had said it could be big, so that he knew there was a whole lot more to it than the eligibility of Maurice Jackson's prospective son-in-law. 'We'll be in the divorce business next.'

The phone rang, and Lorna Day, thankful for the interruption, picked up the receiver. She had overheard considerably more of Maurice Jackson's conversation than she had admitted, but she didn't intend to discuss it with David Grant. Charles Bigrel didn't encourage gossip amongst his personal staff.

'Listen, Lorna – '

'Shut up, David! It's Mr McCann's secretary.'

'Okay, love.' Christopher McCann, CMG, Under-Secretary of State at the FCO, was not to be kept waiting. 'I'll be about

10

my business.'

And before she had put down the receiver Grant was gone, running down the stairs, catching a taxi, on his way to St Catherine's House, the central register of births, deaths and marriages. He had begun his pursuit of Richard Lavery.

Meanwhile Charles Bigrel, his meeting at an end, found himself unable to resist temptation. He ordered his chauffeur to drive to Maiden Lane.

'It's difficult to park along there, sir. Can I drop you and pick you up later?'

'No. I shan't be getting out of the car. I just want to – hover for a few minutes.'

The few minutes stretched into half an hour. A policeman tried to move them on, but desisted when Bigrel produced his identity card. At varying intervals people passed in and out of the building that housed the offices of White, White, Kingston and Lavery, solicitors. Most of them were obviously clients, or clerks from other firms, their briefcases stuffed with documents. Bigrel suppressed each disappointment.

Then, shortly before a quarter to one, two giggling girls went out to collect armfuls of sandwiches and plastic coffee. Bigrel swore gently. He had work to do; he couldn't stay here for the rest of the afternoon. He was a fool to have thought . . . But, as he leaned forward to tell his driver to go back to Century House, a young man came out of the lawyers' office. Clearly it was Richard Lavery.

He stood in the doorway, glancing up at the sky. Above average height, with a thin, clever face and narrow shoulders, he seemed taller than he was. Bigrel could see what Maurice Jackson meant. There was no doubt about the resemblance, especially as the sun gleamed on the fair hair and made Lavery screw up his deep-set eyes.

For a moment the years rolled back, so that Bigrel no longer saw the young lawyer, but a different man, a man he had known well over a long span of time, had admired, envied for his brilliance, loved. Suddenly Bigrel felt old and slightly sick. It could be coincidence, but if not . . .

'We can go now.'

'Very good, sir. Your club? For lunch?'

'No. The office.' He didn't want lunch. But he needed a drink, badly. He thought of the bottle of malt whisky in his desk. 'Be as quick as you can.'

He settled himself in the big car and shut his eyes. Assuming Maurice was right, he still found the situation difficult to comprehend. Why hadn't he been told? Why hadn't the official investigation or, for that matter, some enterprising journalist sniffed out Richard Lavery's existence when the scandal broke nine years ago? Why hadn't the undoubted resemblance been noticed when photographs were splashed across the world's press?

Of course, there were explanations. According to Maurice, Richard would have been an undergraduate then, his features perhaps less formed, his fair hair less gleaming, the likeness to an older man less noticeable. And, as far as the investigation was concerned, the connection with the Laverys could only have been made at the time of Richard's birth twenty years in the past – a long time by any reckoning. What was more, if reputation was anything to go by, the affair could have been brief, casual, one among many, and unremembered.

In any case it was water under the bridge. Bigrel didn't like interfering in other people's lives, especially when Emma, who couldn't fail to be affected, was his only goddaughter. But, having seen the young man, he knew he had to take advantage of the situation. If David Grant's enquiries confirmed his belief, he would have no choice.

And while back in Century House Bigrel tried to concentrate on other work, Richard Lavery – happily unaware of all the interest that was being taken in him – was enjoying an excellent lunch with Emma in one of their favourite Soho restaurants. He finished his whitebait and wiped his mouth.

'Of course I'll drive you out to Heathrow on Thursday, darling, but we'll have to leave early if we're to pick up Betty on the way.'

'Wonderful!' Emma beamed at him. 'Thanks, Richard. That'll be a big help.'

'My pleasure. I suppose it's impossible to persuade you to let your admirable partner go to this toy fair by herself?' Richard grinned, knowing the answer.

'Not a hope!' Emma Jackson shook her head fiercely, and then laughed as she realized Richard was teasing her. An attractive girl, tall, athletic and strong-willed, she was deeply in love with him. 'Betty's got a fine business instinct, but no real flair for toys *per se*, and it's terribly important, just when we're beginning to make a name for ourselves, that we don't fall flat on our faces by buying a heap of goods that won't sell or – worse still – that will sell and then be returned as shoddy or dangerous or plain dull. Toys are expensive these days, and people must know that whatever they buy at our shop is excellent and exciting and good value for money.' She paused, sipped her wine and said, 'Sorry, Richard. I didn't mean to give you my Grade A lecture.'

'Darling, it makes a nice change from the law. And I'm all for your business, providing it doesn't take you away from me too often or too long. What time will you be back next Tuesday?'

'About noon. But we'll have to go straight to the shop and there'll be a lot of work to do, so I'll be late home that evening.'

'Okay. I'll see it's a supper that won't spoil. Incidentally, when I lunch with Dad shall I say that we'll spend the following weekend with them?'

It was a slightly tentative question. Richard hadn't enjoyed his visit to the Jacksons. Maurice, whom Emma said was good fun, he had thought over-formal and over-inquisitive. Helen had been on edge. He hoped the weekend with his own parents would be less of a strain.

'Surely,' Emma said at once. 'And when I've met your ma we'll make a firm date for our marriage. Yes?'

'A firm date, Emma.'

Laughing together, they lifted their glasses and toasted each other. Their world was rose-coloured, as near perfect as it could be. They had no doubts, no fears, no uncertainties. Emma, of course, had known Charles Bigrel all her life, but she had no idea of his job, and on the rare occasions she thought of him it was as a benign figure who never failed to produce a present on her birthday. If she had mentioned him to Richard, he had forgotten. Neither of them had ever heard of David Grant.

But David Grant was working hard and, by the time he rang the bell of Charles Bigrel's flat that evening, he was feeling moderately satisfied with himself.

Bigrel, in a black velvet smoking-jacket that had seen better days, opened the door and led Grant into the book-lined room where he had spent most of his leisure since his wife's death. He gestured to a chair.

'You've eaten?'

'Yes thanks, sir.'

'Brandy, then.' It was a statement, not a question, and clearly Bigrel expected no answer. He poured the brandy and, balloon glass in hand, seated himself opposite Grant. 'Well, David, what have you got for me?'

'Richard's birth certificate. John Lavery's birth certificate, and Veronica's. She was born Veronica White. Incidentally, sir, Richard joined what amounts to a family firm. The senior partner is Veronica's brother.' As he spoke Grant was producing the relevant documents from his briefcase and laying them on the table beside him. He slapped the last one down rather hard. 'And John and Veronica's marriage certificate.'

'Yes.' Bigrel was unmoved. 'I'll look at them later.'

Grant swallowed. 'From the register I went to a newspaper morgue, sir. Naturally the birth was announced in *The Times*. Richard John White Lavery was born in the private wing of one of the big teaching hospitals, and this posed a problem for me. I was torn between legality and discretion.'

'Which did you choose?'

'I posed as a solicitor. It seemed appropriate. I said I was required to assure an American law firm that Richard was indeed Veronica Lavery's son and so entitled to a substantial inheritance from a cousin recently deceased in the USA. No one doubted me. Here are photocopies of the hospital records.' Grant added them to the growing pile.

Bigrel stood up. 'Some more brandy?'

Grant glanced at his glass. He had scarcely touched his drink. 'Thank you, sir. Not – er – just yet.'

Bigrel helped himself and, returning to his seat, said briskly: 'And now, David, stop farting about. Tell me. Did you or didn't you find any sort of skeleton in the Lavery cupboard?'

'I think so, sir, but –

'What?'

'It's possible – no actual proof – that Brigadier Lavery is not Richard's natural father.'

'A – ah!' It was no more than an expulsion of breath. If Grant had expected Bigrel to show surprise, he was disappointed. 'Go on.'

'Richard was born to Veronica White only six months after she married John Lavery. The baby wasn't premature. He was a bouncing nine-pounder. What's more, when her son was three Mrs Lavery went back to the hospital for gynaecological tests. The doctors found no reason at all why she had failed to have another baby. Yet Richard has remained an only child.'

'I see. You're implying that Lavery is sterile, in which case Richard can't have been his son. That may be difficult to prove. I doubt if he consulted an army medic.' Bigrel mused for a moment. 'You could find out where he was when the baby was conceived. He might have been abroad. The War Office would know that. But I'm not sure it's worth bothering about, and it might excite curiosity.'

'There's one other point, sir. Richard won an open scholarship to Oxford. He read Russian and German. He was said to be a brilliant linguist and he intended to go into the diplomatic. No one doubted they'd be delighted to have him. Then suddenly John Lavery objected. He said Richard couldn't take up a career which meant being abroad so much because of his mother. She's an invalid, crippled with arthritis. According to his tutor Richard was pretty bitter about it at the time – and who wouldn't be? – but eventually he agreed. Anyway, sir, it occurred to me that Lavery's real reason for putting a spoke in the poor sod's wheel was because he didn't want any dirt about his birth turning up in his security vetting.'

'Yes – yes. You may well be right.' Bigrel nodded absently. 'Tell me what else you got.'

Grant did as he was told and Bigrel listened, politely but without comment. Grant sensed that he had lost his attention. So Lorna Day's hint had been a good one, he thought, and Bigrel's interest was in Richard Lavery's paternity. He yearned to ask questions, but he knew better. Instead he made a mental note to stand Lorna a drink.

15

' . . . and that's all, sir,' he concluded.

'Good. Then I won't keep you any longer.' Bigrel stood up abruptly. 'We'll talk about it tomorrow.'

'All right, sir.' Grant hurried to drain his glass. 'I'll say goodnight.'

Stifling his curiosity, Grant departed and Bigrel returned to the quiet of his book-lined room. He poured himself another brandy, but didn't touch it. He just sat – and stared, unseeing, at the Bokhara rug on the floor.

After a while he got up, collected his briefcase and took out a file. Contrary to every security regulation at Century House, he had brought it from the office. For several minutes he held it on his lap, unopened. It was as if the cover mesmerized him. But there was nothing revealing on the outside of the pale green folder, no name, no reference number, no kind of mark – only the Cyrillic letter 'D'.

At length he stirred and opened the file. He began to read, though the contents were slight and he knew them by heart. Perhaps, he thought wryly, the file was a kind of requiem for a brave man. Dmitri Sholatov had been a very brave man.

A Muscovite, an outstanding scientist and a professor of physics at Moscow University, Sholatov had cherished a deep love for his country, and a deep hatred of its régime. His mother's father had been a Jew, and he had married a cousin who clung to the old religion. His wife had died in childbirth, and Sholatov, with little to lose and increasingly disgusted by the treatment the Soviet authorities meted out to Jews, had contacted the West. After some years he had become one of Charles Bigrel's most trusted agents – one of the few Soviet citizens in positions of responsibility that Western intelligence had been able to recruit in place.

But two months ago the KGB had come for him in the night. Rather than reveal information under torture he had managed to take his own life. Sholatov had been fortunate.

Gently Bigrel closed the file. He sipped his brandy. He tried in vain to silence his thoughts. Dmitri Sholatov was dead and he, Charles Bigrel, had lost a vital contact, a contact he had so far failed to replace in spite of the utmost effort. There was no alternative. Only one person filled the bill, only one person had the remotest hope of success. Somehow he would have to be persuaded to go to Moscow, and very soon.

TWO

That was Monday. It was Thursday when Bigrel caused Richard Lavery's world to disintegrate.

Thursday was a day of low cloud and drizzle in London, a day for misery. People in raincoats, huddling under umbrellas, hurried along muddy pavements, queued for buses that never came, swore at cars that splashed them as they stood at the kerb waiting to cross the street, ran for taxis already occupied. And at Heathrow all flights were delayed, some cancelled. Emma Jackson, who by now should have been en route to Prague, was still sitting with her friend and colleague, Betty Acheson, in an airport lounge.

Brigadier Lavery had been luckier. His train had been on time. He had caught one of the few taxis available at the station and had spent an engrossing hour in Hatchards bookshop before walking through to his club, the Army and Navy in St James's Square. His trouser legs were damp, but otherwise he was fine. He was looking forward to his lunch with Richard. He always enjoyed the two Thursdays a month he spent in London.

He nodded to the porter as he passed through the lobby. 'Morning. I'm expecting my son about one. I'll be in the upstairs bar.'

'Very good, sir.'

John Lavery didn't hurry. He was early; it would be half an hour before Richard appeared. He got rid of his raincoat and umbrella in the cloakroom, washed his hands, read the latest notices on the board, glanced at the ticker-tape, and made his way to the stairs. At sixty-five he still preferred to walk rather than take a lift.

The bar had just opened. The lights were on and, in contrast to the gloom outside, the room was bright and cheerful, though nine-tenths empty. A club-size whisky to hand, John Lavery settled himself in his favourite corner seat. Here he

17

was close to the bar and in sight of the doorway. He would see Richard as soon as he arrived.

He sipped his drink and thought of Emma Jackson. He had met her once, by chance, when she and Richard had been doing some Christmas shopping. They had all had coffee together and he had liked her. She was an attractive girl, warm and outgoing. He was glad she was to marry Richard. They would make a good pair. He hoped they would have children. He and Veronica would enjoy grandchildren.

Subconsciously he noticed the porter showing someone into the bar and pointing in his direction. His thoughts dissolved. The man was coming across, standing in front of him.

'Brigadier Lavery?'

'Yes.' Lavery took in the good suit, the well-shone shoes, the plain silk tie. A pleasant enough man, with brown eyes behind heavy-rimmed spectacles, and a rather blank face, not someone you would notice in a crowd, and obviously not a club member or the porter wouldn't have escorted him. 'And you are?'

David Grant didn't volunteer his name. 'I'd like to speak to you for a few minutes, if I may, sir.'

'All right. I'm expecting my son shortly, but – ' He left the sentence unfinished. 'Sit down. What's it about?'

'It's about Richard Lavery, sir.'

'Richard?' Lavery was startled. 'Has something happened? Has he had an accident?'

'No, no, sir. Nothing like that,' Grant said quickly, cursing Bigrel for giving him such a bloody job. He didn't know how to begin. He found himself gazing at the Brigadier's empty glass. He gestured towards it. They could both do with a drink in front of them. 'Sir, I wonder if perhaps – '

'Yes. Of course.' Lavery's reaction was automatic. 'What will you have?'

'A pink gin, please.'

Frowning, Lavery went to the bar and ordered the drinks. The chap had said there was nothing wrong with Richard, so why, he asked himself, should he suddenly feel so disturbed? He wished that Richard would come. And in the next instant changed his mind. He must get rid of this character before Richard arrived.

'Here you are.' He put the pink gin down beside Grant. 'You haven't told me your name yet.'

'Thank you, sir. My name's not important.'

'Then what, may I ask, do you want of me – apart from a free drink?'

Grant lifted his head slowly and looked Lavery in the eye; he didn't resent the studied insult. The Brigadier's aggressiveness made his task less difficult.

Without any preamble and in a matter-of-fact voice as if he were commenting on the weather, he said, 'I want you to tell Richard Lavery, today, who his real father is. And please don't pretend it's you, sir, because I know it isn't.'

For a long minute John Lavery stared at him, his mouth slightly open, the colour drained from his cheeks. 'Who – who the devil are you?' he whispered and, when Grant didn't answer, 'What is this? Blackmail? I – I – My God! I'll have you put behind bars. You – you – ' He choked.

David Grant waited. He was sorry for the old boy, half-scared he might have a heart attack, but he showed no emotion. He said calmly, 'No blackmail, sir. Just do what I've asked you.'

'But why? Why after all these years? What good will it do to anyone?' Lavery said at last. He was still rattled, but he had got over the first shock. He had himself under control.

He leaned forward so that his face was near to Grant's.

'Richard is my son. You'd not find it easy to prove the contrary, you know.'

'Easier than you would to tell him a direct lie about it, sir,' Grant said. 'Besides, there are your medical records.' It was a bluff; he hadn't seen any records.

'My medical records would be highly confidential, especially – ' Lavery stopped as Grant allowed himself to smile. 'I see. Not to you. You have access to everything. Who are you? And why? It must be blackmail. Not me – Richard. You intend to blackmail Richard. You – '

He had been speaking to himself rather than Grant, but Grant interrupted. 'No, sir. No one has any intention of blackmailing you or Richard Lavery.'

John Lavery shook his head. 'Then why? Why? I don't understand.'

'There s no need for you to understand, sir. Richard Lavery is having lunch with you today. Just tell him the truth.'

'Between the soup and the fish, I suppose?' Lavery was bitter. 'My God, it makes no sense! If it's not blackmail, what – And if I refuse your demand?'

'He'll be informed by other means. Please don't be in any doubt about that.' Grant stood up. 'It would be much – kinder if you told him yourself, sir, and with the minimum of delay. Goodbye.'

Grant went without a backward glance, leaving John Lavery to stare blankly after him. Slowly Lavery lowered his eyes to the table. The chap, he saw, hadn't touched his drink. He picked up his own glass and gulped the whisky. It made a thin core of warmth inside him. He felt old and tired and defeated. After all these years . . . He couldn't believe it. Why? Why? He tugged at his moustache, a habit when he was upset. He couldn't think straight. What in God's name was he going to say to Richard?

The bar was full when Richard Lavery arrived. Sandwiches and bread and cheese and pickles were now being served, and some members were lunching off them. Richard wouldn't have minded doing the same, but John Lavery always preferred the dining-room; conversation was easier there, he said, and it wasn't as if he and Richard saw so much of each other these days. Richard smiled to himself as he spotted his father in his usual corner seat, back turned, watching something out of the window. He made his way across to him.

'Hello, dad. Sorry I'm late. One of my rich widows wanted to change her will again. You'd think she had something better to do on a filthy day like this, but she's always coming in. Emma says she has designs on me.'

Expecting to get a grin at this remark, Richard was startled by the haunted look he received instead. He took in the drooping mouth, the pallor of the skin, the watery eyes. For a split second he thought the old man had been crying, but that was absurd.

'Dad, what is it? Are you ill?'

'No. No, Richard, I'm all right. A fit of coughing, lost my breath. Nothing more.' His voice was hoarse and it was a fairly convincing lie. He forced himself to smile.

'I'll get you a whisky.' Picking up the glass, Richard noticed David Grant's abandoned drink. 'Is someone with you?'

'No. Take it away.' A violent gesture almost upset the pink gin.

'Okay, dad.'

Thoughtfully Richard went across to the bar. It was clear something was badly wrong. He couldn't remember ever seeing his father so fraught before. Waiting to be served he watched him anxiously in the wide mirror behind the counter.

John Lavery was making a great effort. He blew his nose, gave a couple of experimental coughs, and visibly straightened his shoulders. Then, borrowing a surplus paper napkin that one of his bread-and-cheese-eating neighbours had discarded, he mopped the spilt gin from the table. By the time Richard returned, a glass in each hand, he was to all appearances his usual self.

Richard, undeceived, didn't press. He asked after his mother, talked about Emma's visit to the Prague Toy Fair and described the weekend he had just spent with her family. When they had finished their drinks they went in to lunch. Richard continued to chatter and John Lavery did his best to respond, but eating was beyond him. He pushed his food about his plate until Richard could no longer ignore it.

'You don't seem to have much appetite, dad.'

'No, not much. Would you like cheese, or shall we go and have coffee in the smoking-room?'

'Coffee, please.'

The words were stereotyped. They must have exchanged them a hundred times. Nevertheless, Richard had a sense of occasion. Puzzled and apprehensive, he waited while his father paid the bill.

They went downstairs in silence. It was still early and the smoking-room was almost empty. In a corner, once coffee had been brought, they had complete privacy. Yet John Lavery hesitated. He couldn't bring himself to start.

Richard said: 'Much as I'd like to, I can't stay long today, dad. I've an appointment with a client at three, and I must look through some bumph on the case first.' As he had intended, the remark acted as a catalyst.

'Very well. Then I mustn't waste time.' John Lavery took a deep breath and expelled it slowly. 'I've something to tell you, Richard, as you've probably guessed by now, something I should perhaps have told you years ago. I hoped it would never be necessary.' He paused, tugged at his moustache and continued: 'Please listen without interrupting. You can ask questions afterwards if you want to.'

'All right. I don't know what this is about,' Richard said gently, 'but whatever it is I'm on your side, dad. Remember that.'

'The point is – I'm not your dad.' John Lavery's bitterness was intense. 'I'm not your father, Richard. I'd known your mother since she was a schoolgirl and always loved her, but I was fifteen years older than she was and she wasn't in the least in love with me. She refused to marry me. Then she met someone – he was young, attractive, brilliant and she adored him. But to him it was a brief affair. He'd passed on to the next girl before Veronica even suspected she was pregnant. She didn't know what to do. Even for those days she was pretty innocent. She hadn't a clue how to get an abortion, and anyway the idea was abhorrent to her. She couldn't face her parents. Her mother would have died of shame, and her father' – he gave a short, barking laugh – 'her father was about to be made a bishop. So she came to me and we got married. It was the obvious thing to do. I might add that I've never regretted it.'

'And I'm damn sure she hasn't either.'

Richard spoke instinctively. He was torn between laughter and tears. He found it difficult to take the story he had just heard seriously. It simply wasn't on, no part of the real world, at any rate not his world. Most of his friends were married, some for the second time; others lived together as he and Emma did. He couldn't imagine any of the men behaving as John Lavery had done, or any of the girls being as helpless as his mother. But the inclination to laugh was short-lived. Father or not, he was very fond of John. He didn't want him hurt.

'Ma was lucky – and that goes for me too. I couldn't have been luckier,' Richard said positively. 'And it makes no difference to you and me, or – or anything, dad. I suppose you thought you ought to tell me because I'm getting married, but it really wasn't necessary.'

'Don't be so bloody naïve, Richard!' John Lavery was savage. 'I'd never have told you, and nor would your mother. Never. But someone's found out and, for a reason he failed to explain, he's determined you should know. The choice was to let you be told in some brutal, anonymous fashion or tell you myself. I – I believed you'd rather hear it from me.'

'Yes. Of course. But what does it matter after all this time and why on earth should anyone – ?' Richard stopped, suddenly conscious of a tight ball of apprehension in his guts.

'What does it matter after all this time? Richard, your mother and I weren't just behaving like Victorians. Try to understand. At first there were her parents to consider. And then we wanted to forget for our own sakes. Later we were thankful we hadn't told you. We prayed you'd never have to know. The truth is – ' John Lavery hesitated, groping for the right words when there were no right words. 'The truth is your father – your real father was – is – Guy Carey-Ford.'

'Guy Carey-Ford – my father?' Richard heard his own voice, cold and disbelieving. It seemed to come from a long way away. That sod, that shit, he thought. His mind repudiated the idea. It was absurd, ludicrous, not to be taken seriously. Aloud he said: 'No. No, it can't be true. Not him.'

'It is true. I'm sorry, but it is.' John Lavery yearned to soften the blow. 'He was an – an exceptional man, Richard, one of those people blessed by the gods. He was goodlooking, attractive – charismatic, they call it today – and exceptionally gifted. He was considered for a scientific Nobel Prize. He had a myriad of other talents too. He could have been anything he chose. But seemingly there was a flaw in him and – '

'And he chose to be a traitor.' Richard couldn't hide his bitterness. 'Guy Carey-Ford's one of the most infamous traitors this country's ever produced and – and you say I'm his son!'

It was after three-thirty when John and Richard Lavery came out of the club. The rain had ceased but it was still a glowering day. They stood on the top of the steps, sheltering, while a

23

porter went to find them a taxi.

David Grant was delighted to see them appear. Hungry, since he had had only a sandwich and an apple for lunch, and bored with sitting in his car and watching the doors of the Army and Navy, he was thankful the long wait was over. Hurriedly he picked up a pair of field-glasses from the seat beside him and focused them on the faces of the two men.

'Good-oh!' he muttered to himself. The bleakness of their expressions told him what he wanted to know; John Lavery had done as bidden. 'And now what?'

The porter had found a taxi. The Laverys were getting in. Grant started his car and backed out of his parking space. St James's Square was one-way. The taxi would have to go north. And north it went, with Grant on its tail, stopping and starting in the congested dirty-weather traffic, to Paddington.

Both the Laverys went into the station. Grant hadn't seen them pay the driver and the taxi showed no signs of moving, but he didn't dare risk it. He abandoned his car in a no-parking zone, said 'Keep an eye on it for me, love' to a predatory traffic warden, and hurried after them. From a safe distance he watched them say goodbye. Richard waited until John Lavery had got into the train, waved to him and returned to the taxi. Grant followed, cursing softly when he saw the parking ticket tucked under his wiper blade.

They drove south, through the Park where the trees dripped disconsolately and the beds of tulips looked battered and slightly drunk, and along Knightsbridge to a quiet square behind Harrods. Here Richard Lavery paid off the taxi and went into a block of flats. Grant, who knew Richard lived here, gave him fifteen minutes before going in search of the telephone.

When he got through to Charles Bigrel, Grant said: 'Mission accomplished, sir, and everyone's gone home. May I do the same?'

'Certainly not,' Bigrel said firmly. 'It isn't five o'clock yet. I'm expecting you in the office. I want a personal report.'

'I'm on my way, sir.' Grant soothed him.

His way, however, took him via a Wimpy Bar where he ate two giant hamburgers with a double helping of chips and some extra onions on the side. Hunger assuaged, he was careful not to breathe over Lorna Day as he went through to

Charles Bigrel's office.

Bigrel wasted no time with courtesies. 'Tell me what happened, David, and be quick about it. I'm expecting Maurice Jackson any minute. I was fool enough to say I hoped to have news for him by Thursday and consequently he's been on the phone all day. I had to agree to see him.'

Grant assembled his thoughts and then spoke rapidly, while Bigrel sat and fondled his alabaster egg. When Grant had finished Bigrel had a clear picture of events. They were, he decided, quite satisfactory. It was especially gratifying that Richard Lavery hadn't known of his true parentage till now; otherwise, the threat that Grant represented would have lost much of its impact. As it was, the young man should now be in a state of some anxiety. Given the right moment only a little pressure should be necessary.

'That's fine, David,' Bigrel said, producing a thin smile. 'I think we'll let Richard Lavery stew until Saturday morning. You'd better catch him good and early while he's still bleary-eyed and unshaven. I'd prefer Monday – after all, he's not going to bolt – but we can't afford to leave it. Thomas Penryn has just been kind enough to inform me that Carey-Ford has disappeared from the Moscow scene and no one knows where he is.'

Grant grinned. Penryn was Head of the East European and Soviet Department at the FCO. A smooth, oily man who couldn't help but patronize, he and Bigrel did not get on together. 'What did you say to Mr Penryn, sir?'

'I said, "Really? How interesting." ' Bigrel snorted angrily. 'What do you expect me to have said? – "My dear Thomas, Carey-Ford's in hospital and has been for over two months. What's more, he's in strict isolation. No one's allowed to get near Russia's favourite British traitor. Indeed, the last man who got within spitting distance is now dead, thanks to the KGB." ' As he remembered Dmitri Sholatov, Bigrel's spurt of anger subsided like a pricked balloon. 'David, I may not exactly love Thomas Penryn, but I don't want him to have a heart attack. Dear God! I'm responsible for too much as it is. Imagine what Richard Lavery must be feeling like after his lunch party.'

'Like hell,' Grant said softly. 'Poor bastard. And he doesn't know what's hit him yet.'

THREE

Richard had returned to his flat in the blackest of moods. He felt emotionally unstrung. As far as he was concerned John Lavery was and always would be his father, but questions gnawed at his mind. The real mystery was the source of the pressure on John Lavery. Who could gain from raising the matter in this way after all this time?

His thoughts turned to Emma and her reactions if he told her. Suddenly a simple answer came to him – Maurice Jackson, Emma's father, who had behaved so oddly towards him last weekend, insisting on his resemblance to an unknown someone. Could the someone have been Carey-Ford? As a senior civil servant in the Ministry of Defence it was not unlikely that Jackson would have known Carey-Ford, though if so it was the world's worst luck. No man would want his daughter to marry the son of a traitor, but few would have chosen such a devious way of bringing matters to a head. Richard felt dirty, humiliated.

Viciously he stabbed his front-door key in the lock and let himself into the hall, kicking the door shut behind him. Then he stood stock-still. He wasn't alone in the flat. Just before the door banged there had been a sound from his bedroom as if something had been knocked over.

Emma! Her flight to Prague must have been cancelled because of the filthy weather and she had come back for the night. Richard swore. He couldn't face her, not at the moment. But had he any choice? She must have heard him. He would have to tell her he wasn't well and pray she would believe him.

'Emma! It's me, Richard.' He tried to make his voice light.

There was no answer, and he called to her again – but hesitantly. When the silence lengthened, his mind began to function properly. No one had any right to be in the flat except Emma and possibly the janitor, and either of them would have said something to reassure him. The alternative was an intruder, a thief. He felt his nerves tighten, but he wasn't afraid. It didn't occur to him to let himself out of the flat and go for help. Instead, he advanced purposefully along the passage.

The sound had come, he thought, from his bedroom, which was the second room on the right. The door was ajar. He flung it back on its hinges so that it paralleled the wall, or should have done. In fact, it swung forward again, given violent impetus by someone hiding behind it, slamming into Richard and catching him off balance. Richard staggered sideways and fell.

A man was leaping for the passage and a safe escape. But he was fractionally too slow. As one flying foot grazed Richard's head, Richard shot out his arm and, seizing an ankle, brought him crashing down.

For a second or two they lay in a tangled heap. Then they began to grapple with each other. Richard, half winded, clung desperately to the ankle. He dug his nails through thin socks into skin, while his opponent kicked with his free leg. They rolled together over the carpet, grunting and gasping, but not speaking.

Eventually their efforts took them to the end of the bed and to a point when Richard was getting the better of the fight. He had his hand cupped under his opponent's chin and, exerting all his strength, was able to bang his head once, twice, three times against the brass bedstead. He felt the body beneath him go slack and managed to struggle upright. He was breathing hard and for a moment he just stood there, looking down at the man who lay unconscious at his feet.

He was not Richard's idea of a professional thief. He was thin but wiry, with a small moustache and a narrow face that gleamed white under dark hair. His badly cut suit, dishevelled neatness and general air of respectability made him look more like a clerk in some insignificant office. Quixotically Richard felt sorry for him, but his main emotion was curiosity.

He knelt beside him and began to go through his pockets. They didn't yield much – no money, no keys, no diary, only a plain white handkerchief and a Minox camera.

Richard was frowning over the Minox when he became aware that some change had taken place in the room. It was scarcely more than a shifting of the air. He made to turn but he was too late. The cosh hit him under the right ear, hard and accurately, and he plunged forward into blackness.

The second intruder, who had been standing behind one of the bedroom curtains during the struggle, pushed Richard contemptuously aside with a foot and bent over his colleague. The man's eyes were open and he was grinning broadly.

'I've got thick hair,' he said, 'but the bastard hurt.'

'Shut up! And let's get out of here.'

'The camera?'

The second man stooped and prised it from Richard's hand. 'I've got it. Come!'

They went, ignoring Richard Lavery, but shutting the front door of the flat carefully behind them. The language they had been speaking was Russian.

It was some time before Richard regained consciousness. Even then he had no inclination to move. The carpet tempered the hardness of the floor, and he wasn't aware of discomfort as long as he kept still. He lay, not thinking, letting himself float on a cloud of apathy. Time passed.

At length his stomach began to cramp and he realized he was going to be sick. Reluctantly he got on all fours and from there, by means of the brass bedstead, managed to pull himself upright. He ran, staggering, into the bathroom and knelt in front of the toilet, resting his head on the back of the seat. A stream of vomit poured from his throat into the pan.

After a few minutes he felt better. He washed his face in cold water and swilled more water around his mouth. He could taste the club claret he had drunk at lunch, a long time ago – before he knew of Carey-Ford and the world fell apart. Gingerly he touched the swelling behind his ear. He wished his head didn't throb so much. He needed to think, and to think straight.

Because it was simplest and really not important, he concentrated first on the burglary. The intruder, or rather intruders – there must have been more than one of them –

would be gone by now, but he ought to see what they had taken. There wasn't much of value in the flat; a colour television set, some stereo equipment, a lot of clothes – and the brass bedstead which had been so useful. Richard was surprised to catch himself grinning.

He walked slowly from room to room. Nothing was missing but the place had been searched. Various things had been misplaced. A letter he had found on his return home from the airport that morning and thrown carelessly onto his desk had been read; he was positive he hadn't folded it back into its envelope. What sort of thief read letters? Suddenly Richard remembered the Minox camera he had found in the intruder's pocket. For that matter, what sort of thief came equipped with a camera and stole nothing? It made no sense. Yet why should anyone want to search his flat?

Finally Richard went back to the bedroom. At once he noticed the disarray on the dressing-table. The photographs of himself and Emma, framed in a silver diptych, had been knocked over, scattering one or two other objects. Presumably this accounted for the noise he had heard when he let himself into the flat.

Automatically he picked up the diptych and set it upright. As he did so the photographs shifted in their frames. They had been removed and put back carelessly, hurriedly. The intruders must have been replacing them when the slam of the front door startled them. But what did they want with them? To photograph them with their little Minox? Why? Surely it couldn't be some clumsy attempt of Maurice Jackson's to compare his – Richard's – likeness with that of Carey-Ford. If that were the case there would have been no need to take out Emma's photograph – each half of the frame was quite separate.

Richard groaned aloud. His head was splitting. All right. Two people, at least, had broken into his flat; the lock on the front door was a routine Yale and not too difficult to trip with a piece of plastic. They had stolen nothing and done no damage, except to himself. What could he do about it? It would probably be a waste of time to go to the police. He would get the lock changed for something more substantial and forget the whole matter, if he could. There were other problems, more important problems, to be resolved.

First he needed a pain-killer. As he got the aspirin from the bathroom cabinet he caught sight of his reflection in the glass of the door. For a full minute he stared at it. He had always known he was good-looking. It was something he had accepted, as he accepted the quickness of his mind. Now he regarded his handsome face with distaste. It was, he realized, a similar face that Veronica White must have seen when she lay on her back for Carey-Ford to . . .

Slamming the cabinet door, Richard went along to the kitchen. He would not think of his mother in those terms. He put on the kettle and, while he waited for it to boil, swallowed two aspirin. He made the tea. Then he sat at the wooden table where he and Emma always had breakfast, and brooded, his depression wrapped around him like a heavy grey shawl.

Bitterly he resigned himself to the fact that he could not marry Emma. The odds were against it but, if Maurice Jackson had guessed his relationship to Carey-Ford, so might someone else. And unexpectedly he recalled an incident at his prep school; he hadn't thought of it for years.

In an isolated corner of the playing field, Richard had come on a circle of boys ragging another. Hands joined to prevent escape, they were dancing round their victim, chanting: 'Your father's a bankrupt, a bankrupt, a bankrupt. Your father's a . . . '

Probably none of them knew what a bankrupt was. They just knew it was something undesirable. But the more they chanted the more the small boy in the middle of the circle grew hysterical with fear and anguish.

Kids didn't change. Nor did their gossipy mums. Those words could so easily be: 'Your grandad's a traitor, a traitor, a traitor. Your grandad's a . . . '

It wasn't going to happen to any child of his. Maurice Jackson had been right. Intellectually Richard was prepared to acknowledge this, but emotionally it wasn't so easy to accept. He loved Emma. He wanted her, for always. It wasn't some passing infatuation. They both knew that by now, which was why they had decided to marry.

Richard told himself to be practical. A clean break with

Emma was the only answer. He would write to her, say he had changed his mind, couldn't face marriage, wanted to be free to live his own life again. She was going straight to the shop from the airport on her return from Czechoslovakia. He would send the letter there. He would suggest she move out of his flat as soon as possible, before he – came back.

Yes, that was a good idea. He would go away, take some leave. They were busy at the office, but the last of his cousins had just joined the firm and he could take some of the work-load. He would arrange it tomorrow and be gone by Tuesday, when Emma was due home.

That way he wouldn't have to face her. She was sure to know he was lying. Yet he couldn't tell her the truth. He dismissed the bitter possibility that if Emma knew he was the son of Carey-Ford she wouldn't be prepared to marry him. That wasn't like Emma. She would be more likely to argue, say they should marry and not have children, but that wasn't what either of them had wanted. It wouldn't be fair to her. Besides – 'Haven't you heard? Her father-in-law's that traitor, that traitor . . . ' It wasn't only schoolboys who were cruel.

Richard Lavery pillowed his aching head on his arms, and wept.

FOUR

'Poor Richard. God help him.' David Grant was unaware that he had spoken aloud.

'What d'you say?' A slurred voice asked him from the bed.

'Nothing, love.' Grant scrambled back into his underpants. In his first attempt he had put them on the wrong way round. 'Go to sleep, there's a good girl.'

'Why d'you have to go to work on Saturday?'

Grant didn't answer. He was late. Either the alarm had failed or the bloody girl had turned it off in the middle of the night. He pulled on his socks. There was a hole in one toe. What a life. Then he thought again of Richard Lavery. He oughtn't to complain.

There wasn't time for breakfast and, though the girl kept an electric razor for her gentleman friends, he never liked to use it. His car was fifty yards along the street. He started it carelessly, flooded the engine and cursed. Bigrel had said, 'Get to Lavery's early while he's still bleary-eyed and unshaven.' Ironically the boot was on the other foot. It was he who was bleary-eyed and unshaven – and breakfastless. Grant heaved a sigh. He doubted whether it would make much difference; the odds against Lavery were heavy.

Nevertheless, when he reached his destination he got out the battery razor he always kept in the car and began to shave. From where he was parked he could see in his rear-view mirror the entrance to the flats where Lavery lived. A taxi that had followed him into the square had stopped in front of it; the driver remained in his seat. Guiding the razor carefully over the planes and crevasses of his face, Grant continued to watch, more from habit than interest. He was unprepared when Richard Lavery suddenly ran down the steps and got into the cab.

Furious with himself at having missed Lavery by so little, Grant tossed the razor on to the seat beside him and set off to follow the taxi. Lavery had been carrying a largish bag and a briefcase. Presumably he was going away for the weekend, maybe to visit a client. But why hadn't he taken his own car? There it was in the square, a blue Ford Capri with a resident's permit, sitting in a legal parking zone opposite the block of flats.

The taxi turned a corner and stopped abruptly. Richard Lavery leapt out, thrust a letter into a postbox – it was to Emma, a cold, stilted letter informing her that he no longer wished to marry her, though Grant was not to know this – and leapt in again. Grant swore. His reactions had been slow. He had nearly gone into the back of the damned cab.

The journey continued. They were driving west now. Grant had hoped that the taxi might make for a railway station but it hadn't, and once they reached the M4 there was little doubt where it was heading. It was making for the airport, and at a rate of knots. Grant had to keep his foot down not to be left behind.

As he drove Grant chewed on his lower lip. Worry was jumping in him. This was all his fault. If he hadn't overslept he would have caught Lavery at the flat. As it was, he could only hang on and pray. Bigrel would be savage. He would want to know why Grant had been late, where he had been and with whom. There was no private life in this job. He often wondered why he didn't resign, but what would he do? He couldn't stand a nine-to-five routine. Besides, the pay and the perks were good, and the pension – if you lived long enough.

He groaned aloud as the taxi ignored the ramp for Terminal One. There had been a chance that Lavery was taking a domestic flight, Edinburgh, Manchester, even one of the Channel Islands, but only an outside chance. This wasn't his lucky day. The wretched man was going abroad. Where? Not Moscow! Christ! Surely he wasn't about to visit his traitorous dad? Ignorant, unbriefed, completely at risk, he would end in the Lubyanka without a doubt. But it couldn't be Moscow, not direct. He couldn't have got a visa so quickly. Grant felt himself begin to sweat. Bigrel would have his skin for this.

Caught in a confusion of vehicles, porters, luggage, people, all milling round in front of Terminal Two, Grant was some twenty yards behind the taxi when it stopped. Immediately the door swung open. Lavery scrambled out, pulling his bag after him. He must have paid the driver during the journey for there was no delay. He dashed for the entrance, pushing his way fiercely through a package of tourists who were erupting from a coach.

Grant double-parked his car and started after him, but he didn't get far. His path was blocked by a young, over-enthusiastic policeman.

'You can't leave it there, sir.'

'SB,' Grant said, beginning to edge round him.

'Special Branch?' The policeman grinned; he had heard that one before. 'Your pass, please – sir.'

There wasn't time to argue. Grant thrust his car keys into the constable's hand. 'Take it as a bribe,' he said, and ran.

He half expected to hear the shrill of a whistle and the pound of feet coming after him, but the copper must have had second thoughts. No one pursued him. He burst through the doors into the building and looked around for Richard Lavery. His heart sank. The place was a morass of people and there was no sign of his quarry.

Weaving and dodging through the crowd, nearly knocking down a child, obstructed by a porter with a chain of trolleys, Grant hurried from check-in desk to check-in desk. Most of them had queues, but Lavery must have been lucky and not had to wait because he wasn't anywhere to be seen.

Grant's mind was spinning. Lavery had taken an extravagant taxi all the way to Heathrow and it had gone like a bat out of hell. The obvious conclusion was that he was late, afraid to miss his flight. Which meant he wouldn't be waiting here in the concourse. He'd be at passport control, or the security check, or in the departure lounge, or boarding his plane.

Which plane? According to the departures board there was an Air France flight to Paris, an Austrian Airlines flight to Vienna and a KLM flight to Amsterdam, all boarding. Grant hesitated. Everything had gone wrong. Even if it were at all possible to stop Lavery from leaving the country – and he had no authority to do that – Lavery would be in a foul mood, and Bigrel had stressed that he was to be persuaded, cajoled, not bulldozed. They needed Lavery's cooperation.

As he watched, the lettering on the departures board clicked over. The flight to Vienna was expunged. The aircraft would be trundling out to the runway. Grant turned. He went straight to the Austrian Airlines desk. The girl was charming. Yes, his friend Mr Lavery was on the Vienna flight. He had arrived very late. Indeed, they had held the flight for a minute or two for him. She was terribly sorry she couldn't be of more help.

Grant gave her his best smile. 'Well. I'll have to try to get in touch with him in Vienna. I do hope I can. It's not just a stop-over, is it?'

'No. Of course, he may be going on, but his ticket was an ordinary London-Vienna and return.'

'Thank you very much indeed.'

Steeling himself, Grant went in search of a telephone. Now he had to break the happy news to Charles Bigrel, and he was not looking forward to it.

In the event the conversation was brief. Stark would be a more apposite description, if one excluded the pungency of Bigrel's vocabulary. Grant was shocked. To use such words on a public phone line had to be illegal. He would have cried with laughter if he hadn't been responsible for the whole bloody mess.

As it was, he jumped to obey orders. Bigrel had told him to report at once and, though he thought yearningly of breakfast, he hurried off in search of his car. Fully expecting it to have been removed to some pound, he was relieved to see it parked against the kerb. The key was in the ignition, the policeman standing near.

'Thanks. Thanks a lot,' Grant called, and meant it; it was the first good thing to have happened to him that day.

Bigrel heard Grant out in silence. Though his right thumb worked steadily on the rounded end of his alabaster egg and his lips were a thin, straight line, his anger seemed to have subsided.

'I'm having Lavery's flight met. We should know what he's up to by lunch-time. Meanwhile, David, I suggest you go home and pack a bag. You're booked on the British Airways afternoon flight.'

'Yes, sir.' Grant plucked up his courage. 'Why Vienna, do you think, sir?'

Bigrel shrugged. 'He may like the city, or he may prefer to wait there rather than in London till his Soviet visa comes through. I don't know. I must admit I'd be happier if he'd gone to Paris or Amsterdam.'

Bigrel picked up his telephone. Grant was dismissed. On the whole, he thought, he had got off more easily than he deserved. He could have been removed from the job completely. Instead he was being sent to Vienna. Probably it would only be for a day or two, but it was a change. He was tired of home duty. It was time he got out into the field again. Grant was whistling as he walked to the lift.

'Hello, David. You look more cheerful than when you went into the sanctum.'

'I'm off on a little swan, Lorna my love.'

'So I gathered.' Lorna Day hummed a few bars from the Merry Widow waltz and Grant grinned at her.

'Right first guess.' Waving her ahead of him into the lift he noticed the pathetically thin shoulders and the bright red hair drawn back into a bun. She could have done something with that hair when she was young. Poor old Lorna! He owed her a drink for the tip she had given him about Richard Lavery. 'What about a quick visit to the local before I go and pack?'

'Just what I need, David.'

The Cock and Feathers was a pleasant pub. It had been modernized without losing its character, and the service was friendly and efficient. During the week Grant avoided it because it was always full of his colleagues from Century House, but if he was on duty over the weekend he often went there.

Today being a Saturday, and not long after opening time, the place was almost empty. Grant installed Lorna in a corner seat and went to get their drinks, a whisky for her and a pink gin for himself.

'Cheers, love.'

'Thanks, David. Cheers – and best wishes for your new assignment.'

'My new – ' Grant shook his head. 'No such luck. It's still

36

the same old assignment. Friend Richard has decided to take an impromptu holiday.'

'In Vienna?' Lorna Day sounded amused. 'You don't mean he's walked out on that nice girl of his?'

'Could be.' Grant hesitated. He wasn't sure how much Lorna knew. Probably more than he did himself. He said: 'I was to break it to him that we wanted him to do a little errand for us, but I overslept this morning and he lit out as I arrived.'

'Poor David,' Lorna Day laughed. 'That's why our lord and master was so displeased, was it? I thought Mr Penryn might have been annoying him again.'

'That arrogant bastard,' Grant said. 'A mere Head of Department and he behaves as if he's Permanent Under-Secretary. Whereas Chris – Christopher McCann . . . '

Grant had stumbled over the name and he made himself repeat it. He heard the liquor on his tongue. He had had only one drink, but he was short on sleep and food, and last night . . . He smothered a yawn. He wished Lorna would finish her drink.

'I'd like to offer you the other half, love, but – '

'You haven't the time.'

Lorna was already picking up her handbag, smiling at him, preparing to stand up. She really was an understanding woman. The bird he usually dated would have turned sour at such short shrift. Nevertheless, he was glad when they got outside the pub and she said goodbye. It was a relief to be alone.

He collected his car and drove straight to his flat in South Kensington. He felt tired, dirty and hungry. From necessity – a living-in girlfriend was a disadvantage in his profession – he had become a reasonably good cook. Now he opened a tin of lobster bisque, made himself a three-egg omelette with bacon and mushrooms, and followed that with cheese and fruit. He drank black coffee, cup after cup of it. When he had finished his meal he washed the dishes. He was a tidy man and he wasn't sure when he would be home again.

An hour later, showered, re-shaven and clean clothed, he was back at Century House. Lorna Day waved him through and, leaving his bag with her, he went into Charles Bigrel's office.

'Ah – David.' Bigrel gave him a thin-lipped smile. 'We've

had a stroke of luck. The man I sent to meet Lavery's flight is an Attaché at our embassy in Vienna. He reports that Lavery was met at Schwechat Airport by a colleague of his called Peter Denville, one of the First Secretaries. It seems Lavery and Denville are old school chums and Lavery has gone to stay with him for, and I quote, a few weeks.'

Grant blew out a long breath. 'Thank the Lord for that! Of course it doesn't rule out the possibility that he's planning to go to Moscow.'

'No, indeed. He can't be sure when he'll be able to get a visa, and anyway, a delay won't seem important to him.'

'You mean he doesn't know that Carey-Ford – '

'No. Why should he?'

'Denville may be able to hurry things up for him in the visa line. That could be why he chose to go to Vienna.'

'Possibly. On the other hand perhaps he just felt the need to get away for a while. There may be no more to it than that. Let's not jump to conclusions, David. It's not a good idea.'

'No, sir,' Grant said meekly. He was to remind Bigrel of his words.

FIVE

Richard Lavery woke slowly and for a moment he was disoriented. He was in a square of patterned green, a room unfamiliar to him. Green paper on walls and ceiling, green carpet, green curtains, green duvet. Everything matched. Even the light, shining through half-open shutters, was a dappled green. It was like being under water. Then he remembered.

There was a tap on the door and Peter Denville came in, carrying a tray. He was already dressed. 'Good morning, Richard. Hope you slept well. I've brought you some coffee.'

'Thanks.' Richard propped himself up on the pillows and took the tray. 'Just what I need.' He yawned hugely. 'This is luxury.'

'Bacon and eggs in the refrigerator when you want breakfast. But go back to sleep if you like. No one will disturb you. You're lucky Louise isn't here.' Louise was Peter Denville's French wife, who was in Paris visiting her parents. 'She'd insist on taking you sightseeing.'

Richard grinned. 'You're off to the Embassy now?'

'Yes. Monday's always busy. Work tends to accumulate over the weekend. So – ' He returned Richard's grin, but doubtfully. He was aware that Richard was under strain and he wanted to help if he could. But Richard hadn't confided in him, and he couldn't pry. 'See you around six tonight then. And we'll be going to that party later. Okay?'

'Great – if you're sure the Ambassador won't mind.'

'He won't notice, and Her Ladyship'll be delighted. She's always glad of an extra man.'

When Peter had gone Richard poured himself a second cup of coffee and wondered what to do with his day. He had never been to Vienna before and he was determined to enjoy the visit. That was why he had come – not to forget his relationship to Carey-Ford, which would be impossible, but to learn to disregard it, and to keep his mind off Emma. She would be flying back to London tomorrow, going to the shop, finding his letter . . .

Richard thrust aside the coffee-tray and got out of bed. He would go and inspect St Stephen's Cathedral, stroll around the old city inside the Ring, have lunch in one of the many cafés.

The doorbell rang. Frowning, Richard stopped in his tracks. Peter had said he could lie in, no one would disturb him. Yet five minutes later someone was intent on doing precisely that. The doorbell rang again, a long, imperative ring. Richard shrugged on a robe and slid his feet into a pair of slippers. He couldn't ignore the bell. It might be the postman delivering a parcel, the laundry returning, some cleaning that Peter had forgotten. Richard combed his fingers through his hair and went to the door.

'Good morning.'

The man didn't seem to fit into any of the categories that Richard had considered. He wasn't a postman. He wasn't delivering anything. He could be a neighbour but he had spoken in English and his intonation had been perfect. He could be from the Embassy.

'Mr Denville's not here,' Richard said.

'I know. I waited for him to leave. It's you I want to see, Mr Lavery.'

'Me?' He was startled.

'Yes. May I come in?'

It was a rhetorical question. David Grant was already in. As if it were the most natural thing in the world he had taken a step forward, and Richard, almost without noticing, had given way.

'What do you want?'

'My name is David Grant. I work for the branch of the Foreign and Commonwealth Office. If you'd like to look at my passport – ?'

'No. I doubt if that would serve any purpose. Are you here on official business?'

'Yes, but that doesn't mean – ' Grant was adept at the unfinished sentence and he managed to imply far more than he said.

'Doesn't mean what?

It wasn't going to be easy, Grant realized. 'Listen. I need to talk to you, but it's not very comfortable standing around in the hall. Can't we go into the living room, or better, the kitchen. I'm pining for a cup of coffee.'

'You've still not told me what you want. Why is it necessary to talk to me? Is this some sort of security check?'

'No. Nothing like that.'

'But you are from the Foreign Office, you said? The Embassy? You know Peter Denville?'

'Yes to the first question and no to the others. I'm from the FCO in London. I missed you on Saturday morning so I had to follow you to Vienna.'

'You've come all the way to Vienna because of me? You're joking?'

'No.'

'Then either you're crazy or you've made a hell of a mistake, confused me with someone else. I'm Richard Lavery. I'm a lawyer. My firm is White, White, Kingston and Lavery of – '

'I know that, and a lot more about you, believe me. For instance, you're a Gemini. Your birthday is in June. You're an only child. You were engaged to Emma Jackson.'

'*Were* engaged?'

He was quick, Grant thought, which was a good thing. He would need to have his wits about him. His chances wouldn't be very high otherwise.

'I thought you might have broken off the engagement since you were informed of certain facts last Thursday.' Grant let the silence lengthen, but he didn't like the way Lavery was looking at him – as if he were some kind of rotten garbage. He felt compelled to add, 'I'm sorry.'

'Sorry!' It was a shout of derision.

'Yes. Now can we talk?'

'No. There's nothing to talk about. Just tell Maurice Jackson he's achieved his objective. I've already broken with Emma. He could have saved himself the price of your air fare to Vienna. Or is the poor bloody tax-payer buying your ticket? Whichever it is, it's madness.'

'I don't think you understand. Maurice Jackson – '

41

'Oh, don't I? Get out, Grant, and to hell with you!'

Grant didn't move. He gave what he hoped was a deprecatory smile and adjusted the horn-rims on the bridge of his nose. Lavery had sounded unpleasantly aggressive, but he wasn't the type to hit a man who wore glasses, at least not without considerable provocation. And Grant had no wish to provoke him. Persuasion was the big thing. 'Get him to cooperate,' Bigrel had said. Grant intended to obey orders.

But the present conversation was getting them nowhere. Grant decided to act. The door of the living-room was open and he walked past Lavery and sat himself down in an armchair. Richard followed him and stood in the doorway.

'Get out, Grant!'

'Not until I've told you why I'm here, which has nothing to do with Maurice Jackson or Emma. It concerns Guy Carey-Ford. He's desperately ill. It's probably terminal cancer,' Grant said levelly.

There was a pause while Richard absorbed the shock. When he spoke it was without emotion. 'And you expect me to say how sorry I am?'

'No. But I think you owe it to yourself to find out what's happening. There are various implications, as you must realize.'

'Yes.' Richard's voice was taut. 'All right. Wait there. I'll be a few minutes.'

Grant drew a deep breath and let it escape in a long whistle. He was, he thought, over the worst hurdle, but he didn't relax. He listened for tell-tale sounds; running water, the buzz of a razor, the thud of a cupboard door and, happily, the burp of a percolator. He wasn't surprised when Richard Lavery returned, washed, shaved, dressed and carrying a coffee-tray.

'Black, please,' he said in answer to a glance.

Richard poured the coffee. 'I have a lawyer's mind, and before you begin there are one or two things I'd like to get clear. Maurice Jackson recognized my likeness to Carey-Ford, and got a chum in the FCO to investigate. When Jackson's suspicions were confirmed, said chum ordered you to force my father to tell me of the relationship, so that I'd break with Emma.' Richard paused. 'Is that the sordid story in a nutshell?'

'More or less. Strictly speaking I wasn't personally concerned with your love-life.'

'Really? Well – it's your turn now. You've been sent all this way to talk to me. I'm listening. Talk.'

'Thank you. But first I have to tell you that what I'm going to say is secret. You must treat it as if you were a priest and I was in a confessional. Is that understood?' Grant spoke apologetically, but he was watching Lavery carefully and he didn't like the derisive grin which greeted his remark. He repeated, 'I mean it, Lavery. Is that understood?'

'Perfectly. To my knowledge I've not inherited any traitorous genes. Your secrets should be safe.'

Grant let the gibe pass; the poor guy was entitled to his bitterness. He said, 'It's two or three months since Carey-Ford was last seen around Moscow, and the rumour is that he's working on some high priority project. We know that's a lie, put out by the Soviet authorities. He's ill, very ill in hospital. We believe he's dying, though we're not sure. For some reason he's being kept strictly incommunicado, no visits from friends, nothing.'

Grant waited as if at this point he expected Richard to ask a question, but when Richard gave no sign he continued. 'We don't really know why. The Russians are a secretive lot. Often they go to immense trouble to hide something that's either already common knowledge or seemingly not in the least important. So there's probably nothing to the fact that they're making such an effort to keep Carey-Ford in what amounts to solitary confinement. However, it does complicate things for us.'

Again Grant waited for a question, a comment, but none came. Lavery continued to regard him in sardonic silence. His attitude was beginning to rile Grant, who felt he was losing control of the situation.

He said sharply, 'Aren't you interested enough to ask why?'

'Should I be?'

'Yes.' Grant told himself not to press. He leant forward confidentially. 'Listen. It's vital that someone from the West should get to talk to Carey-Ford. We know he's got information he wants to pass on to us. It seems that, believing himself to be near death, he's had a change of heart and wants to make amends for his past treachery. But – you see the problem?'

'I see the problem. But if you're thinking what I think you're thinking, the answer is definitely no. I couldn't do it, and even if – '

'You could try. Why not? You've got the perfect cover. John Lavery decided that because you were getting married, you should be told the truth about yourself and Carey-Ford. Naturally it made you curious. You're indifferent to politics but you do want to meet your father. It's very reasonable that you should. The Russians will appreciate that. With luck they'll give you a visa, let you see him and – and the rest would be up to him.'

'How simple you make it sound.'

'It is simple – for you. For some obscure reason, as I said, they won't let anyone near him. But there's a good chance you'd be the exception.' Grant smiled wryly. 'It means only you can help us, and you will, won't you?'

Richard shook his head. 'No. I will not. For several good reasons. I'm not qualified for such a job. I suspect it's far more complex than you're prepared to admit. And I resent the way you've tried to involve me in it.'

'I'm afraid you are involved whether you want to be or not. Guy Carey-Ford is your father.' There was an edge on Grant's voice. 'Nine years ago he went over to the Reds, taking with him a mass of information, future Western technical programmes – laser systems, particle beams, anti-satellite weapons – all the things that make for strong positions in these days of international bargaining. Obviously the communists would eventually have got the data for themselves, just as they could have done the work the atom spies supplied. But time is of the essence in this business, and there's no doubt that Carey-Ford did more damage to the West in the last decade than the atom traitors or the secret service infiltrators did in their time. And if you care about people, it's arguable that hundreds of thousands of lives have been lost in a host of small wars that wouldn't have started if the communists hadn't been so confident as a result of the information Carey-Ford gave to them. Now you've got a chance to compensate – to make up for a fraction of the enormous wrong your father did. Don't you think you owe it – ?'

'No! I owe nothing to him or to you.' Richard got to his feet and stood over Grant, his hands clenched at his sides. 'I don't like your methods. I don't trust you. And, for the last time, I have no intention whatever of going to Moscow to see Guy Carey-Ford. If your masters don't like my refusal, that's too bloody bad. They know where they can put it.'

'Are you afraid?'

Richard laughed without mirth. 'I won't bother to answer that one. You've not managed to persuade me to do what you want. You're not going to shame me into it either. Or black-mail me. So there's something you'd better understand. If there's the slightest hint in the press or any of the media of a connection between the names of Lavery and Carey-Ford I shall make public what you've told me this morning – and to hell with the Official Secrets Act. Do you believe me, Grant?'

'I believed him,' Grant said, a half-hour later. He was in the Embassy, talking to Charles Bigrel in London. It was a scram-bler line, but all the same he wasn't indulging in careless talk. 'He convinced me, sir. To judge by appearances he could be the thinking girl's heart-throb, but there's more to him than that. He's got guts.'

'And you're certain it's useless to try again?'

'Yes. He won't accept it as a duty and he won't be pressured into it. I don't know why we assumed he would. You said yourself that we oughtn't to jump to conclusions about him.'

'Quite. My mistake. I'm sure you did your best, David.' Even at this distance the bitterness in Bigrel's voice was apparent. 'But God knows what we do now.'

'And me, sir? Do I stay with him?'

Bigrel's hesitation was minimal. 'No. What's the point? We'll forget him. If he won't play, he won't. We can't force him. We can't even blame him for refusing. You catch the first available flight home, David, and I'll see you tomorrow.'

'All right, sir. Goodbye till then.' The old man had sounded very depressed, and not surprisingly. Time was running out fast. It was most improbable that anything would turn up now. The odds were all in favour of Guy Carey-Ford going to his Russian grave without a chance to right any of the wrong he had done.

Richard's thoughts were complementary to Grant's. He too was thinking of Carey-Ford, though without regret. He wasn't unpatriotic. If he had been approached differently, he might at least have questioned his own decision. As it was he had no doubts.

Richard knew nothing of Intelligence except what he had gathered from the movies, television, an occasional novel and the not infrequent lurid story in the press. What he did know didn't impress him. He couldn't believe in the intrepid amateur and, fiction apart, the professional seemed to be tough, unscrupulous, amoral and often inefficient – adjectives he didn't hesitate to apply to David Grant. He strongly suspected that, because he was Carey-Ford's son, Grant considered him fair game, an expendable pawn, and he was damned if he was going to be used in some hare-brained scheme.

But it wasn't easy to rid his mind of the unpleasantness engendered by his argument with Grant. Again and again, while he was forcing himself to eat a belated breakfast and catching a tram to the centre of the city and wandering around St Stephen's Cathedral, Richard unwillingly recalled scraps of their conversation.

It was to distract his thoughts, rather than from any particular interest, that he attached himself to a group about to be conducted through the catacombs. The group was small, not a dozen people, and the guide, forseeing little in the way of tips, was slow to start. When at length they did move off he stopped almost at once. He had noticed a young man standing, back turned, near the sacristy, and he went to invite him to join the party. The man shook his head. The guide repeated the invitation. The man again refused but, apparently embarrassed by the guide's continuing persistence, finally agreed.

The incident amused Richard and made him look at the unwilling sightseer with some attention. To his surprise the man was familiar. Black slacks, dark green shirt, a jacket folded neatly over his arm, he might have been any tourist, but Richard could have sworn he had seen him before, and recently. There was something about the easy flow of his limbs as he went down the steps into the crypt that snagged a memory.

46

Five minutes later the memory crystallized. The guide, having finished his dissertation on the urn of some Austrian emperor, had turned rather abruptly and the man had moved out of his path with the quick, light movement of an athlete. And Richard remembered. He had seen him less than an hour ago. They had been on the same tram but, whereas Richard had been waiting at the stop, the other man had appeared out of nowhere and only by running hard and taking a great leap had managed to catch the tram. He had been wearing his jacket then, and a floppy hat that had covered his shaggy brown hair.

Satisfied to have placed him, Richard lost interest. He left the Cathedral and, strolling around the Stephansplatz, set off to explore the old quarter. He walked aimlessly. Enjoying the picturesque Strobelgasse, admiring the sixteenth- and seventeenth-century houses on Bäckerstrasse, and losing himself in a succession of little covered passageways, he was pleased to come unexpectedly on the Church of the Jesuits. He was feeling happier now and more relaxed; the residual memories of the meeting with Grant had at last faded. Then, suddenly, at the sight of a shaggy brown head bowed devoutly in a pew, his spirits plummeted.

Richard told himself not to be a fool. The man had as much right to be there as he did. The Jesuitenkirche was a tourist attraction, like St Stephen's Cathedral. Of course the man wasn't following him. But they did seem to be bumping into each other a lot.

Richard wasn't happy about it. He hadn't liked David Grant but he had been impressed by him. Grant, he thought, wasn't the sort to give up easily, and he would have resources. He might have arranged for Richard to be shadowed until he could have another try at making him go to Moscow. It was an unpleasant idea.

Deciding to find out if it had any basis, Richard left the Jesuitenkirche and continued his exploration. He walked casually, as if he was without a care and time was no object. On Schönlaterngasse, which was busy with sightseers and Viennese going about their daily business, he stood on the edge of the pavement as if he were about to cross the street, and looked back. His pulse quickened. Some twenty yards behind him was a man in a floppy hat. He was the right height and build, but he was wearing a bright yellow sweater and he seemed to be in conversation with an elderly woman. He was carrying a plastic shopping bag.

Richard changed his mind about crossing Schönlaterngasse. Instead, he walked on, idling, until he spotted the entrance to a narrow side-street. He was almost past it when, without warning, he changed direction and dived into it. He ran. There was a turning off to the left, no more than a passage. He took that, surprising the embrace of a couple of lovers, turned left again and found himself in a small deserted courtyard. He hid in the shadow of an archway. He didn't have to wait long.

It was the same man, the one who had taken that flying leap on to the tram and had followed him from St Stephen's Cathedral to the Church of the Jesuits. He had pulled a thin silk sweater over his green shirt and, while Richard watched, he took off his floppy hat and thrust it into the plastic bag that must already have held his jacket. He shook his shaggy head. He seemed glad to be free of the restricting hat. Then he looked slowly round the courtyard and made for the archway.

Richard didn't wait. As the man came from the light into the shadow he grabbed him by the shoulders and slammed him back against the wall. Immediately he felt the knee jack-knifing into his groin and, realizing his own stupidity, flinched from the anticipated pain. But no contact was made. The man had slumped to the ground.

He lay there cowering. '*Nein. Nein,*' he said. 'Don't hurt me, *mein Herr*. If it's money you want, here you are. Take it.' He held out his wallet. 'But please don't hurt me.'

'Stand up!'

The man stood, pressing his body against the wall so as to keep as far from Rictard as possible. He seemed to have shrunk into himself. He was a pathetic, cringing object. Only his eyes betrayed him. They were hard, shiny boot-buttons, without expression.

'Why have you been following me?' Richard spoke in German as the man had done.

'But I haven't. You're mistaken, *mein Herr*. I'm just a

tourist. I manage a small hotel in Bonn. I'm taking a vacation. I know I was with you in the Stephansdom catacombs and in the Jesuitenkirche, but I wasn't following you, *mein Herr*. I swear it. Why should I follow you?'

'What are you doing in this courtyard?'

'I lost my way. I was trying to find the Heiligenkreuzer Hof, the place where writers and artists go. Please, *mein Herr*, I assure you – '

It was a plausible story, but Richard was unconvinced. He regarded the man warily. The German – from his accent he probably was what he claimed to be – was about his own age, slightly shorter but broader, strong, well-muscled and certainly no weakling. Yet, apart from his first instinctive reaction, he hadn't put up the slightest resistance. On the contrary, he had collapsed like a pricked balloon. It was out of character.

'Would you take a message to David Grant?' Richard said, watching him closely.

'David Grant? Who is he, this David Grant? I know no one of that name, *mein Herr*.'

The response was quick, natural. But a flicker of the almost expressionless features told Richard what he wanted to know. The man was lying.

Richard said, 'Tell Grant he's wasting the tax-payers' money. I am not going to Moscow. Carey-Ford will have to die without any consolation from me.'

'But, *mein Herr* – '

'Goodbye.'

Richard turned on his heels and walked out of courtyard. Horribly conscious of the hard, button eyes boring into his exposed back, he forced himself to walk slowly. The German didn't move. But it was fortunate for Richard's peace of mind that he didn't hear the threat spat after him.

SIX

Angrily Charles Bigrel pulled off his black bow-tie and threw it on the bed. It was the second he had ruined; the first was already lying on the floor. And he owned only three that were respectable. Before her death his wife had always tied his black ties for him and seen to it that he had a good supply. Things were different now, he thought morosely.

He sighed. He didn't want to go to this Lancaster House reception tonight. It would have been much pleasanter to put his feet up on the sofa and listen to some Bach. But there was no option. It was a duty thinly disguised as pleasure and, since a minor Royal would be present, he mustn't arrive late. He approached his last tie with extreme caution.

The car was waiting at the door. The right to a chauffeured limousine was one of the perks of his job that Bigrel really appreciated. It made life infinitely easier. As the car began to move he leaned back and shut his eyes. For once, however, his habitual trick of blanking his mind and taking a cat-nap failed. His brain continued to click over like an old first-generation computer and, not for the first time recently, he wondered if he too was out-dated and should be scrapped.

The day had brought nothing but indecision and frustration. There had been no joy in Grant's report on his meeting with Richard Lavery in Vienna. According to Grant Lavery was adamant. In no circumstances would he go to Moscow. Which left Bigrel with only one alternative, to infiltrate someone – possibly David Grant himself – into the trade mission that was due in Moscow at the end of the week. He didn't like the idea a bit but, as hard as he tried, he could think of no other possibility.

'Good evening to you, Charles.' A voice hailed him as he got out of the car.

'Ah, Thomas, good evening.' Reluctantly Bigrel waited while Penryn helped his wife from the taxi and turned to pay the driver. 'Good evening, Mrs Penryn.'

'Poppy, please,' she corrected him, and offered her hand. 'Good evening, Charles.'

Charles Bigrel smiled politely. Each time he met blonde, pretty, sharp-featured Mrs Penryn – nothing on earth would make him call her by that incredibly stupid first name of hers – they went through the same rigmarole. And he knew exactly what she would say next.

She said it. 'Charles, we haven't seen you for ages. You must come and have dinner with us. Very soon. We should have asked you before this, I know, but we've been so busy with the family. We've not been entertaining at all recently. Have we, sugar?'

'No, dear, no. I'm afraid not,' Thomas Penryn agreed.

Bigrel smothered what had become a genuine smile. It was worth the minor irritation of receiving yet another never-to-be-consummated invitation from the Penryns in order to hear Thomas addressed as 'sugar'. Mrs P., he thought uncharitably, couldn't have chosen a less suitable pet-name for her husband.

As she went off to put her stole in the cloakroom, he seized the opportunity to be rid of them. 'If you'll excuse me, Thomas. I'll see you later.'

'A moment.'

One foot already on the bottom step of the grand staircase, Bigrel stopped. Penryn was plucking at his sleeve, drawing him aside, looking carefully around to make sure they couldn't be overheard. Bigrel hoped the confidence was going to be worth these precautions.

'I've some information re our friend C–F.'

'Who?'

'Charles, you know perfectly well I'm talking about Carey-Ford.' Penryn did his best to smile; Bigrel's vagaries could be very annoying sometimes. 'It appears the story going the rounds is that he's working on some top secret project. It's false. He's ill. A member of the Politburo told our ambassador at a reception last night. Quite casually. He didn't even say it was under cloaks. In fact, H.E. got the impression *Pravda* and *Izvestia* will be breaking the news any day.'

'Really?'

Bigrel was interested, more interested than he cared to show. Obviously it was a deliberate leak on the Russians' part. But why now, after all the past secrecy? He wondered if their change of policy would include allowing Carey-Ford to have visitors. If so, his immediate problem could be solved. But somehow he didn't like it. The whole thing smelt.

'Chris McCann thinks Carey-Ford's dying and the Reds intend to milk his death of everything they can get in the way of publicity,' Penryn murmured. 'He suggests a meeting tomorrow to consider the situation.'

'Right. I'll expect to hear from his secretary.'

Bigrel nodded and left Penryn, he hoped not too abruptly. Out of the corner of his eye he had sighted Mrs Penryn returning from the cloakroom, and he felt he had already done his duty by her. From now on he should, with luck, be able to avoid both the Penryns. But he would appreciate a word with McCann.

The opportunity didn't arise at once. The reception was one of those large, glittering affairs, and Bigrel knew too many people. It was some fifty minutes later, after two glasses of champagne and a peculiar conversation with the minor Royal — peculiar because a Cabinet Minister who should have known better had introduced Bigrel as 'one of our cloak-and-dagger merchants' and the Royal hadn't known how to interpret this – that he saw his chance. Chris McCann, holding his attractive young wife by the elbow, was steering her across the room to meet someone. Bigrel intercepted them.

'Charles, how very nice to see you.' Anita McCann kissed him on both cheeks. 'I'm glad you spotted us in all this crush.'

McCann smiled on them both. 'My dear, unless I'm much mistaken, Charles's eagle eye has been on the look-out for us. He wants to tell me he's too busy to attend a meeting Penryn's planning for tomorrow. Am I right, Charles?'

'Penryn? I thought it was you who – ' Bigrel began.

McCann shook his head and permitted himself a wink. 'Not guilty. But I thought we might lunch together afterwards. Just you and me?'

'That would be very nice.' Bigrel grinned his pleasure as a waiter interrupted them. 'Excuse me, sir. Mr Bigrel? Mr

Charles Bigrel?'

'Yes,' Bigrel said.

'You're wanted on the telephone. If you'll come with me, please.'

Apologizing to the McCanns, Bigrel followed the man down the wide shallow stairs and into an anteroom. He waited until he was alone and the door shut before he picked up the receiver. An irascible voice was saying 'Hello, hello, hello.' Bigrel frowned. Whatever the crisis, he couldn't imagine any of his staff sounding so impatient.

'Charles Bigrel here,' he said.

'Charles! Thank God I've got hold of you at last. It's me, Maurice Jackson. Charles, I must know. What is Richard La – '

'Be quiet!' Bigrel felt the shock waves from his own command. Biting off each word, he said, 'Maurice, this is an open line. Anyone could be listening to our conversation. Think before you speak. Better still, don't speak!'

'Yes. But – it's Emma!'

'All right.' Charles Bigrel controlled his anger. Clearly Jackson was upset, too upset to be discreet. Something would have to be done about him. 'Where are you, Maurice?'

'At the office. I was working late when Betty phoned. Why she didn't have the sense to get in touch with me as soon as she got back to London I'll never know, but –'

For a moment Bigrel couldn't place any Betty. Then he remembered; she was the girl who ran the toy-shop with Emma and presumably she knew Richard Lavery. He stopped himself from speculating. Long ago he had learnt that it was a waste of time. He said, 'Listen, Maurice. Take a taxi and go to my flat. I'll be with you as quickly as I can.'

He replaced the receiver without giving Jackson a chance to argue, and glanced at his watch. Protocol demanded that no one should leave the reception before the Royal. But to hell with protocol. His failure to return was unlikely to be noticed and if anyone did comment later he could always plead a giddy spell.

He came out of Lancaster House and hesitated under the portico. The plain-clothes man standing beside the Royal Rolls looked at him curiously. A uniformed constable stepped

53

forward, saluted and said, 'Can I help you, sir?'

'No. No, thanks. I'll be all right when I've had a breath of air. I'll go and find my driver. He'll be parked in the Mall.'

'Very good, sir.'

Bigrel walked slowly out of the courtyard and turned right. Now he was out of sight and he quickened his pace. He was trotting as he came out of Stable Yard into the Mall. Any one of a long line of parked cars might be his but he relied on the fact that Tyler, his driver, always had his wits about him. He stood under the light and waved. The response was almost immediate. Headlights blinked, and a dark shadow drew away from the kerb. Bigrel was home inside fifteen minutes.

The doorbell rang as Bigrel was putting on his old velvet smoking-jacket. He brought Maurice Jackson into the living-room, made him sit down and gave him a large whisky. He was shocked by Jackson's appearance, the heavy frown-lines on his face, the glowering anger; Maurice was usually an easy-going man. He sat himself opposite.

'You were lucky to find me, Maurice. How did you manage it?'

Jackson took a gulp of his whisky. 'Not through your bloody duty officer. He was no help. But luckily I remembered the name of your assistant, Lorna Day. Nice woman. I looked her up in the phone book and eventually I got the right Miss Day. She told me you were at Lancaster House.'

'And you thought it urgent enough to contact me there during an official reception?'

'I'd have contacted you at Buckingham Palace. Charles, Emma has disappeared. She's supposed to have joined Richard Lavery somewhere. I don't know where. It all sounds terribly unlike her and – and I don't trust that young man. Not anymore. It may be illogical but – '

'You'd better tell me exactly what's happened,' Bigrel said gently.

'I only know what Betty – Betty Acheson, the girl who runs the toy business with Emma – told me. She and Emma have been in Prague together, at the Toy Fair. They were due home today. They got to Ruzyne – that's the airport for Prague, about 10 miles outside the city – in good time, and they were waiting in the departure lounge. Everything had gone well.

Emma was in high spirits, talking about seeing Richard tonight.' Maurice Jackson paused. He was breathing heavily. 'Then a stewardess came up to them.'

'From British Airways?'

'No. From CSA. The girls were travelling on the Czech airline. She said Emma was wanted on the telephone, and Emma went off with her. She – she never came back. The flight was called. Naturally Betty got very worried. She thought Emma was going to miss the plane. She went to the enquiry desk and tried to make them grasp what had happened, but either they couldn't or they wouldn't. They told her she must board with the other passengers and she refused. She's got a lot of guts, has Betty. She said she intended to go to the British Embassy.'

'And that brought some action?'

'Seemingly, yes. There was considerable chatter, which Betty didn't understand because of course she doesn't speak the language, and some telephoning. Then the stewardess, the one who had first approached Emma, reappeared – all smiles and apologies, and with a message from Emma. According to her, Emma had changed her mind about return·ing to London and had decided instead to join her fiancé, Richard Lavery, who was on holiday in Europe.'

'Lavery knew she'd be at the airport at that time?'

'Yes. He knew which flight she was meant to be on.'

'So Betty accepted that he had phoned Emma and Emma had gone to meet him somewhere.'

'Yes, though she thought it extraordinary.'

'Why should she think it extraordinary?'

'Because it was utterly unlike Emma. She's not a casual, inconsiderate person. They'd been away a week already and she knew how much work there'd be at the shop when they got back. She and Emma had been discussing all they had to do, while they were waiting for the plane. And just to send a message was somehow terribly off-hand. Maybe she had a good reason, but why didn't she come and explain to Betty herself?'

Bigrel ignored the question. 'Anyway, Betty flew back to London, without Emma. Presumably there wasn't much else she could do. But she didn't telephone you at once. She waited until this evening. Why?'

'God knows! She said she was busy and didn't want to make a fuss unnecessarily. I think myself she was bloody stupid, but I suppose she felt Emma would be all right as long as she was with Lavery. She likes Lavery.' Jackson sounded disgusted at the idea. 'Later she began to have doubts, and got in touch with me.'

Jackson drained his glass and held it out. Charles Bigrel stood up. He poured Jackson another double whisky and helped himself to a brandy. Still standing, he warmed the bowl of the brandy balloon in the palm of his hands. He said nothing. He seemed lost in thought.

'For Christ's sake, Charles!' Jackson burst out angrily. 'Stop being so bloody enigmatic and tell me what you think has happened.'

'I think she's gone to Vienna, where Richard Lavery's spending a couple of weeks with an old school friend,' he said quietly.

'Vienna! But you told me everything was going to be all right. You said once Lavery knew about Carey-Ford he'd leave Emma alone. Now you tell me he's persuaded her to go to Vienna. He'll have her in Russia next, with that unspeakable father of his.'

As if to emphasize what he was saying Jackson swallowed the rest of his whisky and banged the glass down on the table beside him. Bigrel wondered how much he had had to drink before coming to the flat. At least the spare bed was made up. Jackson could stay overnight.

He said, 'Maurice, I made you no promise. I arranged for Richard Lavery to be told about his father, and he reacted as – from what I'd learnt about him – I foresaw. He broke off his engagement to Emma. I know that definitely. I suspect there's a letter waiting for her at the shop. Then he went off to stay with the Denvilles. Peter Denville's a First Secretary at the British Embassy in Vienna. Why Lavery's changed his mind and asked Emma to join him there, I've no idea.' A fleeting thought of David Grant crossed Bigrel's mind. Grant had admitted that he and Lavery had clashed. Possibly there was a connection here. But he didn't intend to discuss it with Jackson. 'However, I'm certain of one thing. Richard Lavery has no intention of departing to Moscow, either with or without Emma. You can rest assured of that.'

'Well, thank God! But something's going on in your intelligence racket. Don't pretend there isn't, Charles. I know! And if it concerns Lavery, it concerns Emma, and I've got a right to be told.'

Bigrel sipped his brandy, covering his hesitation. This was a twist he didn't like. He reminded himself that Maurice Jackson, who was nobody's fool, knew him very well. They had been friends for a long time. He would have to be careful.

He said, 'Honestly, I don't know what you're talking about but, whatever it is, we'll get down to it in a minute. First, there are some things to be settled. Have you told Helen you're spending the night in town? You'll stay here with me, of course. Have you had any dinner? And would you like to help yourself to a drink while I rustle up some food?'

Jackson gave him a long, quizzical look. 'I would like drink and food and to spend the night. Helen's not expecting me. I told her I had to work late and would sleep at the club. I didn't want to worry her. But what I'd like most is to telephone these Denville people and speak to Emma myself. That would make me feel a lot happier, Charles.'

'I dare say, but I haven't their number. And it won't be easy to get it so late in the evening. Maurice, leave it till tomorrow, there's a good chap. Emma won't thank you for interfering, you know, and the less fuss you make, the better.'

Maurice Jackson sighed and pinched the bridge of his nose as if he had a headache. 'I suppose you're right,' he said at last. 'At least I know where she is. That's a blessed relief.'

'Good. I'm sure it's a wise decision.' Bigrel nodded, pleased. 'I'm off to the kitchen. Help yourself to whatever you want and make yourself comfortable. I won't be long.'

'Thanks.'

If Bigrel had hoped for a minute or two by himself to consider what Jackson had been telling him, he was disappointed. He had scarcely cracked the eggs for the omelette when his guest appeared. Glass in one hand, Jackson lounged in the doorway.

'Charles, are you or aren't you prepared to tell me what's going on? Why, for instance, is Thomas Penryn interested in

Richard Lavery?'

With great care Bigrel pulled the edges of the omelette away from the sides of the pan. This was the difficult bit, and he concentrated on his cooking. When he spoke it was casually, over his shoulder. His voice was quite level.

'I didn't know he was.'

'I can assure you he is. I was in the Garrick yesterday. I'm not a member. I was waiting for a friend. And they called me over, offered me a drink.'

'They?'

'Chris McCann was with Penryn. Actually, I think he was the host. They were talking about that dissident Russian scientist, Dmitri Sholatov. There was a sort of obit on him in *Pravda*. I expect you saw it. He died, weeks ago – took his own life, according to officialdom – but the news has only just been released.'

'Yes. I saw it.' Bigrel was making a great commotion, laying two places and muttering to himself. 'Knives, forks, bread, butter, cheese, and the omelette. We'll eat in here if you don't mind, Maurice. I often do when I'm busy. It saves trouble. Now – we need some wine.'

Throwing off his butcher's apron, Bigrel produced glasses, opened a bottle of Tavel and sat himself down at the kitchen table. He didn't bother to taste the wine, but he sampled the omelette carefully. It was very good, crisp on the outside, moist in the middle. He smiled across at Maurice Jackson.

'You were about to tell me why you thought Penryn was interested in Richard Lavery,' he said.

'Sorry. My mind went off at a tangent. You know – Lavery, Carey-Ford, Russian scientists, people like Sholatov, so many of them Jews.' Jackson grinned ruefully. He had drunk too much. It was foolish of him. But then he'd been bloody worried about Emma, still was, for that matter. 'Funny thing, that's the way Penryn's mind seemed to work, in reverse. We were talking about Russian science and what it owed to the Jews and from there he went on to Carey-Ford and Richard Lavery. He asked me a hell of a lot of questions about the Laverys. McCann told him not to be so inquisitive. I think he saw I was embarrassed. Of course, it could have been just curiosity, but . . . '

It was the 'but' that kept Charles Bigrel awake long after Jackson was snoring his head off in the guest room. Thomas Penryn was a curious man and he had few social graces. His idea of being friendly was to ask personal questions. Bigrel had suffered this trait of Penryn himself; an intensely private person, it was one of the reasons he disliked the man. Nevertheless, it was a very big 'but'.

SEVEN

Peter Denville regarded his **ambassador** with round-faced disbelief. 'He wants to ask *me* some questions?'

'He does.' Sir William was terse. 'You know who Charles Bigrel is?'

'Yes, sir. He's the Director-General of – '

'Then pick up at that receiver and say good morning to him. And, Peter – '

'Yes, sir.'

'You're not only to tell him the truth, you're to be as helpful as you can. Is that understood?'

Peter Denville nodded miserably. A normally well-contented and self-possessed young man, His Excellency always made him feel as if he were back at his prep. school, either being reproached by Matron for having wet his bed, or threatened with dire consequences if he dared to commit such an offence. He wished he could be left alone to speak to Charles Bigrel, but there wasn't a hope of that. Sir William showed no sign of moving from behind his desk.

Denville sat on the straight-backed chair to which Sir William was pointing, picked up the phone, and said good morning. A female voice asked him to wait, but he didn't have to wait long. Charles Bigrel came on the line almost immediately.

Wasting scant time on pleasantries, Bigrel said: 'I need to ask you some questions, Denville. Some of them may be unexpected, but I assure you they're important, extremely important. First, is Emma Jackson staying with you?'

'Emma Jackson?' Peter swallowed his surprise. 'No, sir.'

'Are you expecting her? Do you know where she is?'

'No – no, sir. She's been in Prague, at a toy fair, I understand, but she ought to be back in London by now.'

'I see.' There was a pause. 'Then you've no reason to believe she has come or intends to come to Vienna.'

'No.'

'But Richard Lavery's your house guest. When's he leaving you?'

'Richard? I – I'm not sure. I expect him to stay for at least a week, and he only arrived on Saturday.'

'Did you know that he telephoned Emma Jackson yesterday morning while she was waiting at Prague airport and asked her to meet him – presumably in Vienna?'

'No! No, I didn't. What's more, I don't believe it. He – ' A warning cough from Sir William reminded Peter that he wasn't being exactly tactful. He added hurriedly, 'I'm sorry, sir, but – but I find it very difficult to accept what you've just said.'

'Why?'

'Because – ' Denville hesitated, trying to assemble his thoughts, sensing that his answer was vital, but determined to say nothing that might harm Richard. 'My wife's away at present, sir, and last night Richard and I stayed up talking until the small hours. Naturally we talked about Emma. He was – worried about her, wondering how she'd react to his letter. He'd written to her before he left London to say he'd changed his mind and wasn't prepared to marry her after all. He was pretty upset, himself. He – sir, everything he said would have been a nonsense if he'd already made plans to meet her somewhere.'

'Yes.' It was almost a sigh and was followed by an appreciable silence.

'Could you – could you tell me what's happened, sir?'

'I was asked to make enquiries by Emma's father, who's a friend of mine. He's concerned about her because she seems to have disappeared. She was called to the phone at Ruzyne Airport, failed to catch her flight and hasn't been heard from since.'

'And you thought Richard – Christ!' Denville was too upset to be aware of Sir William's disapproval of the expletive. 'He knows nothing about it. I'm sure, sir. Can I tell him? He's terribly in love with her still and he'll be demented, but I think he ought to know.'

'Ye – es. All right.' Bigrel's hesitation was minimal; whatever he said, Denville would still tell Lavery. 'But don't let him panic. She's probably been held up by emigration or customs. The Czechs are a fussy lot. It's very easy to do the wrong thing as far as they're concerned. The telephone call could merely have been a pretext to stop the friend she was travelling with from interfering. Anyway, I'll sort it out.'

That was pretty weak, he thought to himself as he put down the receiver, but it was the best he could do. He hoped and prayed he would be able to sort it out. Misled by the mention of Richard Lavery's name he had already jumped to one wrong conclusion. He couldn't afford to make another mistake, not where the girl who wanted to marry Carey-Ford's son was concerned.

Richard Lavery sat in the glassed-in apron of the restaurant where he had arranged to lunch with Peter Denville. Peter was late, and while he waited Richard ordered himself a bowl of Lugenstrudel soup. He was savouring its delicacy when he was suddenly aware of being watched. The watcher, a small boy in jeans and a T-shirt, was standing almost at Richard's elbow on the pavement outside the restaurant. Their eyes met and the urchin, nose pressed against the glass that separated them, licked his lips with a long, pointed tongue. The gesture was unmistakable. Richard had to laugh.

Taking this as an invitation the boy sidled along the front of the building to the door of the restaurant. Here he lingered until all the waiters seemed occupied. Then he whisked among the tables and slid into the chair that awaited Peter Denville's arrival.

'Good?' He pointed at the soup. 'Very good?' He spoke in English, guessing that Richard was either American or British.

'Very good indeed.' Richard grinned. 'Here. Why don't you finish it for me?' He passed the plate across the table.

The boy started on the soup, eagerly and noisily. Richard watched him with amusement. He was a skinny child with a thin, pale face, but he wasn't uncared for. His hair was well-brushed, his clothes clean. He didn't look like a professional beggar.

There was a roar of anger from across the restaurant. In one concerted movement the boy swallowed his last mouthful, wriggled out of his chair and bolted, seizing a sweet pastry from the trolley of *Mehlspeise* as he passed. The waiter, encumbered by a laden tray, was helpless. He swallowed his wrath as best he could and hurried over to Richard.

'*Mein Herr*, I apologize. He's incorrigible, that rascal, incorrigible. I hope he didn't annoy you too much.'

'You know him?'

'Alas, yes, *mein Herr*. He is the son of the chef, a good man but a widower, and he cannot control the boy who is always in trouble.' The waiter balanced his tray on the edge of Richard's table and made to reach underneath. 'You have dropped something, *mein Herr*.'

Richard Lavery pushed back his chair and picked up the picture postcard lying at his feet. It was brightly coloured, of the kind that tourists buy by the million every year to send home to friends and relatives. This one depicted the famous Johann Strauss monument in the Stadtpark.

About to deny that it was his, Richard turned the postcard over. In the space reserved for the address two words were written – 'Herr Lavery'. The boy must have been bribed to deliver it to him.

'If there is anything you want before your friend arrives, *mein Herr* – '

Richard's eye flicked over the message beside his name. 'No. No. Nothing, thanks.'

The waiter departed to his other customers and Richard reread the postcard. 'If you still care for Emma Jackson you should be at the foot of the great Ferris wheel in the *Prater* at 15.30 hours today. Emma is in danger and needs your help. Grant.'

Fear for Emma flared, and died in disbelief. Anger filled Richard. This was some stupid trick of Grant's. The man was mad, unreal. He wouldn't accept that Richard wasn't going on any ludicrous errand to Carey-Ford. He persisted, only proving how right Richard had been in the first place to refuse to take part in his wild schemes.

Again and again Richard tore the postcard across until he was left with a kaleidoscopic heap of coloured pieces. But it did little to relieve his feelings. He was still seething with irritation when he saw Peter Denville come through the door of the restaurant. Hurriedly, not wanting to explain, he swept the bits on to the floor. The waiter could think what he liked.

'Sorry I'm late, Richard. I couldn't get away.'

'That's all right. I've ordered – *Tafelspitz mit Apfelkern*, and no fried potatoes for you. Okay?'

'Fine. Let's have a bottle of wine with it.'

Normally Peter never drank with lunch; he said it made him sleepy during the afternoon. Richard didn't comment. He was too absorbed by his own problems to notice his friend's tension and anxiety. And Peter had decided to wait until the coffee stage before telling Richard of his conversation with Charles Bigrel. The result was a silent meal, broken by sporadic bursts of superficial conversation. Neither of them enjoyed it or appreciated the food or the wine.

Oddly enough it was Richard, the more closely involved of the two, who provided the catalyst. Peter, monotonously stirring his sugarless coffee, was startled when Richard asked if he had had a bad morning.

'It shows, does it?' He tried to smile. 'Yes. It's been ghastly. But I thought we'd better eat before I told you about it.'

'Your usual nice sense of priorities.'

Peter ignored the pleasantry. 'Richard, do you know who Charles Bigrel is?' he asked abruptly.

'Never heard of him.'

'He's the head of SIS – the head of the secret service, if you like. Officially he's attached to the FCO but, in many ways, he's a law unto himself. He's very high-powered indeed. He telephoned me this morning to ask questions about you and – and Emma. He seemed to think you might have asked her to come to Vienna.'

'Really?' Richard's voice was contained and cold. 'I hope you denied it.'

Peter stared at him. 'You don't sound madly surprised.'

'I'm not. As I said, I've never heard of Charles Bigrel, but I know a guy called David Grant and, if Bigrel's the big white chief, Grant must work for him.'

'He never mentioned any Grant, but he told me – Richard, Emma's disappeared. No one knows what's happened to her. Yesterday . . . '

Richard Lavery listened, his thin intelligent face set, his mouth a determined line. Under the table his shoe moved against the torn bits of the postcard the small boy had delivered. The postcard had said Emma was in danger. He hadn't believed it. He didn't believe it now. It was nonsense. There was a limit to how far Bigrel and his minions would go. But she was probably being inconvenienced and caused distress. Damn them to hell! How dared they interfere with Emma in any way. He would have to convince them, once and for all, that he would not do what they wanted.

He would go to the Prater this afternoon, though it was unlikely much good would come of it. Grant hadn't believed him before, and the message he had sent by the shaggy-haired German who had followed him around the city on Monday had achieved nothing. But at least he knew now that Charles Bigrel was the man in charge. Richard looked speculatively at Peter Denville's round, anxious face.

'Do you know how to get in touch with this Bigrel?'

'There's no point, Richard. You must be worried sick. I realize that. But he's promised to sort it out and we'll be told as soon as there's any news.'

'Very kind of him.' Richard made no attempt to hide his sarcasm. 'The truth is he's playing games with me, Peter. Emma's all right. Bigrel may or may not be a friend of Maurice Jackson as he claims, but Jackson's a senior man in the Ministry of Defence and Bigrel wouldn't dare put her at any risk.'

'Bigrel wouldn't – What on earth are you talking about?'

'Blackmail.'

'What?'

'Blackmail. I'm sure they'd avoid the word, but that's what it amounts to,' Richard said bitterly. 'This man Grant has been doing his best to cajole me into taking on a job for them. I've refused. Now – '

'What job? You never mentioned a job last night.' Peter's voice was a mixture of curiosity and disbelief. 'Is it – is it something to do with Carey-Ford?'

'Why should it be?'

'Because why should they be interested in Richard Lavery, solicitor, otherwise?'

Richard looked at Peter in exasperation, regretting his confidences. He said coldly, 'What I told you last night was personal. This is different. I can't talk about it, so please don't ask questions. But, if you're prepared to do me a favour, ring up that shit Bigrel and tell him I will *not* be blackmailed into going to – to – ' He drew a deep breath. ' – into cooperating in his crazy scheme.'

'Richard – for Christ's sake! I can't do that.' Peter Denville was aghast. He didn't know what to think. 'Look, you may be right. Bigrel may be a shit. But you can't seriously believe he's kidnapped Emma so as to force you – '

'Why not?'

They argued with surprising acrimony until Peter suddenly became aware of the time. 'I'll have to go, Richard. I'm late already and I've a mountain of work to do. Will you pay the bill and we'll settle up tonight. Is that okay?'

Richard nodded, tried to grin. He was more angry with himself than with Peter. None of this was Peter's fault. 'Sure. Don't work too hard.' He signalled to the waiter. '*Herr Ober!*'

Five minutes later Richard was in a taxi on his way to the Prater.

It was a beautiful afternoon, the sky pale blue with an occasional white billowy cloud, the sun surprisingly warm. Richard Lavery, early for his appointment, dismissed the taxi and walked about the park. In other circumstances he would have enjoyed it. Today he repeatedly caught himself darting suspicious glances around him. It was a reflex action. It didn't really matter if someone was following him. He had every intention of being under the giant Ferris wheel at precisely half past three.

His anger had abated, and he was aware only of tension, nervousness. But his determination hadn't faltered. He just wished that thoughts of Emma wouldn't keep intruding. She would have loved the gaiety, the fair-like atmosphere of the Prater. She would have insisted on doing everything, the roundabout, the dodgem cars, the ghost train, the centrifuge and – greatest thrill of all – the sick-making Ferris wheel.

Turning sharply away from the pavement artist he had been watching, Richard knocked against a small child clutching an ice-cream. The cone went flying. It landed squarely on the artist's drawing, spattering the whole picture. The child began to cry, loudly and violently. The mother protested at Richard's clumsiness. The artist demanded recompense for his ruined work. A small, unfriendly crowd began to gather.

Richard, embarrassed and on the defensive, handed out money. The mother went off with her screaming child to buy another ice-cream cone. The artist wasn't so easily satisfied. He said he hadn't been given enough. There was an angry argument, some of the bystanders now on Richard's side. It ended when Richard thrust more money at the man in order to escape.

The incident had consumed time. Glancing at his watch Richard saw that it was a few minutes to three-thirty. A spasm of anxiety seized him. He didn't want to draw attention to himself by running, but he walked fast, and he was sweating when he reached the foot of the Riesenrad. Here he came to an abrupt halt. He had no idea who he was to meet; it didn't have to be Grant, in spite of the postcard's signature. He stood, feeling conspicuous and scanning the faces of everyone who strolled past for a sign of recognition. No one paid him any attention.

Nearby the great Ferris wheel was revolving very slowly as its cars were filled with eager thrill-seekers. Richard didn't envy them. It wasn't his idea of fun. He disliked heights. For the fifth or sixth time he looked at his watch.

It was three-thirty-five and the last car had come round ready for loading. The wheel was still. The attendant seemed to be arguing with some would-be passengers. He too was consulting his watch. Richard decided that as soon as the wheel started to revolve again he would leave.

'Come, *mein Herr*, I have paid for us.'

A hand gripped Richard's elbow and he felt himself being propelled forward, up the steps and into the waiting car. He had barely collapsed on to the seat, his companion beside him, when the Ferris wheel began to move. Within seconds they had swung thirty feet above the ground and Richard grabbed the rail beside him. He gritted his teeth. He wasn't going to enjoy this.

'Damn you,' he said. 'I might have known it would be you.'

The German laughed. 'What have you to complain of, *mein Herr*. A free ride on the Riesenrad. Many would envy you such pleasure.'

'Not if they had to share it with you.'

'Ah, naturally you would prefer to be with Fräulein Jackson, but she is—otherwise occupied. You'll have to be content with me.'

The wheel gathered speed, and the remark Richard had been about to make was cut short. The German appeared unperturbed. He ran his hand through his shaggy hair and grinned unpleasantly at Richard. His teeth were very white.

'This is a good place for us to talk. Most private.'

'I did my talking to you yesterday morning, when you were pretending to be a tourist.'

'That was different. I had my instructions. Today we are — shall I say? — on more equal terms. I no longer have to pretend.'

Richard half turned in his seat and fixed his eyes on the German. Anything was better than looking outwards, where earth was giving way to sky and ground rushing away from him. There was nothing he could do about his inside. He was already feeling queasy. The bloody man had the advantage of him. He concentrated his anger.

'I don't know who you are and I don't care. You're not important, *mein Herr*. You're only a messenger-boy. And I want you to take a message, the same message I gave you on Monday afternoon. Tell your master I will not go to Moscow for him.'

'You can tell him yourself when we get off the Riesenrad—if you still wish to do so. Somehow I don't think you will, not when you've heard what I have to say about Fräulein Jackson.'

'I'm not interested.'

'No? I can't accept you mean that, *mein Herr*. The prisons in Czechoslovakia are not pleasant places. The Czechs don't believe in pampering their prisoners. When she's released in ten or fifteen years, you won't recognize Fräulein Jackson. Your Emma won't be the beautiful, healthy girl she is now.'

Richard tried to laugh, but bile rose in his throat and he

gagged. 'You're wasting your time. I don't believe Emma Jackson's in prison in Prague or anywhere else. This is a disgusting little trick your master has thought up and I'm not – '

'Going to Moscow.' The German finished the sentence for him. 'I know. You're a stubborn man, *mein Herr* – and wrong-headed. Perhaps you won't go to the USSR. That will be up to you. But if you refuse, Emma Jackson will suffer. Make no mistake about that. At present she is charged with infringing Czech currency regulations. It's a serious offence, but it could be smoothed over – put down to an error on the part of some petty official, maybe. However, if the charge of drug-smuggling is added, everything becomes more complicated and of a magnitude of importance fifty times greater, including the penalty.'

'Don't be absurd!' Richard said.

He glared at the German, hating him. Somehow, in spite of the ludicrousness of what the man had said, his words carried conviction. Butterflies of doubt fluttered in Richard's mind, only to be suppressed. However powerful Charles Bigrel might be and whatever strings he might pull, he neither could nor would arrange to have Maurice Jackson's daughter incarcerated in a Czech prison on a trumped-up charge. The whole thing was phoney, a stupid attempt at blackmail.

'I repeat what I've said before, to David Grant and to you. The answer is *no*.'

'Emma Jackson means nothing to you?'

'The pack of lies you've just told me means nothing to me.'

'They're not lies, *mein Herr*. I swear it. What more can I do? How can I convince you?'

'You can't! But you could try to convince Charles Bigrel. For the last time, I'm not going to change my mind. I'm not going to Moscow. Tell him that.'

'Charles Bigrel?'

Richard scarcely heard the words, though there was no doubt what they were. The thick lips had formed them perfectly. And utter astonishment illuminated the German's face. Then it went blank, wiped of all expression. Richard shut his eyes.

Their car had reached its apogee. It was at the top of the

giant wheel, the ground seemingly a mile below. It swung over the top, hesitated and started to fall back to earth. The occupants were shrieking and screaming with delight, but Richard sat in grim silence, eyes tightly closed, teeth clenched, body tensed, praying he wouldn't be sick.

'*Mein Herr! Mein Herr!*'

The German was shaking his arm. Richard swore and pulled free. He swallowed his saliva. There was sweat on his brow and upper lip. He wiped it away with his wrist. He forced himself to take long, deep breaths. They were nearer the ground now, the motion like that of a lift uncertain which floor to stop at.

'Didn't you hear what I said?' The German was impatient.
'No!'

'You're not well? The Riesenrad doesn't agree with you?'
'Vertigo. I've no head for heights. You didn't know?'

The German shook his head contemptuously. 'We are efficient, *mein Herr*, but not omniscient, and there's not been much time to enquire into your likes and dislikes. I chose the Riesenrad because it was a private place to talk and you couldn't walk off in the middle of our conversation.' He pulled the red sweat scarf from round his neck and waved it from the window.

'What are you doing?'
'Signalling. I made an – arrangement before we started.'
'I see.'

'Of course, we've not had our money's worth yet. If you'd like to go round again . . . '
'Christ, no!'

The German chuckled. Suddenly he seemed to be in a good humour. Richard didn't care. The bloody wheel was slowing, coming to a halt. Thankfully he allowed himself to be helped from the car and down the steps. He felt like an old man or a drunk, unable to control his legs. He was glad to lean on the German.

People were staring, wondering why the Riesenrad had stopped to let off two men and then restarted. Richard looked away as it began to gather speed. Now he was on the ground he felt better almost at once, but he didn't argue when the German suggested they should sit on the grass.

70

'It's better we should finish our conversation here, *mein Herr*, where you can concentrate on what I'm saying. We are a little early for our appointment.'

'What appointment?'

'I told you we were to meet – my master, as you like to call him. He will confirm everything I've told you about Fräulein Jackson, and you can tell him whether you are prepared to cooperate with us or not.'

'Do you mean that Charles Bigrel is actually in Vienna?'

'Bigrel? No. Not Bigrel.' The German was amused, though his amusement didn't reach to his hard brown eyes.

'Who then? Grant?'

The German shook his head gently, as if he were enjoying himself. '*Mein Herr*, we've been at cross purposes. I didn't realize you still thought I worked for the British intelligence service. I don't. I come from the DDR – the *Deutsche Demokratische Republik* – East Germany, as you call it. I am a good communist. And the man you are about to meet is Comrade Igor Goransky, a most senior officer of the Russian KGB. I'm afraid you will have to rethink some of your ideas, *mein Herr*.'

EIGHT

Richard Lavery walked through the Prater with the German from the DDR. His mind was in a turmoil. Although he knew with a cold, despairing fury that it was the truth, he didn't want to believe what he had been told. It made no sense that the communists should have seized Emma in order to persuade him to – do what? The West had wanted him to go Moscow and talk to Carey-Ford. What did the East want? That too had to be connected somehow with Carey-Ford. Silently Richard cursed the man who was his father.

Whatever it was they wanted he would have to go along with them. There was no alternative. The German had meant what he said about Emma. She would spend years in prison if he told them to go to hell. It didn't matter that she was innocent. He had read in the newspapers of people to whom this sort of thing had happened and he had been indifferent. But this was Emma. Torture. Solitary confinement. Hunger. Thirst. Degradation. Absolute despair. The words were real to him now. The pain of them was in his head.

'There's the café, *mein Herr*. You'll find Comrade Goransky inside.'

'How will I know him?'

'He'll recognize you, the same way as I and others have recognized you – and Fräulein Jackson. From copies of the photographs in your London flat.'

'You mean it was you who broke in and – '

'Not personally. My associates.' The German grinned mockingly. 'Did you blame Herr Bigrel for that as well?'

Richard didn't answer. It was true he had accused David Grant. Grant had denied it, swept the accusation aside as irrelevant, and Richard hadn't believed him. Perhaps more important, he hadn't believed what Charles Bigrel had said on the phone to Peter this morning. Misled by Grant's supposed signature on the postcard and his own stupidity, he had

72

jumped to the wrong conclusion and, in spite of Peter's arguments, stuck to it. Not that it made any difference now.

Conscious of the German's hard brown eyes probing the back of his head, as if to anticipate him should he decide to make a run for it or throw himself into the murky waters of the Danube, Richard walked the last twenty-five yards to the café alone. The tables under the red and white striped canopy were busy with eager patrons, but he ignored them. As he hesitated in the doorway of the building itself a man lifted a rolled-up newspaper from the chair beside him and waved it to draw Richard's attention. Richard went across to him.

'Good afternoon, Mr Lavery. I'm so glad you've come.' His English was almost accentless. 'Do sit down. You'll have coffee and cakes?' Without waiting for an answer he signalled to a waiter.

Igor Goransky was in his early fifties, a small, dapper figure, his neat beard tinged with grey. There were laughter wrinkles at the sides of his eyes and his mouth was generous. One could picture him in private life as a kind, indulgent husband and father, and in public life as a distinguished diplomat. He was in fact, unmarried and an ambitious, ruthless KGB officer. And, though he didn't show it, he was afraid. He thought it possible – not probable, but possible – that he had made a terrible, ghastly mistake, the sort of mistake for which there could be no forgiveness.

'Franz explained the situation to you?'

'If Franz is the name of that shaggy-haired, boot-button-eyed East German who's been following me around Vienna, yes.'

The Russian permitted himself a small smile at the description. The Englishman wasn't lacking in courage, and he admired that. The girl too, he had heard, had expressed her feelings vociferously and without fear. He held up a warning hand as Richard opened his mouth to speak. The waiter was approaching with the glasses of water that inevitably precede every order in a Viennese café.

When they were alone again, Goransky said, 'It's not as bad as it seems, Mr Lavery. A little cooperation from you, and Emma Jackson will be released immediately with profuse apologies for the inconvenience she has been caused. Meanwhile, though very angry, she's being well cared for.'

'What sort of cooperation?'

Goransky nodded approvingly. 'Good. You're being sensible. You didn't bother to ask what would happen to her if you decided to wash your hands of the whole affair.'

'Your comrade, Franz, explained.'

'Ah, yes. Crudely, I'm sure. Franz Baucher is apt to be crude.'

'You haven't answered my question.'

'About cooperation? No.' Goransky took a sip of water. 'It's really extremely simple. Your father, Guy Carey-Ford, is ill. He has terminal cancer and, not unnaturally, he would like to see his son – his only son – before he dies. Since we've obtained so many benefits from his work in the past, we would like to arrange for his last wish to be gratified. That's all there is to it.'

Goransky spoke gently and with quiet sincerity, but his gaze never left Richard's face. He hadn't needed the photograph. The physical likeness between this young man and the English traitor was extraordinary. Goransky smiled ironically to himself. He had his own set of morals, and any man who betrayed his country, whatever advantages the Soviet Union might gain from it, was to him a traitor. He wondered if the son resembled the father in more ways than appearance. And suddenly, thinking of treachery, he remembered the other traitor – the Russian Jew, Dmitri Sholatov. It was a pity, a great pity that Sholatov had succeeded in killing himself before he could be made to talk.

Richard tried to hide his astonishment. It was unbelievable, the blackest of black jokes, that the Intelligence services of both West and East should be so keen for him to visit Carey-Ford. He said, 'And what about Emma Jackson? When will she be released?'

'As soon as you agree to do what we ask.'

'Is it really as simple as that?'

'Not quite, perhaps.' The Russian gave a shrug. 'You're an intelligent man, Mr Lavery. You'll appreciate that there are certain practicalities which will have to be attended to.'

The arrival of the waiter with the *Jause* saved Richard from answering, and he took his time choosing among the rich cream cakes. He was trying very hard to think clearly and logically. He knew that he was out of his depth, that he was dealing with people he didn't understand, whose values were different from his, whose motives were incomprehensible. He couldn't hope to outsmart them. Nevertheless, he had to try to bargain, not for himself but for Emma, and that meant seeking every advantage he could. Perhaps he could get Goransky to talk a little more . . .

Playing with the cake on his plate, Richard said, 'It should have been simple, Mr Goransky. Surely the only problem was a visa, and you could have provided that. Why didn't you just get one of your people to explain that my – my father was dying and wanted me to visit him?'

'That's what we intended to do, but we were told that you had refused to go at Mr Bigrel's request, and it seemed unlikely that you would oblige us.' Goransky stirred the whipped cream into his *Einspanner* and sipped it. 'Or was that different? Was that because you didn't want to be a spy?'

'I – I don't know what you mean.'

'Come, Mr Lavery. Let's not play games. Your SIS suspect that Guy Carey-Ford has had a change of heart – or should I say a change of politics? They're wrong, of course, as they are so often. He hasn't repented of his treachery. He's not going to reveal some great Soviet secret on his deathbed, to you or anyone else from the West. He'll die, as he's lived for most of his life, a good communist. Bigrel's a fool if he believes the contrary.'

Goransky, who had been leaning across the table towards Richard, made himself sit back and relax. He had been horrified by the overtones of frustrated anger – or was it fear? – that he had heard in his own voice. He would have to watch himself. Luckily young Lavery was inexperienced. He managed to smile.

'You must be surprised how well informed I am,' he said genially. 'I'll let you into a secret. David Grant has a girlfriend with expensive tastes, and sometimes he talks in his sleep.'

Richard didn't respond to this wolfish humour. Goransky was right; he was shaken by the extent of the Russian's knowledge. But somehow he didn't believe that Grant was its source.

Pushing away his coffee-glass and the plate with its

uneaten cream cake, he said, 'What do you want me to do?'

Goransky gave him a searching look. 'Ah, yes, the practicalities I was talking about. They're not complicated. We'll drive you back to Peter Denville's apartment so that you can pack up your clothes and leave him an explanatory note. We'll spend the night with Franz. Then tomorrow we'll fly to Moscow. Your father is very seriously ill, and we don't have time to waste.'

'Go on.'

Goransky shrugged. 'What more do you want to know?'

Richard didn't reply at once. Momentarily he had forgotten what he intended to say. A sudden thought had come to him. Emma had been kidnapped in order to put pressure on him, but it would have been just as easy and much less complex not to have bothered with her, but merely to have seized him and taken him forcibly to Moscow. Why hadn't they done this? He wondered that the question hadn't occurred to him before.

'Are you thinking of Emma Jackson, Mr Lavery?'

'Yes. Earlier you talked of cooperation. Okay, I'll cooperate. I'll go to Moscow with you. I'll visit the hospital. I'll be as nice to Carey-Ford as I can bring myself to be – nicer. I'll do all this willingly and cheerfully. I give you my word on it. But –'

'Ah, the but. There's always a but.' Goransky stroked his bearded chin thoughtfully. 'Tell me what yours is, Mr Lavery.'

'You must satisfy me, before I leave Vienna, that Emma is free and absolutely safe. Otherwise, Mr Goransky, I don't go with you – not voluntarily.'

Richard was shocked by the hard, brittle edge on his voice. He hadn't intended to challenge the Russian. It wasn't that he lacked the courage, but the situation had seemed so hopeless. Now, having found a possible weakness in his opponent's strategy, he had rammed home his attack without considering the consequences. He hoped Goransky couldn't hear the pounding of his heart in the silence that followed.

At last Goransky said, 'You don't trust me. Why should I trust you? Because you've given your word?'

'I shall be under your orders, in your country. If I don't behave myself when we're in Moscow, you can always have me thrown in the river.'

Goransky spluttered with laughter. 'I like you, Richard. I really do. I may call you Richard?' He didn't wait for an answer. 'And you must call me Igor. But, you know, you read too many books.'

'I never read fiction,' said Richard.

'All right. All right,' Goransky said, laughing again. 'I'll arrange for Emma Jackson's release today, and you can speak to her on the telephone yourself. In return you'll come to Moscow with me and do your best to comfort your poor, dying father. If not I have your permission to push you into the Moskva. Is that a gentleman's agreement, Richard?'

It was such a ridiculous question, here in a Viennese café, amid happy family parties enjoying their *Jause*, and the world apparently normal. Richard felt unstrung. But unbelievably he heard himself say, 'Yes – a gentleman's agreement.' And over the remains of the cream cakes and coffee he shook hands with Igor Goransky.

Peter Denville got home soon after seven. He let himself into the apartment and was surprised to find everything in darkness. Automatically he switched on the hall light and called out to Richard, thinking he might have fallen asleep. When there was no answer, he went though into the living-room, turning on more lights.

He saw the envelope immediately. It was a heavy cream envelope and had almost certainly come from Louise's writing desk. It was propped up on the long coffee-table that stretched in front of the sofa. He stared at the one word on it – Peter – and wondered why he had such a sense of apprehension.

The letter written on matching paper wasn't short. Yet it seemed to have been written in a hurry. It read:

Dear Pete,

Forgive me for departing somewhat unexpectedly but I'm feeling terribly restless and I thought it would be a good idea if I continued my travels. I'm sure you'll understand. Many thanks for your hospitality, which I've enjoyed immensely. I'm sorry to have missed

Louise. Please give her my love and say I hope to see her – and you again – soon. Perhaps we can all get together on your next leave.

Yours ever, Dick.

The seconds ticked away as Peter Denville sat frowning at the letter in his hand. His reaction was that Richard had had an irresistible urge to go to Prague to see if he could find out anything about Emma. This would have been understandable. Even his failure to be explicit could be put down to the fact that over lunch they had almost quarrelled about the reasons for Emma's disappearance. Richard, accepting that he was part of the establishment, might not have wanted to involve him anymore.

But why had Richard signed himself 'Dick'? Never, during all the years they had known each other, had he called Richard anything but Richard, nor had Richard called him anything but Peter. Suddenly he peered at the curiously stilted note. He couldn't be sure, but what he had taken to be an 'r' at the end of his name now looked like a scrawled comma. Picking up the envelope that had fallen to the floor he saw that it was clearly addressed to 'Pete'. He had read it as Peter because that was what he had expected to see.

Why? What was Richard trying to tell him? Thoughtfully Peter got up and poured himself a whisky. As he added the soda his hand shook so that the glass juddered against the nozzle of the siphon. He could only think of one faintly credible explanation. Richard wanted him to know that this wasn't a normal letter – that he had been coerced into writing it, before he disappeared like Emma.

Scarcely aware of what he was doing, Peter wandered, drink in hand, through the apartment. In the guest-room he stood and stared about him. Everything looked neat, tidy, impersonal. There was no sign that Richard had ever occupied the room. Nevertheless Peter began to make a thorough search.

At first it was unproductive. The drawers allotted to guests were empty, as was the space in the fitted cupboard, mostly taken up by the overflow of Louise's clothes. Idly he pushed the hangers along the rail so that her dresses, several of them

78

long, wouldn't be squashed. At once he spotted the briefcase in the corner. Crouching, he pulled it out.

The initials 'R.L.' showed it was Richard's. It wasn't locked, but the contents were surprising – a book of travellers' cheques and a bottle of prescription capsules.

Peter's fears were confirmed. Richard wasn't a careless man, casual about his possessions. Even if, for some reason, he hadn't wanted to carry two bags, he wouldn't have abandoned the traveller's cheques. He couldn't have much spare cash. He had insisted on paying for the tickets Peter had got for the opera next Saturday, and their lunch today hadn't been cheap.

His mind darting from thought to thought, Peter went into the bathroom. Here Richard had overlooked none of his belongings, deliberately or otherwise. He had taken everything, including the soap. There was no doubt about the soap. It had been a bath-size piece of Floris Ormonde, Louise's favourite, and all that Peter could find when Richard had apologetically pointed out that he had no soap. They had laughed about it.

'I'm a rotten housekeeper,' Peter had said. 'Louise would have checked before you came.'

And Richard had said, 'No matter. It's better here, even without Louise, than in a Moscow hotel. You might have expected me to bring my own soap, but at least you didn't expect me to bring a plug for the bath.'

Plug for the bath? That was in place, but the basin plug was missing. Presumably Richard had taken it. A broad hint? Moscow? Somewhere else behind the Iron Curtain? The only explanation of these anomalies was that Richard had left the apartment under some kind of duress. Which meant that he, Peter, had to do something about it. But what? It was a hell of a situation. Charles Bigrel was the man to cope with it.

NINE

It wasn't until the following morning that Bigrel heard about Richard Lavery. Peter Denville had made up his mind to telephone Bigrel as soon as he could but, since his only means of doing this was through the ambassador, it hadn't proved easy, and there had been considerable delay.

Bigrel was in his office with David Grant when the call from Vienna came through. They were discussing the trade mission with which Grant was to leave for Moscow the next day, and Grant's chances of locating some associate of the dead Sholatov to help him contact Carey-Ford. Neither of them was over-hopeful, and the interruption didn't come at a good moment.

'He says it's very important and he has to speak to you personally, sir.' Lorna Day smiled her apology.

'All right. I'll take it.' Bigrel didn't try to hide his impatience. He picked up the receiver and motioned to Grant to listen on the other phone. 'Peter Denville? Yes, Charles Bigrel speaking. I can guess why you've telephoned. I tried to get you yesterday evening, but you were having a long conversation with someone.'

'My wife, sir. She's – '

'Yes. Quite. Denville, I've excellent news for you and your friend Lavery. Emma Jackson's safe and well, having spent a day and a half in the custody of the Czech authorities. It seems they had a tip-off about some young woman smuggling heroin and they confused her with Emma. Anyway, it's all been sorted out. Profuse apologies from the Czechs, of course. Our ambassador's away, but the chargé has coped with everything. He and his wife put Emma up for the night, and he's seeing her on to the London flight this morning. In fact, she should be boarding in about ten minutes. The crisis is over.'

'No, I don't think it is, sir. I mean – it's great as regards Emma, but – but Richard has disappeared.'

'What?'

Peter explained – about the letter Richard had left him, about 'Dick' and 'Pete', the briefcase, the travellers' cheques, the pills, the soap, the plug. Somehow, knowing that fears for Emma had been unfounded, he couldn't take seriously what he himself was saying, and waited for Bigrel's scornful reception of what now seemed to be a flight of fancy. To his surprise he was subjected to a series of raking cross-questions. Bigrel wanted to know when he'd last seen Richard, what kind of mood Richard had been in, how he had reacted to the news that Emma was missing, whether he had ever implied he was considering a trip to Moscow, and a host of other details. Peter felt bludgeoned by the demands made upon him. He was thankful when Bigrel put down the receiver with a promise to keep in touch.

'Which would you bet on, sir, Prague or Moscow?' Grant asked.

Bigrel picked up his alabaster egg and ran his thumb fondly over its comforting surface. He didn't bother to answer Grant's question. If Richard Lavery had left Vienna under some form of pressure – which was a fair assumption, considering the pointers he had been clever enough to leave behind him – there was no reason for him to have gone anywhere but Moscow. The only importance he had, except to his family and friends, was his connection with Carey-Ford. But who had known of their relationship? Suddenly Bigrel recalled the curiosity that, according to Jackson, Thomas Penryn had shown in Lavery.

He said, 'David, think carefully. When you were talking to Richard Lavery did he give you any reason to suspect that someone, other than ourselves, was taking an undue interest in him or interfering with him in any way?'

'No.' Grant shook his head slowly.

'Nothing unusual happened to him recently?'

'Discounting his on-and-off engagement and our activities,' Grant said sardonically, 'no.'

'Are you certain?' Bigrel put down his egg and was shuffling through a file. 'Here's your report. Reread it and see if a bell rings.'

Grant read, came to the last page, handed the report back

to Bigrel. He was frowning, trying to recreate the scene. Lavery had said he didn't like their methods, something about – A broad grin spread across his face.

'Got it!' he said. 'Lavery accused me of breaking into his flat. I denied it, but I don't think he believed me. Anyway, it got lost in the rest of our argument.'

'Ah!' Bigrel expelled his breath. 'Right.' He looked at his watch. 'This is what I want you to do. Get everything you can on the break-in. Then go to Heathrow and meet Emma Jackson. Lorna will arrange a VIP room for you. Time's going to be tight, so take my car and report in en route.'

Tempted to point out that there were other members of the staff who could share the workload with him, Grant nodded his understanding. At least he would enjoy the luxury of the chauffeured limousine. He decided to go first to the block of flats where Lavery lived. If there had been other burglaries in the neighbourhood the porter should know.

The porter pocketed the pound note Grant had slipped him and prepared to be helpful. Break-ins were endemic in central London and there wasn't much one could do about them. Of course, it was up to people to have effective locks on doors and windows – Grant was posing as an insurance man – and to let him know when they would be away, but he couldn't be everywhere at once. They had been fairly lucky in the square. He hadn't heard of any trouble recently, and none of his tenants had complained.

At the offices of White, White, Kingston and Lavery, Grant was told that Mr Richard Lavery was abroad, but that Mr Andrew White might be able to help him. And indeed he did. Bored with the dull chores given to the youngest and most newly qualified member of the firm, Andrew White was glad of the interruption. Led on by David Grant, still pretending to be in the insurance business, he was talkative to the point of garrulousness. Grant made a mental note never to employ him as a solicitor, but he listened with gratitude.

'Terribly annoying thing to have happen. Richard was furious. But, Mr – er – Grant, I understand nothing was actually taken?'

Grant regarded him owlishly through his horn rims. 'It's a question of security, for future insurance purposes. Do you know how the man got in?'

'Men,' White corrected him. 'There must have been two of them. Richard caught them red-handed. He managed to down one of them. Then the other, who'd been hiding behind a curtain, knocked him out, most likely with a cosh. Richard had a dreadful lump behind his ear. Lucky he wasn't killed, in fact.'

Grant nodded sympathetically. He guessed the young solicitor was exaggerating, but that wasn't important. Bigrel would be interested, very interested. The break-in, which seemed to be an isolated incident, was sounding more and more like a search of the flat rather than an attempted burglary.

'You wanted to know how they got in,' Andrew White continued. 'It must have been through the door. The lock's not up to much.' He stopped abruptly. 'Oh, dear, I shouldn't have said that to you, should I? But Richard's having a new lock fitted as soon as he gets back. There wasn't time before he went.'

'No time – for something so important?'

'No. It was Thursday when he caught them. He got home particularly early. He'd not been in the office that afternoon. I remember because – '

But Grant had heard all he needed. Making hurried excuses, he bade the somewhat surprised Mr White goodbye and bolted for the car. Normally, when he was by himself, he sat beside Tyler, but today he got in the back seat in order to use the telephone. His call to Bigrel was brief, the bare bones of what he had learnt, and afterwards, during the drive to Heathrow he did some hard thinking. His thoughts were not pleasant.

The plane from Prague was landing as Grant reached the airport. He was taken straight to a small VIP lounge where Maurice and Helen Jackson, Emma's sister Jane, and Betty Acheson were waiting. He introduced himself as from the Foreign Office.

'Chris McCann sent you?' Jackson didn't wait for a reply. 'Very good of him. He's been most kind over this stupid business, most kind. Would you tell him we're grateful?'

'Yes, sir. I will. Incidentally, I hope you won't mind if I ask Miss Jackson a few questions when she arrives. With a drink, perhaps.' Grant gestured towards the bar in the corner of the room.

'Questions? Now?'

'Yes, sir.'

'Surely they can wait.' Helen Jackson objected. 'Without wanting to flap, I do feel Emma must have had a harrowing experience and – '

'That's just it,' Grant said quickly. 'Mr McCann's wondering if we should make an official complaint to the Czechs, and we need all the facts while they're clear in Miss Jackson's mind.'

The Jacksons accepted the lie without further protest and Grant gave them his best smile. He hadn't expected such a large welcoming committee for Emma. It wasn't going to be easy to question her in these circumstances. He hoped she would be cooperative.

He watched with interest as she came swinging through the door, a tall, dark, pretty girl, who showed no sign of her ordeal. Richard Lavery was a lucky man, he thought, and caught himself up as he remembered. Keeping in the background, he waited while Emma was kissed and hugged by her family and Betty Acheson.

'Darling, this is David Grant from the FCO,' Maurice Jackson said.

'I'm glad to see you home safely, Miss Jackson.'

Emma offered him her hand. 'I'm glad to be safely home, Mr Grant.'

'Grant wants to ask you some questions, darling.' Jackson had gone to the bar. 'I shall pour the drinks while you get on with that, and then we'll all go out to lunch to celebrate.'

'Can we listen, Mr Grant?' Jane Jackson – a sixteen-year-old version of Emma – was enjoying the drama. 'I won't tell anyone. I swear.'

Grant grinned at her. 'It's not top, top secret, Jane, but please don't spread it around.' He turned to her sister. 'First, Miss Jackson – Emma – what about your luggage?'

'That's it.' Emma held out a large Gucci bag. 'God knows what happened to the rest.'

84

'It's at the shop!' Betty Acheson flushed as everyone looked at her. 'I asked about it at Ruzyne airport – I thought you'd need it – and the CSA girl promised they'd take it off the plane. But they didn't. It arrived at Heathrow, and I collected it with mine.'

'Super! I thought I'd lost it.'

'So you only had one bag, Miss Jackson,' Grant interrupted. 'I imagine the authorities examined it very carefully?'

'Not a bit. I watched the woman who did it with a sharp eye in case she pinched something, and she missed two of the pockets. I could have had half a pound of heroin in them.'

'Did they do a body search?'

Emma wrinkled her nose in disgust at the idea. 'No. I'd have hated that. They were very – correct, and really quite pleasant. But they kept on contradicting themselves, which was horribly frustrating. First they said there was a telephone call and – '

'From Richard. "Your fiancé", the stewardess called him. She said you were joining him on an unexpected holiday,' Betty burst in. 'I wouldn't have left you otherwise, Emma. I'd have made much more of a fuss.'

'It wouldn't have helped.' Emma smiled at her friend. 'There was no arguing with them. It was infuriating. They accused me of breaking their currency laws. They never mentioned drugs. But when they were apologizing to me, as I was going, they said they'd confused me with someone who was suspected of smuggling heroin. The whole thing was mad.'

While Emma, prompted by Grant and the curiosity of her family, was telling the rest of the story, Betty Acheson produced a somewhat crumpled envelope from her handbag. When Emma paused for breath she tossed it into her lap.

'It came to the shop. It was there when I got back. From Richard, isn't it?'

'Yes. It's his writing, but – '

Glancing up in puzzlement from the envelope, Emma looked by chance straight at her father. Guilt and apprehension were painted on Maurice Jackson's face. Grant, who appreciated the situation, would have caused a diversion, but it was too late. Emma was already ripping open the envelope and reading the letter that Richard had written before he left for Vienna.

Grant saw her mouth tighten and she swallowed. Then her chin came up. She crumpled the letter into a ball in her fist. Her eyes were very bright.

'Do you know what this is about?' Again she looked directly at her father.

'No, darling. How – how could I?'

It was a palpable lie. Maurice Jackson gulped down his drink and went to pour himself another. He kept his back turned to Emma.

'It's from Richard saying we're – we're through.' Emma's voice broke. 'He doesn't intend to marry me and he wants me to clear out of the flat. But it's not true. It can't be. He phoned me last night – he said he'd traced me through the Embassy – and he was as loving and concerned as ever. I expected him to be here to meet me. I – I just don't understand.'

'But regrettably, it's crystal clear,' Charles Bigrel said. 'Some time after Denville left Lavery at the restaurant yesterday, Lavery was made to realize that Emma's disappearance was not some ploy of ours but a grim fact. Of course, the communists were only using Emma to put pressure on Lavery. She wasn't important to them herself. Obviously they never intended to make the charges against her stick. But Lavery couldn't know that and, for her sake, he agreed to go to Moscow.'

'Moscow? Is that definite, sir?'

'Yes, David. I've just heard. He caught the *Aeroflot* flight first thing this morning. We were too late to stop him even if he'd wanted us to, and I don't think he did. I think he just wanted to warn us that he'd gone to visit his father, at the earnest bidding of our communist friends. Ironical, isn't it?'

'It's too damned much of a coincidence.' Grant was vehement. 'Assuming that break-in was a KGB search job, they must have started taking an interest in him about the same time we did.'

'Quite.' Bigrel looked him straight in the eye. 'And neither of us believes in coincidences. So the Russians must have an informant amongst our chums. Remember that, David. They may be expecting you when you get to the USSR.'

TEN

Richard Lavery's arrival in the Soviet Union was no different from that of any tourist. He landed at Sheremetyevo airport after an uneventful flight from Vienna, went through immigration, made currency and customs declarations and caught a bus into Moscow, where in due course he was delivered to his hotel. There were no difficulties. If the official who inspected his passport gave him a more than cursory glance it wasn't obvious. But sitting beside him on the plane and constantly at his elbow during the journey was that shaggy-haired East German, Franz Baucher.

Igor Goransky travelled separately. He sat in a reserved part of the aircraft, ignored Richard when their paths crossed at Sheremetyevo and was whisked away from the airport – as befitted an important KGB officer – in a black, chauffeur-driven Zil. Richard, who had found him far more civilized than his fellow communist, was almost sorry to see him go.

'We lunch in the hotel,' Franz Baucher said as the ornate antique lift carried them up to the sixth floor. 'Afterwards we go to the clinic. This evening we enjoy ourselves. There's much to enjoy in Moscow. It's a great city. You've been here before, *mein Herr?*'

'A brief visit when I was still at school – as I'm sure you know damn well,' Richard said.

The East German tut-tutted, his smile malicious. 'Don't forget what you promised Comrade Goransky,' he said softly, lowering his voice although they were alone in the lift. 'We've kept our part of the bargain. Now you must keep yours.'

'I propose to do just that,' Richard said acidly, and wished he hadn't sounded so pompous.

As the lift doors opened a square-built woman, dressed in a black, indeterminate uniform, rose from behind her desk. Putting down her knitting she took the piece of paper the reception clerk had given Baucher, glanced at the numbers on it, selected two keys and held them out. Her face cracked into what was intended to be a smile.

'Comrades, welcome. If there is anything you lack, please to tell me,' she said in heavily-accented English.

The East German nodded, took the keys and walked ahead down the wide corridor. Richard, thankful they were not to share a room, followed. He was feeling tired, depressed and apathetic. He waited while Franz Baucher unlocked the bedroom doors.

'Take your choice, *mein Herr*.'

Richard, who guessed the rooms were identical, walked into the nearer without speaking. It was high-ceilinged, shabby and full of heavy Victorian-type furniture. There were two doors leading from it. Richard flung his bag on to the bed and went to try them. One, which obviously connected with the room Baucher was to occupy, was locked. The other led into a bathroom. It was a drab place with dangerous-looking plumbing, but the towels were clean, there were new plugs in the bath and basin, and soap had been provided.

Fleetingly Richard thought of Peter Denville. He wondered if Peter had contacted Charles Bigrel. At the time he had felt he should try to give Bigrel some warning of what he was about to do. Now that seemed an absurd, quixotic action, more likely to lead to trouble than anything else.

'I'm sorry if the accommodation doesn't meet with your approval, *mein Herr* – or should I perhaps call you Comrade, since we're in Moscow?' Baucher interrupted Richard's thoughts. 'It's not the *Ukraina* or the *Rossia*, I admit, but it's more discreet than the big luxury hotels, and convenient for our purposes.'

'That's okay.' Richard crossed to a window and looked over the adjoining roof-tops in the expectation of seeing in the distance the onion-shaped domes of old Moscow. His view was totally blocked by a concrete and glass cube of flats. 'I don't propose to be here long,' he said emphatically.

'No.' The monosyllable was flat but peculiarly expressive.

Richard swung round and stared at Baucher, who continued to lounge in the doorway. Slowly shaking his head the

East German grinned, his eyes hard and bright. Richard was chilled.

'No,' he said incisively.

'You may change your mind, Comrade – or someone may change it for you. You could stay here, in Moscow – for ever.'

'What the hell do you mean by that?'

Baucher was at once conciliatory, thinking he might have gone too far with his baiting.

'Nothing. Nothing, *mein Herr*. Just that Moscow's a fine city and you may like it. No need to jump down my throat.' He bent and picked up his bag. 'We shall go to lunch in half an hour,' he said abruptly.

The door closed behind him but Richard didn't move. He was filled with a sudden despairing anger which, as he was honest enough to recognize, was a cloak for his fears. He had no doubt that Baucher had threatened him. He was equally sure that Baucher had immediately regretted it, but that was no reassurance. The East German was, as he had first surmised, of no great importance in the KGB scheme of things. Nevertheless, he knew a lot, possibly more than he was meant to, and the threat had not been empty. Richard knew he had cause to be afraid.

Lunch was a long, interminable meal. The food – borshch, a kebab, and the inevitable ice-cream adorned with a piece of canned fruit – was adequate and probably worth the Intourist vouchers that had to be handed over for it. But the service was abominable and, since they were not a compatible couple, conversation was minimal and sporadic. Time limped along.

Baucher did his best to be pleasant. He insisted on ordering Pilsener from Czechoslovakia, saying that Russian beer was flat and an acquired taste. He addressed Richard as '*mein Herr*' and abstained from the mocking 'Comrade'. Indeed, his behaviour was altogether exemplary. The result was to make Richard even more wary and, as his meeting with Carey-Ford grew nearer, his former apathy was replaced by a state of nervous apprehension.

'When you are ready, *mein Herr*,' the East German said at last. 'The car will be waiting.'

The car, in fact, was a taxi. It drove them to the

Tchaikovsky Street stretch of the ring road that encircles the heart of Moscow, and let them out. They walked for about fifty yards. Then a black Volga came up very fast behind them. The rear door was flung open as the driver braked hard.

'In you get! Quick!'

Richard felt himself propelled across the pavement and half lifted into the car by Baucher's muscular strength. The East German leapt in after him, sprawling across him as the Volga made a racing start. The door slammed and they were away. None of the passers-by showed any curiosity.

'You all right?' Baucher straightened himself and sat back in his corner.

Richard nodded. His heart was pounding but he was determined to appear cool. 'Was that really necessary?'

'Yes. It's important we shouldn't be followed. There are always hostile eyes watching and Comrade Carey-Ford's whereabouts are top secret.'

'I thought he was ill in hospital, dying,' Richard said sharply.

Baucher was quick to allay the sudden suspicion. 'Unfortunately that's true. He's in a clinic. It's a house on what was formerly a private estate in the country, about thirty-five kilometres from the centre of Moscow. It's in a fine park. Very beautiful. And he's getting the best possible treatment. You will see.'

Richard made no comment. He knew it was illogical, but in spite of his extraordinary situation he was at the moment more concerned about meeting Guy Carey-Ford than about anything the KGB might have in store for him.

The Volga was eating up the miles. The driver sat stolidly, his shoulders four-square, his black hair curling over the top of his coat collar, his foot firmly on the accelerator. He seemed incurious. He hadn't once turned his head to look at his passengers. But Richard, catching sight of his face in the rear-view mirror, a dark-skinned face with a heavy moustache, was surprised to meet the man's eyes staring unblinkingly back at him.

They sped through a village, scattering some children and narrowly missing a sleepy dog, to come soon after to a pair of tall iron gates. The driver screamed to a stop and hooted imperiously, but men were already running from the guard-house.

Two minutes later the car drew up in front of a columned two-storey house. Waiting by the door was a man in a white-coat, who introduced himself as Dr Mirov. Welcoming them in Russian, he ushered Baucher and Richard through the hall into a room that was obviously his study, gestured to them to be seated and himself sat behind his desk. A small dark man, he somehow succeeded in being both arrogant and obsequious at the same time.

Without being asked Baucher produced some papers and passed them across. 'Our credentials, Comrade.' He too spoke in Russian.

'Yes, of course. The documentation. I suppose I must – ' He shuffled through the papers. 'You won't be offended, I hope, Comrade Baucher, if I say Comrade – er – Lavery scarcely needs any. The likeness, in my opinion, is apparent.'

'Your opinion's of no importance, Mirov,' Franz Baucher interrupted rudely. 'At least not in this respect. Medical questions are, of course, another matter. How is the patient today?'

'When a man's so near death there's little difference from one day to the next,' the doctor replied bitterly. 'He's under heavy sedation much of the time. It's necessary because of the intense pain. But he's been told that Comrade Lavery is to visit him, and he's prepared.'

'Then I suggest – '

'Very well.' Dr Mirov's prim mouth tightened. He looked at Richard and said in English, 'You are ready, Comrade Lavery?'

'Yes.' So far it was all he had contributed to the conversation and he wondered if Mirov was aware that he understood Russian.

'That's good.'

Immediately the door opened – the doctor must have pressed a bell under his desk – and a girl in nurse's uniform came into the room. She was magnificent – tall, with high full breasts, slim hips and long, long legs. She looked as if she'd just stepped out of a poster publicizing the Olympic Games.

'Ah, Natalya, this is Comrade Lavery.' The doctor indicated Richard. He didn't introduce Baucher. 'You will look after him, please,'

'Most certainly, Comrade.' She gave Richard a wide smile. 'If you will come with me – '

Richard followed her through the hall, up the carpeted stairs and along a corridor. He saw neither nurses nor doctors busy about their work, no patients wandering about in dressing gowns, no blanketed stretchers, no trolleys heaped with obscene reminders of the body's vulnerability. It was all very quiet. Except for a slight smell of antiseptic he could have been in a private house. Then, as he passed a closed door, someone inside the room started to scream. Abruptly the sound was choked off.

Natalya paid no attention. Calmly she continued on her way to the end of the corridor. Here she turned to face Richard. Putting a hand on his arm, she said in excellent English:

'You must prepare yourself for a shock, Comrade. I don't know if you've seen someone dying before, but it's not a pretty sight. He suffers unbearably but still he clings to life, as if he couldn't die before you came. Be kind to him. He can't have much longer, a day, perhaps two. You're only just in time.'

Giving Richard no chance to reply, she knocked at the door by which they were standing, opened it and thrust him gently forward. As he went into the dimness of the sickroom he was aware of the door closing again behind him. He was alone with Guy Carey-Ford. Reluctantly he went over to the bed and stood looking down. And any secret hope he might have had that the traitor Carey-Ford and the man his mother had loved might not be one and the same was at once negated.

The resemblance to himself was undeniable, the deep-set eyes, dark-lashed and dark-browed, the wide mouth – more sensual than his own – the slightly aquiline nose, the whole bone structure of the face. True, Carey-Ford's fair hair was dull and greying, his cheeks concave, his skin tinged with yellow and beaded with sweat, but then, he was in his fifties and desperately ill. There was the smell of death about him. Against his will Richard felt the stirrings of pity.

'So you're Richard, one of my wild oats come to fruition. And to think I didn't know you existed until Goransky told me.' His voice was hoarse. 'Hello to you. Come and sit down.'

'Hello, sir.'

The eyes gleamed with sardonic amusement. 'It's some time since anyone called me "sir".'

'Would you prefer to be – ' Richard stopped.

' – called "Comrade"? No, I think not. Try "Guy". After all, had things been different, we would have been on those terms by now, wouldn't we?'

He was right. Richard knew it instinctively. But he wasn't prepared to admit it. To him John Lavery had always been 'Dad'. It had never occurred to either of them that as Richard grew older he might call his father by his first name. And to accept the implication that, had things been different, he would have had a greater degree of intimacy with Guy Carey-Ford was intolerable.

'How's Veronica Jane?'

'Who?'

'Your mother, dear boy. Isn't that her name?'

'Veronica Mary.'

'Ah yes. I forgot, It's been so long.' He sounded deliberately provocative. 'How is she?'

'What the – ' Richard began. He had been about to say, 'What the hell do you care?' He drew a long breath and expelled it slowly. 'She doesn't have the world's best health but she's – all right.'

'I'm glad.'

There was silence. The courtesies were over. It was point-less to ask Carey-Ford how he was. Richard racked his brain for some safe, innocuous subject that wouldn't be miscon-strued, but he could think of none. He wished Carey-Ford wouldn't watch him so closely, as if he were trying to make up his mind about him, to form some sort of judgement.

'You haven't asked me how they're looking after me here, Richard. Isn't that a standard question when one visits the sick?'

Richard glanced around the room. 'I – I assumed you were being well cared for.'

'Well cared for? That's an understatement.' Carey-Ford

tried to laugh, but his body contorted with pain. When he could speak again he continued hoarsely, urgently, as if what he was saying were vitally important. 'Russian medicine's the best in the world, the most advanced. You don't understand. Because there's not a nurse in sight you think I'm being neglected, but I'm not. I'm being monitored, all the time. They can see me on closed-circuit television – even hear my thoughts, I don't doubt. And it's free. I don't have to pay. I'd never get this splendid treatment on your National Health.'

The long speech had exhausted him. His head fell back against the pillows, his mouth dropped open and his breath came in short, painful gasps. Slowly, as if against his will, his eyes began to close.

Richard, looking desperately for a bell to call the nurse, started up from his chair. Simultaneously there were running steps in the corridor, the door burst open, nurse and doctor appeared, and the fingers of Carey-Ford's right hand seized Richard's wrist in a steel grip.

'Richard!' It required a tremendous effort for him to gasp out the name.

'Yes.' Richard bent over him.

'Come again. Please!'

The nurse was urging Richard to leave. She was a short, dark girl with a broad, flat-cheekboned face, and utterly unlike Natalya. The doctor, also a stranger, had rolled up a sleeve of Carey-Ford's pyjamas and was about to give him an injection in his left arm.

'You must go. At once,' he said across the bed to Richard. 'That is an order.'

If it were possible the pressure of Carey-Ford's fingers tightened around Richard's wrist. 'Please! Promise!' he gasped.

Scarcely knowing what he was saying, Richard murmured, 'I'll come again, I promise. I'll come – if they'll let me.'

'If they'll let you.' It was little more than a breath and only Richard could have caught the words. 'Thank God.'

For a moment Carey-Ford's eyes opened. They were wet with tears. A smile illuminated his face. Then his eyelids fluttered and dropped, letting one solitary tear trickle down a waxen cheek. His grasp on Richard's wrist slackened and fell away. Richard straightened up. He was indescribably moved.

'Go! Go!' The doctor seemed very angry. 'You are impeding our work.' He turned to the nurse and said in Russian, 'Take him outside. Find Natalya or whoever's meant to be in charge of him. Hurry.'

'It's all right!' Richard's spurt of anger matched the doctor's. 'I'm going.'

Storming from the room and along the still-empty corridor, he was met at the top of the stairs by Franz Baucher. There was no sign of the delectable Natalya or of the doctor who had first welcomed them. Baucher seemed agitated.

'Ah, there you are, *mein Herr*. Good. The car's waiting for us.'

Richard said nothing, either then or during the drive back to Moscow. Huddled in his corner of the Volga he closed his eyes and pretended to sleep. It was a heaven-sent opportunity to try to understand his ambivalent feelings towards Carey-Ford and to come to terms with a traumatic experience.

Goransky had two offices – one in KGB headquarters in Dzer-zhinsky Square, and one in the Kremlin. He used the latter to be near at hand for Politburo meetings and to impress special visitors. As Richard thought of his father, Goransky was in his Kremlin room, stroking his neat, greying beard and listening to a tape of Carey-Ford's conversation with his son – a tape delivered by a courier speeding past the Volga on his motor-cycle. When the tape came to an end, Goransky replayed it. It was, he thought, extremely unsatisfactory.

First there was the business of the woman's name. Carey-Ford had called her Veronica Jane and Lavery had instantly corrected him. It could, of course, have been a genuine mistake, a lapse of memory. Or it could have been some kind of test; it wasn't an English practice to call anyone by both their given names. If it were a test, how had Carey-Ford interpreted the spontaneity of Lavery's response? It was impossible to guess.

There were other questions. Had Carey-Ford been innocently praising the care of the clinic, or had he been warning Lavery that their meeting was being watched and recorded? Had his collapse been faked so that Lavery would bend over him and they could whisper together? Above all, how important were those last brief confidences that, thanks to the interference of the fool doctor and his nurse, the microphone had failed to pick up?

Goransky sighed. He knew how easy it was to become over-suspicious and thus defeat one's ends. It was a perpetual hazard in his profession. And he could not believe in Carey-Ford as the repentant traitor revealing some Soviet secret on his deathbed in a last-minute bid to buy his way into a bourgeois heaven. The idea was absurd, such behaviour completely out of character. Nevertheless, Charles Bigrel had made a determined effort to persuade Lavery to visit the dying Carey-Ford, and it wasn't for any altruistic or humanitarian reason. There had to be some valid explanation.

Muttering swear-words he had picked up as a boy on the streets of Leningrad and hoped he had forgotten, Goransky swerved from the track he had been wearing in the carpet as he paced up and down his well-appointed office. At a side-table he greedily spooned caviar into his mouth, poured himself a generous tot of vodka and threw it down the back of his throat. He gasped when the fire hit his belly, but at once he felt better.

He checked his watch. Richard Lavery should have been here by now. But, even as misgiving stirred within him, the intercom buzzed and his personal secretary reported that Comrade Baucher and his companion had arrived. Goransky relaxed. Minutes later, when there was a tentative tap on the door and Lavery came into the room, he was his usual expansive self, whom only the guilty or the knowledgeable would suspect they had reason to fear.

'My dear Richard,' he said with his best English accent that had been perfected at the Soviet Embassy in London many years ago. 'I'm so sorry, so terribly sorry.'

Richard stopped short as if he had run into a plate-glass door. 'He's dead?'

'No. No, you misunderstand me. He's still alive – just. But I understand you witnessed one of those intolerable attacks of pain that are always harrowing for the observer. The doctor telephoned me,' Goransky explained ingenuously.

'Yes. It was – distressing,' Richard agreed.

'And, of course, it meant you didn't have much time together.'

96

'He asked me to come again.'

'And are you prepared to?'

'Do I have any choice?'

'No – not really. Not if that's what he wishes. But there's a saying you have. One can take a horse to water but one can't make it drink. Isn't that right?'

'I'll drink, unless the water's too brackish.'

Goransky laughed. He liked Richard Lavery. He did indeed. The young man was a refreshing change. He was tired of being surrounded by people who grovelled to him. But he regretted even more that he couldn't have been at the clinic himself. Yet it wouldn't have been wise. At this stage, when the traitor was dying and seemed to be no longer of any importance, he couldn't afford to show too much interest.

'Come and sit down,' Goranksy said. 'We'll have a drink together anyway. You like vodka, I hope. It's Stolichnaya, which I prefer.'

'Thank you.'

Richard, who didn't know one vodka from another, allowed himself to be waved to a seat and provided with a mound of caviar, strips of toast and a small glass of vodka. Observing protocol, they drank to each other – and to Guy Carey-Ford.

Goransky made no attempt to probe. He had decided to change his tactics. Carey-Ford and his son were clearly eager for a second meeting. They should have it. Goransky hid his annoyance, his anxiety. It wasn't often he felt as frustrated as this. He forced himself to smile at Richard.

'We both know you had no desire to come to Moscow,' he said sympathetically, 'but since you're here I hope you're going to enjoy at least some of your visit. Do you like ballet?'

'Yes, very much.'

'Excellent. The Bolshoi company are dancing Swan Lake at the Palace of Congresses tonight. I'll arrange tickets for you – and a suitable companion. Somehow I don't think Comrade Baucher appreciates the ballet.'

'That's kind of you.' Richard grinned to show his acknowledgement of a joke against Baucher.

'And now, Richard, I'm afraid you'll have to excuse me. I'm a busy man, alas.' Goransky stood up, saw Richard to the door, shook hands with him. 'We'll meet again before too long – after you've seen your father again.'

'Yes. All right. Thank you.'

Why the hell did I thank the man? Richard asked himself as, seated beside Baucher, he was driven across the Square of the Cathedrals through the Spassky Gate in the forbidding red brick wall of the Kremlin and into Red Square. It wasn't for the chance of seeing a part of the city within a city denied to tourists. It wasn't for Goransky's friendliness, which he utterly distrusted, though the Russian had kept his word and arranged for Emma's release. It wasn't for the vodka or the caviar or the tickets to the Bolshoi or the promise of being spared Baucher's company for a few hours. It was because Goransky had been more than content for him to pay another visit to Carey-Ford.

Sadly Richard smiled at the irony. It was only a matter of days since David Grant – on behalf of Charles Bigrel and British Intelligence – had gone to unspeakable lengths to urge him to go to Moscow and contact his father, and he had refused. Goransky and the KGB had used Emma to blackmail him into reversing that decision. He still had no idea what either of them really wanted. Nevertheless, such was the strength of the affinity he had felt with Carey-Ford in their one brief meeting that he now had this terrible, urgent desire to see him again, to talk to him at length. He wanted to be sure that it wasn't just his imagination, but that Carey-Ford – though obviously very near death – was in desperate need of some kind of help which seemingly only he, his son, could give.

And then what? More vodka and caviar and Igor Goransky waving him goodbye as he boarded a flight for London? It wasn't, he knew, going to be as simple as that.

ELEVEN

The curtain came down on the first act of *Swan Lake* amid
rapturous applause. The Russian audience clapped, stamped,
shouted their approval. Some, too impatient to wait until the
end of the performance, threw flowers which mostly fell on
the musicians as they left the orchestra pit. The dancers
refused to take a curtain call. They were used to such adu-
lation, and unimpressed. They needed the rest before the next
act. And gradually the six-thousand-strong audience
desisted. They too would enjoy the interval. There was still
much pleasure to come.

'Wasn't it wonderful, wonderful?'

'Yes, marvellous.'

'It's a unique experience for you? You have nothing so
splendid in England?'

Despite himself Richard grinned. Because it was true; it
was a unique experience for him. He had seen *Swan Lake*
several times, but never better danced, never in such a
breathtaking setting as this enormous Palace of Congresses,
never with a more educated, more ecstatic audience – never
with a KGB agent.

Igor Goransky had done him proud. Some hours earlier a
tap on his bedroom door at the hotel had heralded, not
Baucher whom he expected, but the black-clad woman from
behind the desk in the corridor. She was followed by a waiter
pushing a trolley. The trolley contained an excellent light
meal with a half-bottle of white wine and, in an envelope,
two tickets for the ballet and a stack of roubles. There was no
accompanying note.

Forty-five minutes later the woman returned to announce
that a taxi was waiting for him. And in the taxi had been
Natalya Meriosova, the beautiful nurse he had met at the
clinic. She greeted him like an old friend, laughed at the dark
suit he had put on for the occasion and insisted on replacing

his tie with a light blue scarf she was wearing.

'Now you are more suitably dressed,' she said. 'We Muscovites don't make a big thing of the ballet. For us it is a happy, informal event. You must be happy and informal too.'

The informality didn't worry Richard, and he would have forgotten the scarf around his neck if it hadn't been redolent of Natalya's scent, a heavy, musky perfume that he found disturbing. The order to be happy wasn't so easy to obey.

The last time he had gone to the ballet had been at Covent Garden; he and Emma had seen the Royal Ballet Company in *Giselle*. Seated beside Natalya Meriosova in the Palace of Congresses, memories of that evening returned to him with a bitter intensity. He yearned for Emma and London and home. And he wondered how Carey-Ford could have abandoned everything that he himself loved to live in this strange alien land and to die here. Happiness was out.

'I would like champagne and smoked salmon,' Natalya announced when they reached the crush bar.

'Of course,' Richard said. 'Isn't that what every good communist lives on?'

He expected her to be annoyed at this remark, but she only laughed and he pushed his way to the bar. He gave the order: champagne and smoked salmon. Why not? Goransky was paying. He waited. The service was good, unlike that in the hotel restaurant, but demand was high. He didn't mind waiting. Natalya had found them two seats and, though she could see him from where she sat, he was – he suddenly realized – for the first time since arriving in Moscow surrounded by ordinary Russian citizens and virtually free of the KGB. His spirits rose.

Someone jogged his elbow. He turned. The girl standing beside him had spilt mineral water down her skirt. She was an attractive girl, dark-haired, dark-skinned, with something of the gypsy about her. He apologized automatically though it hadn't been his fault.

'It's all right. It won't stain,' she said in Russian and, under her breath so that Richard barely caught the words, she added in English, 'When C-F dies blow your nose as you come out of the clinic. Please – for your own sake.'

She moved away. Her place at the bar was immediately

taken by someone else. Richard's order was ready. He paid, left the change and carried the tray carefully through the crowd to where Natalya was sitting.

'Who was that girl?' Natalya asked. 'What did she say to you?'

The questioning wasn't unexpected. Richard gave the Russian girl a long, quizzical look. 'Don't be so suspicious,' he said mildly. 'I accidentally knocked against her and spilt her drink. There's a hell of a crush getting served. I apologized and she said no harm done, it was only mineral water. That's all. I haven't the faintest idea who she is. Why don't you ask her if you're interested?'

'She's gone.'

'Really.'

Richard glanced casually around the room, though he was well aware the girl was no longer there. He had seen her leave the bar. She appeared to be alone. He wished he knew who she was and what her extraordinarily cryptic message meant. But it was no use guessing. He tasted the champagne.

'You don't like it?' Natalya said.

'On the contrary, it's exceedingly good.' To please her Richard exaggerated; he had thought it mediocre.

'Yes. It's Russian. The French believe no one except them can make champagne, but we've proved them wrong.'

Her smugness irritated him, but he didn't argue. The wine was pleasant enough and the smoked salmon delicious. He asked her about the ballet company. She was enthusiastic, and it was a safely neutral subject. She chatted knowledgeably. But he noticed that her eyes kept straying to the clock above the bar and from there to the entrance to which his back was turned.

He wasn't surprised when she suddenly made a show of recognizing someone. She waved. She half stood up. She seemed agitated. She seized Richard by the arm.

'It's Franz Baucher. He's looking for us. Ah – he's seen us. Richard, I hope this doesn't mean – '

She left the sentence unfinished but he knew what she was implying. He felt himself grow cold. If Carey-Ford were dead . . . Then he realized that unless Carey-Ford's death had occurred much earlier, in fact before Natalya had picked him

101

up at the hotel, she would have had no means of knowing about it, and wouldn't have been expecting Baucher to bring the unhappy news to the Palace of Congresses. This was another trick on the part of the Russians, another deception. He stifled a sigh and twisted away as Baucher's hand came down on his shoulder.

'I'm sorry, but we'll have to go, *mein Herr*. He's worse. They're afraid he won't last the night.'

When they arrived at the clinic everything was in darkness. Richard's first reaction was that he was too late. Guy Carey-Ford was indeed dead. He had died while the Volga was still speeding through the countryside. Shivering in the chill of the night Richard reluctantly got out of the car.

Perhaps the driver had also noticed the cold, because suddenly he produced a large white handkerchief and blew his nose. It sounded like a trumpet, reminding Richard of the girl in the crush bar and the enigmatic message she had whispered. Startled, he carefully refrained from looking at the driver.

The front door opened. Dr Mirov came on to the step. He was carrying a lamp which he held high above his head. Behind him in the hall other lamps glowed softly.

'I'm sorry,' he called. 'Our electricity has failed. Please take care, Comrades.'

Richard followed Franz Baucher into the house. He was relieved that the darkness had such an ordinary explanation, but he was still beset with doubts.

These were accentuated when Mirov said, 'The patient's condition has deteriorated sadly since you saw him earlier, Comrade, but he may rally again. It's impossible to know in such cases. We can only hope he regains consciousness and is able to speak to you before the end.'

Making assenting noises, Richard allowed the doctor to show him up the stairs and along the corridor. Fleetingly he thought of Natalya Meriosova – at this moment presumably watching the second act of *Swan Lake*. Except for the lack of light everything was much as it was when Natalya had brought him up here earlier that day. From behind the door where someone had screamed in pain came now the gentle sound of snoring, but otherwise there was the same unexpected quiet, the same lack of presence.

The doctor led the way into Carey-Ford's room. Richard, following, had to suppress a gasp of surprise. The scene before him was extraordinary, like something from the Middle Ages. The curtains had been drawn at the window so that the darkness was unrelieved by a reflection from the night sky, and the eye was drawn directly to the bed. It could have been a catafalque.

A tier of tall candles, their flames steady, was set on either side of the pillow, intensifying the pallor of Carey-Ford's face. A white coverlet hung to the floor and was drawn smoothly up over the sick man's body to beneath his chin. More candles burned along the bottom of the bed. And in the shadows sat two watchful figures like professional mourners keeping vigil.

'Any change?' Mirov asked in Russian.

The taller figure rose. Mirov lifted the lamp he was carrying so that it revealed the man's features, and Richard recognized the doctor who had earlier ordered him from Carey-Ford's room. He guessed the other was the unattractive-looking nurse.

'No change. Not yet, Comrade. It's too soon. The drug isn't meant to wear off for – '

Mirov made an impatient gesture. 'Good!' He turned to Richard. 'It's difficult for us, you understand, Comrade. Without electricity we have no means of observing the patient, monitoring his vital signs, hearing any sound. Until the power returns we are dependant on someone watching over him. But naturally you would prefer to be left alone, and I was wondering if you . . . ' He hesitated.

'Yes, Comrade?'

Richard kept his voice strictly neutral. He knew what their plan was now, and it seemed to him incredibly heavy-handed, unworthy of Goransky. Yet it could have worked. If Natalya's expectation of Baucher's arrival hadn't alerted him, if Mirov hadn't dressed the set quite so theatrically, he might have believed that there was no one to oversee or overhear what transpired between him and Carey-Ford. And Carey-Ford himself, waking to this scene from a drugged sleep

– God knows what he might not blurt out.

'If you wouldn't mind watching over him yourself you would have complete privacy to talk, should he regain consciousness, and there would be no danger. The doctor and the nurse will be on the floor. You would only have to call them. Would you be happy with that arrangement, Comrade?'

'Of course. It sounds perfect.' Richard agreed without hesitation.

Minutes later he was alone with Carey-Ford, his chair close to the bed so that he couldn't fail to notice the slightest alteration in the patient's condition. The silence was leaden, the darkness of the room heavily oppressive outside the perimeter of the candlelight. Time crawled. Richard, too conscious of Natalya's musky scent, pulled off the scarf she had insisted he should wear and stuffed it into a pocket.

An hour and a half later nothing had changed.

Richard's nerves were stretched. He couldn't sit there any longer. He got up and walked to the window, stumbling over a stool that had been hiding in the shadows. He drew the curtains. The sky was dimly luminous, the moon behind the clouds. He looked down. Below him, on the gravel forecourt, squatted the shape of the Volga. He wondered where the driver was, and if it was coincidence that the man had blown his nose at that particular moment.

Behind him there was scarcely more than a disturbance of the air, but he sensed the change. He threw himself towards the bed. Carey-Ford was conscious. His eyes were wide open, staring, full of fear.

'It's all right. All right!' Richard pressed the startlingly thin shoulders back against the pillows. 'The electricity failed and they lit the room in this bloody stupid fashion. But you're okay. Don't worry.'

Carey-Ford relaxed and a smile flickered across his face. He was breathing heavily. He tried to speak but no words came. Richard took a tissue and wiped the sweat from Carey-Ford's brow and around his mouth.

'Take it easy.' He had had time to think what he would say when Carey-Ford regained consciousness, and now he said it, carefully, keeping his gaze fixed on the sick man so as to impress him with its importance. 'The electricity failure

104

makes no difference. You're being as well cared for as you were before. You mustn't think that because the machines aren't working no one's watching out for you. There's a doctor and a nurse nearby. I've only to call and they'll be with you.'

Carey-Ford nodded his head fractionally to show that he understood. His eyes were bright with intelligence, but it was obvious, even to Richard, that his physical condition was extremely poor. Either he was still being affected by the drug he had been given or he was at a very low ebb.

At last he managed to speak. 'Must — must tell you, Richard. I regret nothing – absolutely nothing – except you. If I'd my time over again I – I'd do just the same – come to Russia. Wonderful country. Greatest in the world. But – but sorry if it's made things difficult for you. Truly sorry, dear boy.'

Richard looked at Carey-Ford with pity – and exasperation. He yearned to ask 'Why?' Why did a man who had everything throw it away to become a traitor, a Western defector, one of the Twilight Brigade whom even the communists secretly despised. But it was an unaskable question. Richard sighed. He would never understand.

He said, 'There's no need to worry about me.'

'But there is. There is.' Carey-Ford was suddenly emphatic.

The effort seemed to exhaust him. For a full minute he said nothing. He lay, eyes shut, struggling with pain and weakness. Richard bent over him and again wiped away the sweat. He wondered if Carey-Ford had been trying to warn him. But of what? It was a hopeless situation.

Then, as he brushed the damp hair back from Carey-Ford's forehead and straightened a pillow, he thought he heard him say, 'Ignore one. Pay attention to two. I mean two.' It made no sense. Either he had misheard or the sick man was rambling.

Richard pulled his chair closer to the top of the bed, sat down and waited. After a few seconds Carey-Ford thrust his hand halfway out of the bedclothes. It was an appealing gesture and Richard responded instantly.

'Thank you,' Carey-Ford murmured. 'I mean it.' And he pressed Richard's hand firmly, decisively, twice.

Richard swallowed his surprise. Guy Carey-Ford, he thought, was an extraordinary man. He was stuffed with drugs and subject to bouts of intense pain. He was dying. And he knew he was dying. Nevertheless, not trusting those who were administering to him, he could bring himself to devise a secret means of communication and to use it. It was impossible not to admire him. If only . . .

'Was good of you to come and see me, Richard.' Nothing; a neutral remark.

'I was happy to come.' One press; Carey-Ford would know he had been under some form of compulsion. 'And I'm glad I'm here.' Two; it was the truth or a fair approximation of it.

A sardonic smile played around Carey-Ford's mouth. 'But you should go home now.' Two. 'Can't really talk. Mind's clouded with pain-killer.' Nothing. 'No need – wait for me to die.' Two.

Richard didn't reply. He couldn't explain to Carey-Ford that the decision as to when – even if – he went home wouldn't be his but Igor Goransky's. Their method of communicating was too cumbersome, too exhausting.

As if reading his thoughts, Carey-Ford said, 'I'm tired. Must rest. Stay!'

He pressed Richard's hand twice, pulling it towards him so that it was completely covered by the bedclothes. A natural gesture. And when he began to free his fingers from the clasp Richard, who thought Carey-Ford was merely making himself more comfortable, started to withdraw his own hand. Immediately Richard realized he had misunderstood. Carey-Ford was flattening his hand against the mattress. He left it there and waited.

Carey-Ford lay. He was breathing heavily, grimacing with pain and occasionally tossing his head from side to side. If the movements of the coverlet had aroused any curiosity his restlessness would have accounted for them. No one would have guessed that he had removed his signet ring and was fitting it on the little finger of Richard's left hand. His nails dug into Richard's palm, once, twice.

'Not been a good father,' he mumbled, 'and nothing to offer now – except advice. Don't trust anyone – especially not high-up bastards in the UK – not any of them. Traitor, they call me. Traitor – not the only one.'

Carey-Ford sounded as if he didn't know what he was saying, but his finger nails were biting signals into Richard's palm. Richard concentrated, trying to absorb the message he was being given. Later he would have to decide exactly what it meant and what action he should take – if he had the opportunity.

After a long pause Carey-Ford said, 'Another piece of advice. Never – volunteer. Wait. Other man'll come to you. Then – you'll know.'

The words were getting more and more slurred. Richard had to lean over the bed so that his ear was within inches of Carey-Ford's mouth. He doubted that any bug could pick up what was being said, but his knowledge of electronic surveillance was slight. He dared not take any risks.

He said, as if humouring the sick man, 'I appreciate your advice. I won't forget it. But I'm always a careful chap, you know that. It comes of being a lawyer.'

Carey-Ford just managed to nod before the spasm hit him. This time there was no pretence. He was obviously in agony and he had little strength to support him. There was a sheen of sweat on his skin which returned as soon as Richard wiped it away, and a blue tinge around his mouth. He let go of Richard's hand and clutched at the bedclothes, kneading the coverlet as if the useless action might help him, and grinding his teeth.

'Shall I get the doctor?'

'No.'

Richard sat on the edge of the bed and took Carey-Ford in his arms, holding him tight, suffering with him, trying to bear some part of his pain. He himself was beyond thought, aware only of his own inadequacy.

'It's all right – Guy.' He choked on the name, but he had to say it. He wanted to say it. With every fibre of his being he wanted to say it, to offer what consolation he could to this man he scarcely knew, whom he – hated? loved? It didn't matter.

Gradually the attack passed. Richard laid Carey-Ford back against the pillows. He just caught the exhausted whisper.

'Tell no one – till he – comes – for – ring.' Then there were

107

some words that Richard missed and, 'Bigrel suspects' or 'suspect'? A little later, Carey-Ford said, 'Doctor. Must sleep now.' He smiled at Richard. 'Bless you.' He was quite spent.

The doctor and nurse came running. The nurse brought a lamp so that there was more light. Richard retreated to the shadows, watched the doctor swab Carey-Ford's arm and give him an injection. He prayed that no one would notice the absence of the signet ring.

Suddenly and loudly Carey-Ford said, 'Put out those damned candles.'

It was the last thing he said. Some hours afterwards he died in his sleep. This time Richard, who was staring out of the window, only slowly became conscious of the change in the room behind him. He walked to the bed and stood, gazing down at the body of Guy Carey-Ford. He was drained of all emotion.

After a while he went to the door and reported to the doctor, who confirmed that Carey-Ford was dead. Then miracles blossomed. The electricity came on. The nurses led Richard along the corridor to a comfortable sitting-room. Scalding hot lemon tea and sweet pancakes were produced. And Natalya Meriosova, whom he had left in the crush bar at the Palace of Congresses, reappeared in uniform.

Richard refused to eat anything, but Natalya insisted that he drink the tea, and he was glad of it. Although he had dozed a little during the small hours while Carey-Ford was sleeping, he was desperately tired, far more tired than if he had been at a party or travelling all night. He felt physically and mentally exhausted. But it wasn't until he tried to stand and was overcome by giddiness that he suspected his condition wasn't natural. The lemon tea had been drugged.

Pretending to have noticed nothing unusual he smiled weakly at Natalya and asked if he might go to the bathroom. She acquiesced at once and he allowed her to help him up and take him as far as the door. He was thankful when she said she would wait for him outside.

As soon as he was alone Richard forced himself to act methodically. He thrust home the bolt, turned on both taps in the wash basin and looked around for a glass or cup. There wasn't one. He scooped up the water from the hot tap in his hands and drank as much as he could. It was no more than warm and it tasted revolting. It made him gag. Thrusting his fingers down the back of his throat he staggered to the lavatory pan and managed to bring up most of the tea.

Natalya was banging on the door. 'Are you all right, Richard?'

'Yes. Fine. With you in a minute.'

He urinated, pulled the flush and returned to the wash basin. He ran the cold water and, when the basin was full, plunged his face in it. He came up gasping. The water was icy. That was the best he could do. Natalya was getting impatient.

'Richard! Richard! What is happening?'

He dried his face on a towel and opened the door. 'Sorry to be so long.' Purposely he slurred his words. 'I didn't feel too well. I'm terribly tired.'

'You've not vomited?' She was suspicious.

'Heavens, no!' he said. 'There's nothing really wrong with me, nothing an hour or two of sleep won't cure.'

'That's good. You can sleep in the car.'

'The car?'

'Yes. It's waiting to take us back to Moscow.'

Richard nodded and wished he hadn't. What the hell had they done to him? And why? He forced himself to think, but his brain wasn't functioning properly. His thoughts kept running off at tangents and he wasn't helped by the fact that he had to pretend to be even more doped than he was. Yet surely the why was simple. They were going to cross-question him, to find out exactly what Carey-Ford had said. The drug was to make him more amenable. If it didn't work, they would try – something else. His mouth was suddenly dry and he swallowed hard.

They had reached the top of the stairs. Natalya was on Richard's right side. She took his arm to support him and instinctively he put his left hand on the bannisters. He heard the click of metal as Carey-Ford's signet ring hit against the wood. It sounded appallingly loud, and he caught his breath. Natalya paid no attention. But every step of the way down the stairs he was conscious of the ring on his finger, and when he reached the hall where Dr Mirov and Franz Baucher were waiting he had to restrain himself from burying his left hand deep in his trouser pocket.

He listened to Mirov and Baucher discussing the funeral. It was to be held early the following week; evidently Carey-Ford had expressed a wish to be cremated. Baucher ignored him, but he was aware of the doctor's professional appraisal, and purposely he showed no interest in their discussion. He stood like a dummy with a vapid smile on his face while Natalya fetched her nurse's cloak. Somehow he doubted whether he would be attending Carey-Ford's funeral.

Then Mirov was saying goodbye to them, and they were outside in the cold morning air. Richard shivered, sniffed, fumbled in his pocket and produced a handkerchief. He blew his nose, taking his time about it, making Natalya and Baucher wait for him, putting all his trust in the unknown girl in the crush bar at the Palace of Congresses.

And nothing happened – not one bloody thing.

TWELVE

The Volga went down the driveway at a steady pace. The guardhouse had been alerted and the gates were open. The car turned on to the road, heading for Moscow. Its speed increased, but not by a great deal.

'Can't you go any faster?' Baucher demanded.

'Yes, Comrade. But the engine's got a knock and it would be wiser to nurse it.'

Baucher sighed and muttered something about 'usual inefficiency', but he didn't press the point. The car speeded up a little as if the driver wanted to show willing, and then slowed again. In the back, sitting on Natalya's right, Richard half-closed his eyes and tried to feign drowsiness without actually falling asleep.

In due course, as on the previous afternoon, the Volga was overtaken by a motorcycle courier, bearing the latest tapes from the clinic to Igor Goransky in the Kremlin, and not long after the car reached a part of the road leading through a birch wood. It was definitely not running well. The driver slowed to a crawl and stopped.

'What is it?' Natalya asked authoritatively. 'Why are we stopping?'

Baucher turned round. 'You heard him before. There's something wrong with the engine.' And to the man, he said, 'Take a look. See if you can fix it.'

'Yes, Comrade. I'll try, but the car needs a good overhaul I'm not sure if – '

'And hurry up about it,' Baucher ordered. 'It's important we get to Moscow as quick as we can.'

'You'll be the one responsible if we're delayed,' Natalya added. 'So hurry, as Comrade Baucher says, or you won't like the consequences.'

'I'll do my best, Comrades,' the driver said obsequiously, 'my very best.'

He had been bent double, groping under the seat. Now he straightened himself. There was a small snub-nosed automatic in his hand. He gave Baucher no warning. He didn't threaten; he shot him through the heart with the same swift deliberation that he might have used for shooting a clay pigeon. Baucher died instantly, unaware of what had happened.

Natalya Meriosova was a different matter. An instinct must have warned her. Even as the driver swung round her hand came up from under her cloak. They fired simultaneously. By some miracle neither of them was killed outright. Natalya was saved by flinging herself sideways. The bullet hit her in the top of the chest. Richard saved the driver. With a chopping movement of his hand he knocked the girl's wrist, sending her gun flying and spoiling her aim. The bullet nicked the top of the driver's ear and smashed its way through the Volga's windscreen. The glass tinkled on to the road.

The driver swore volubly. Richard didn't understand Hebrew, but it was clear the man's concern was for the damage to the car. He seemed indifferent to Baucher's dead body or the suffering of the wretched Natalya, who was whimpering uncontrollably as she fumbled on the floor for the weapon she had dropped. Before Richard could stop him the driver leaned over Baucher, put the barrel of his gun against the girl's temple and pulled the trigger.

'She had to die, anyway,' he said in English, 'and the car's not much use to us now, so it's unimportant where.'

Richard felt the bile rise in his throat. Choking, he flung himself out of the car and vomited on the ground. He had once witnessed a bad traffic accident in which three people had been seriously injured and one had died. But he had never seen anyone killed in cold blood. The fact that Natalya Meriosova and Franz Baucher had been enemies made no difference. He was appalled.

'Come and help me, please. There's no time to waste.' The driver had pulled Baucher from the front seat and was stripping the leather coat from his body. 'I'm sorry about all this but I expected to deal only with the man. I didn't think the girl would be returning to Moscow with you.'

Richard wiped his mouth on his handkerchief. He knew the

112

Russian was trying to help him and he knew he needed that help. He was ashamed of his own weakness.

'What do you want me to do?'

'Help me get this coat off. You must wear it. It'll hide your suit and make you look less – less conspicuous. It's a pity about the bullet-hole but it doesn't show much, and when one's life's at stake one can't afford to be choosy.'

The Russian's matter-of-factness steadied Richard. He regarded the coat with distaste but he didn't argue. Finding Natalya's scarf in his trouser pocket he used it to scrub off the worst of the blood, and once he was wearing the coat he was thankful for its warmth.

He helped the driver to carry what remained of the shaggy-haired East German across the road. Together they heaved him into the ditch. There was a splash as the body landed, and a sucking noise as it sank out of sight.

'I'll deal with the girl,' the driver said, to Richard's relief. 'You clean up the glass and the rest as much as you can. The KGB will be on to us soon enough. We needn't make it easy for them.'

They worked fast. Within five minutes there was no obvious sign that anything untoward had occurred. Both the bodies were safely hidden. Dust had been kicked over the bloodstains. The glass had been picked up or dispersed. In the back of the Volga an old copy of *Pravda* covered the fragments of blood and brain that had once been part of Natalya Meriosova. Richard got into the front. The seat was still warm from Franz Baucher.

For the last time before driving off the Russian looked anxiously up and down the road, which throughout had remained silent and free of traffic. Always lonely, it was as yet too early for the odd military convoy or member of the Politburo on his way to his *dacha* in the country. Everything was very quiet and peaceful and picturesque. The driver grunted his satisfaction.

'I'm grateful to you for saving my life,' he said to Richard, 'but I wish you'd deflected the bullet somewhere else. If the windscreen was whole we might have driven into the heart of Moscow with impunity, but now we're sure to be noticed and when the hue and cry starts someone will remember us.'

Richard, who had been doing the Russian's bidding automatically, found himself reanimated by the words 'hue and cry'. As the Volga sped towards Moscow, his mind began to function again and bitterly he realized that he was in a worse mess than ever. At least before he had been able to kid himself that Goransky might take pity on him and let him go, or that the British Government might take some action. But neither was a possibility any longer. He was as guilty of the killing of the two KGB agents as the man sitting beside him, and he couldn't expect the authorities openly to countenance murder.

'Incidentally,' the driver interrupted his black thoughts. 'I should introduce myself. My name is Misha Kemenev. You know my young friend Tamara. It was she who told you to blow your nose as a signal when Carey-Ford had died.'

'Yes. We met at the ballet last night,' Richard said sardonically, remembering the pretty girl who had reminded him of a gypsy.

'And what is your name?'

'My name?' Richard thought he had misheard the question.

'Yes. Who are you?'

Richard turned in his seat and stared hard at the Russian. A plan had been devised, enormous risks accepted, at least two people killed, all in order to rescue him from the KGB – and the rescuers didn't know who he was. It was unbelievable.

'I'm Richard Lavery.'

'So. And how are you related to Carey-Ford?'

Richard hesitated, and decided on a counter-question. 'What makes you think I am?'

'You're English and you've been visiting him.'

'Very logical,' Richard murmured.

'And I've cultivated one of the cooks at the clinic, who heard Mirov talking to a woman doctor.' The Russian gave a deep, throaty chuckle at his own cleverness. 'Mirov believes you're Carey-Ford's natural son.'

'Yes. I am,' Richard said slowly. There seemed no point in denying it and possibly causing antagonism. Besides, he wanted to learn more. He explained about Emma and how he had been forced to come to Moscow, and asked, 'Why did you and Tamara decide to rescue me?'

114

'It was for Sholatov's sake!' Misha Kemenev spoke with a passion that surprised Richard. 'And for your sake too, of course,' he added lamely.

'Who is Sholatov?'

'You don't know who – who Dmitri Sholatov was?' It was Kemenev's turn to be amazed.

'No,' Richard said, noticing the Russian's use of the past tense. 'Who – was Sholatov?'

'He was a great scientist, a great Jew, a great patriot – and my very dearest friend. I would have died for him,' Kemenev said mystically, 'but I wasn't given the chance. Instead he died for me. After the KGB seized him Franz Baucher got to work and when he couldn't hold out anymore he took a suicide pill rather than betray his friends, his fellow Jews.'

'Baucher got to work – tortured him?' Richard said.

'Yes. It's my big regret that I had to kill Herr Comrade Baucher so quickly. I had promised myself that his death would be slow – very, very slow – and that he would remember Dmitri Sholatov every second of it. But that was not to be, alas.' Kemenev was frowning fiercely. He turned his frown on Richard. 'And you say you've never heard of Sholatov?'

'No. I'm sorry.' It was an inadequate response, Richard knew, but he couldn't think what else to add.

'Ah well!' The Russian shrugged hugely. 'There'll have to be some explaining, but it must wait until we're safe and I've changed my mind about that. Since it's still so early I've decided to drive to the Metro station nearest to where we want to go and leave the car right outside the entrance as if we had abandoned it in a hurry. With luck the KGB will assume we've taken a tube train and gone somewhere far away.'

'What about the shattered windscreen?' Richard asked tentatively.

'It's one risk against another, but the less you're seen by anyone the better. You agree?'

'Whatever you say. I'm in your hands.'

And that, Richard thought, was literally true. He had no option. He had to rely on the big, burly Russian Jew whom he more than half-distrusted. Resentfully he stared out of the car window. By now they were in the outskirts of Moscow. There were a few people about, a party of workers going on an early shift, a small queue beginning to form outside a shop, some street-cleaners. But traffic was almost non-existent. He saw a couple of buses and a tram but only one car – a Zhiguli, old and dilapidated.

Kemenev took off his cap and passed it to Richard. 'Put it on. As we get nearer the city centre there'll be more activity and your fair hair's very noticeable.'

Obediently Richard tried on the cap. It was too small for him. It balanced on his head and made him look absurd, but he wasn't conscious of the fact. He had sensed the sudden increase in the Russian's tension and his own nerves tightened.

'And listen,' Kemenev continued. 'Listen carefully. Very soon I will say to you "Out". You must be ready. I'll stop for a mere second. You jump out and you walk – walk, not run, but with purpose, in the same direction as we are going. Then you take the first turn to the right and the second to the left. Don't wait for me. Don't hang about. I'll catch you up. Do you understand?'

'Yes. First right. Second left.'

'Then you follow me. You don't come with me. You follow me – but not too closely, because I'll stop just short of the entrance to a block of apartments. I'll sneeze, make a big thing of it – and blow my nose. That's the signal for Pavel – you've not met him yet – to distract the attention of the concierge. Luckily she's a drunk so it won't be too difficult. You walk in as if you lived there, straight up the stairs, three flights, and the door directly opposite you will be ajar. Tamara will be waiting.'

'And you?'

'I'll come – when I can.'

Kemenev braked hard to avoid the swinging tail of a trolley-car. There were more people around now and more traffic. Moscow was awake and getting ready for the day.

'Are you ready? We are almost there,' he said two minutes later.

'I'm ready.'

'Right.'

Kemenev drew in to the kerb. Richard leapt out of the car, slamming the door behind him. The Volga was already moving. He was alone and suddenly horribly conscious of his own vulnerability. For a moment his mind was a blank, all of Kemenev's instructions forgotten. He began to walk.

The Volga had gone straight on, but he turned right and, after perhaps thirty yards, left, to find himself on a broad spacious avenue. Ahead he could see the spires and domes of the Kremlin. There were more people here, but no one paid him any attention. A large black Zil went by, reminding Richard of Goransky. Fear gripped him. What would he do if Kemenev didn't reappear? Involuntarily he slowed his pace and, unable to resist the temptation, glanced over his shoulder. His sense of relief when he saw Kemenev not far behind was enormous.

Letting himself be overtaken, Richard followed Kemenev, who unexpectedly dived down some steps which led by a subway to the other side of the wide street. In the open air again Kemenev took the first to the right and the next to the left. He had been walking fast, but now he slowed. He was fumbling in his pocket. He extracted a large, white square of cotton. He stopped. His shoulders heaved and he buried his face in the handkerchief. Anyone noticing him would have assumed he had been overcome by a fit of sneezing.

Richard, feeling the excitement grow in him, approached Kemenev. As he drew level the Russian put away his handkerchief and walked off. Richard turned into the entrance of the apartment block. So far everything had gone according to plan.

But either because of carelessness or tiredness Richard suddenly slipped on the step and the chauffeur's cap that Kemenev had insisted he should wear shot off his head and slid into the hall in front of him. He stumbled after it. He was on his knees. He reached for the cap, grasped it and put it on.

Sweating, he became aware that he was looking at a pair of cheap shoes. He raised his head slowly. His cheek brushed against rough material – trousers, jacket. He was on his feet. He stared into a hard, angular face, eyes like stones.

'You're drunk, Comrade. Better get to bed.'

The man – presumably this was Pavel – made an angry

gesture towards the stairs and turned back to the concierge. He had succeeded in blocking her view of Richard, but the fall had aroused her curiosity. Richard could hear her high, querulous voice and Pavel's soothing responses as he reached the first floor.

Two more flights. The stairs were uncarpeted but clean. There was no sign of vandalism. From behind the closed doors came early morning sounds, the waking cry of a child, the clatter of pans, the throb of a razor being stropped. Richard hurried, praying that no one would decide to come out on to a landing. He reached the third floor and, as Kemenev had promised, there was a door ajar. Tapping lightly, not waiting for an answer, he went in, shut the door behind him and leant against it. He was safe – at least for the moment.

'I would say "Come in", but you're already in.' Standing in the middle of the room in a white blouse and green skirt, Tamara looked pretty and fresh, and absurdly normal. She smiled a welcome at Richard, waved him to a chair and went to listen by the door. There were quick, light steps on the stairs and Pavel appeared. He was very angry.

Glaring at Richard, he said to the girl, 'It's all right, I think. But not thanks to this fool. He fell into the place, drawing attention to himself, making the concierge take an interest, advertising his arrival. I only hope it's been worth while, that he's got something really important for us.'

'Quiet, Pavel.' She smiled at Richard. 'Do you speak Russian?'

'Yes, though by no means perfectly.'

'Perhaps we should talk English. But keep your voice down. The walls aren't very thick. First, do you have a message from Misha Kemenev?'

'And what have you done with that swine Baucher?' Pavel was still angry and impatient and his accent was heavy. 'Tell us!'

Richard told them – everything that had happened since he left the clinic, everything that Kemenev already knew, including Richard's name and his relationship to Carey-Ford and his reason for coming to Moscow. He was surprised that it took such a short time, but there were few interruptions. The two Russians listened eagerly, serious-faced, intent.

118

When he had finished Tamara said she would make some coffee and went into the kitchen. Pavel followed her but lounged in the doorway where he could keep an eye on Richard. They muttered together, Pavel doing most of the talking. Richard strained his ears, but he couldn't catch what they were saying, so he looked round the apartment.

It consisted of the room he was in, which was small but pleasantly furnished with a polar-bear skin on the floor and ikons on the wall. Of the four doors one, he knew, led directly on to the outside landing. The others gave into a kitchen, and presumably a bedroom and a bathroom. By Western standards it wasn't wonderful, but in Moscow only someone of comparative importance would be allowed to rent such a place, and it seemed an unlikely hide-out for a group of dissident Jews. Richard sighed. As Kemenev said, there would have to be a lot of explaining.

'You're tired,' Tamara said. 'When you've had your coffee you can sleep. You'll be quite safe here. Pavel has to go to the hospital, but I'll stay with you. He'll send a message to the laboratory where I work to say I'm sick and there'll be no trouble for me. This evening, when he returns, he'll bring you some clothes – yours aren't suitable – and as soon as Misha comes we can talk.'

It was all arranged and Richard saw no point in arguing. Clearly Misha Kemenev was the one in command, the one whom he would have to persuade, bribe, somehow force to help him get out of the Soviet Union. At least, that was the purpose to which he must cling, and not only for his own sake. Surreptitiously he touched the signet ring that Carey-Ford had given him. He had never wanted to come to this bloody country, never wanted to meet the traitor who was his father, never wanted to be involved with people like Goransky and Baucher. But now that it had happened to him, he intended to do his damnedest to see the thing through.

He swallowed the last of his black, bitter coffee. He yawned loudly. Suddenly he felt dizzy. His head was enormous, too heavy for the neck to support. It seemed to be rolling around. And his eyes were closing. With an effort he returned the cup to its saucer – or hoped that he had. The spoon fell on the floor. As he bent to pick it up he was overwhelmed by tiredness. Nothing mattered except sleep.

He was grateful to the two Russians who helped him into the bedroom. They stripped off his clothes and laid him in the bed and he was able to sink deep, deep into oblivion.

Richard woke slowly, conscious of a long passing of time, and not caring. As he moved his limbs he became aware of his nakedness, but it didn't worry him. He often slept in the nude. But the bed was hard, the bedclothes harsher than those to which he was accustomed. Reluctantly he came fully awake.

Although he couldn't remember the bedroom he knew at once where he was. He sat up carefully, quietly. There was a murmur of voices from the next room. He looked around him. His clothes had gone, and his shoes. He glanced at the bedside table. It held a lamp, an alarm clock, two books, but neither his wallet nor his watch.

Heart thumping, he pressed his left thumb hard against the little finger. The ring was still there. It fitted snugly, more snugly than it must have done on Carey-Ford's poor, wasted hand, and if Pavel or Tamara had tried to remove it they hadn't succeeded. Careless in his relief, he stretched luxuriously and knocked one of the books off the bedside table. Immediately the girl was at the door.

'You're awake? Good.' She came and sat on the bed beside him. 'Are you feeling better?'

'Much better, thank you.'

'You were very tired, exhausted, but tense too. Pavel put something in your coffee to help you rest and you've slept all day.' She beamed at him as if he had been clever. 'Are you hungry? Would you like something to eat?'

'Yes, please.' Richard was surprised at the enthusiasm of his response. 'But no more sleeping draughts, thank you.'

Tamara laughed. 'No. It's time to talk now, not to sleep. Misha has come. He says all is well. He's had no trouble. The car has been found, but they're still looking for Baucher. Pavel may have more news. He should be here soon.'

As far as he was concerned Richard didn't care if Pavel never came. He didn't like him, and sensed that the dislike was mutual. Admittedly he had forgotten to mention the drugged tea he had been given at the clinic, but nevertheless he resented Pavel doping his coffee.

A half-hour later Richard – washed, shaved and dressed in the typical Russian clothes that Pavel had brought for him – joined the others in the living-room. Pavel returned his watch and his wallet without comment. Tamara brought him a big bowl of borshch and some black bread. And while he ate, greedily and hungrily – it was the first solid food he had had for almost twenty-four hours – Kemenev talked.

Dmitri Sholatov had been a professor of physics at Moscow University. He was a Jew and spoke out against the régime. He worked secretly to help his fellow Jews, and he organized other dissidents to resist the activities of the Soviet authorities. He had been a truly great man. As he spoke, Kemenev's voice shook with emotion, and Richard remembered the passion with which he had described Sholatov in the car. He sympathized, but he didn't understand how Sholatov could be in any way connected with Carey-Ford.

Kemenev continued, 'Dmitri Sholatov was our leader. When he told us to do something we did it. He told me to become a driver for the KGB and get close to Baucher, Goransky's right-hand man, and I did, though it took time to become Baucher's chauffeur. But Dmitri didn't always tell us why he wanted things done. About two months ago he asked Pavel to drive him into the country. Pavel is a doctor and has a car of his own. It goes with this fine apartment and other advantages. He's one of the privileged people.'

There was a protesting flood of Russian from the young man, and Tamara whispered to Richard. 'Pavel's not a Jew, but he was a pupil of Sholatov and he would have done anything for him. He hates the KGB. We all do,' she ended simply.

Pavel turned angrily on Richard and said in his heavily accented English, 'Twice he asked me to drive him out near the clinic and to wait in the car for him. Obviously it was important or he wouldn't have let me take such a risk. The second time I asked what he was after, and he told me he needed to talk to the British defector in order to obtain some vital information, but the place was heavily guarded and he had to devise some means of getting in. Next night that bastard Baucher came for him and – '

Abruptly Pavel pushed back his chair and stood up. He went to a cupboard and took out a bottle of vodka and some glasses. Tamara fetched a plate of black bread cut into small squares.

'We shall drink to Dmitri Sholatov,' Kemenev said. And when the toast had been drunk – emotionally by the Russians, with some slight embarrassment on Richard's part – he added, 'Now, Richard Lavery, you can guess what we want of you and why we've risked so much to get it. We must finish what Dmitri began but couldn't finish. For us it's a sacred trust.'

Richard nodded his understanding. This obscure group of dissident Jews wanted what Igor Goransky wanted and what Charles Bigrel wanted – the secret that Guy Carey-Ford had only half confided in him. But he wasn't going to tell them, he thought savagely, not any of them, not yet, not unless they tortured it out of him.

THIRTEEN

It was Sunday. During the spring Igor Goransky was wont to spend his weekends in the country but today, although it was unpleasantly warm, he was in Moscow. What's more, he wasn't relaxing in his office in the Kremlin. He was at KGB headquarters on Dzerzhinsky Square – and with him were almost all his senior staff members.

Goransky was in a foul temper. This didn't mean that he shouted and banged his fist on the desk and swore as some members of the Soviet hierarchy were apt to do when things went wrong. On the contrary, he was very quiet. He spoke seldom, and between remarks were long, icy silences. His orders were short and incisive. He either sat motionless or, as a concession to his pent-up feelings, walked up and down the room, pulling gently at his greying beard. It was at times like these, as everyone knew, that Goransky was most to be feared.

So, when the rumour spread that the bodies of Franz Baucher and Natalya Meriosova had been discovered in a ditch beside one of the roads leading into Moscow, a wave of doubt swept through the headquarters. No one was sure how Goransky would take the news. Baucher, though born in the DDR, had in some ways been closer to him than many of his Russian colleagues.

'The assassins will be found, Comrade, I assure you, and with speed.'

'Perhaps,' Goransky said and, after a pause that convinced his assistant he had overlooked some vital clue, added, 'Two bodies, you say?'

'Yes, Comrade. The driver's still missing – but we'll find him, dead or alive.'

'What do you know about him?'

'His name is Misha Kemenev – a Jew, but oddly enough Comrade Baucher didn't seem to mind that. He was his regular driver.'

A Jew! Goransky didn't speak the words aloud, but they rose in his throat and he had to choke them down. Dmitri Sholatov had been a Jew. Dmitri Sholatov had been trying to make contact with Carey-Ford. There was no actual proof of this; Sholatov had died too soon. He had been one of Baucher's rare failures. But Baucher had been convinced of it. Sholatov, Carey-Ford, Richard Lavery and Kemenev – also a Jew. At least it was another possibility.

The alternative – that the SIS were responsible – Goransky found difficult to accept. Admittedly Charles Bigrel would have liked nothing better at this point than to have spirited Lavery away, but he would never have devised such a clumsy plan. He was a subtle man. Goransky had a great admiration for him. Besides, there hadn't been time or opportunity. Forewarned of David Grant's arrival in Moscow as the replacement for a supposedly sick member of a British trade delegation, Goransky had ordered that he be kept under close surveillance, and he was sure Grant couldn't have arranged Lavery's abduction at such short notice, even with help from his Embassy.

Yet if it had been a party of Jewish dissidents acting on their own, why? What had they to gain? What did they intend to do with Lavery – hold him as a hostage? And if Lavery talked to them? The mere thought chilled Goransky.

Lavery had been given a drug before he left the clinic. The idea was to make him drowsy, receptive to suggestion, ready to answer questions – even unexpected questions – and, if that had failed, Baucher would have used other means of persuasion. But it was he, Goransky, who was to have asked the questions and received the answers, not a parcel of dissident Jews. If what he feared was true he would rather the SIS had got hold of Richard Lavery, much rather. He could have bargained with Charles Bigrel.

'You remember the traitor, Dmitri Sholatov?' Goransky didn't wait for a reply. 'Round up all persons known to be connected with him – all persons, Jews or not.' He paused. 'Pay special attention to anyone who might have some form of transport – a car, a motor-cycle – at his disposal.'

'But, Comrade, we did this before, when Sholatov – '

'Do it again!' Goransky said gently. He hesitated, made up

his mind. Until now he hadn't mentioned Lavery. 'At the same time look for a young man, about thirty, tall, narrow shoulders, fair hair, thin face, deep-set grey eyes. He's a foreigner, but he speaks our language well. It's possible he's being held against his will.'

'Very good, Comrade.' The assistant failed to hide his surprise. 'Does he have a name, this young foreigner?'

'He's called Richard Lavery, but that's for your ears only.'

He was gratified. 'Yes, Comrade. Is there anything else?'

'What is the latest report on the Englishman David Grant?'

'Grant cut the formal meeting that Comrade Mischaev was to address this morning. Instead, one of the Commerical Secretaries from the British Embassy picked him up at the hotel and they went for a walk in Gorky Park. They spent some while near the big wheel, watching the chess-players at the open-air boards. We had a directional microphone on them, but they only discussed the chess. At present they're lunching at the restaurant on – '

'Grant's trying to make contact with someone.' Goransky nodded his head in satisfaction. It confirmed his belief that the SIS were not responsible for Lavery's disappearance. 'All right. Don't lose him. But first priority is to round up the Jews and find Lavery.'

In London it was a grey day given to squally gusts of rain. Charles Bigrel shivered as he came out of the Guards' Chapel where he had been attending matins. He wasn't a religious man but, when possible, he adhered to the custom of church on Sunday that had been part of his boyhood. Usually he found it comforting.

Today had been an exception. He couldn't clear his mind of thoughts of Guy Carey-Ford, and the thoughts were grim. He had known Carey-Ford well at one period, before the man had turned traitor and defected to the Soviet Union, and he felt desperately sorry for him. No one had forced Carey-Ford to go to Moscow. He had gone of his own free will – unlike young Richard Lavery – but to suffer for months and to die . . .

Nodding his thanks as Tyler held the door for him, Bigrel got into his car. It was Richard Lavery he should be thinking about now, he told himself, not Carey-Ford. Somehow they had to get young Lavery out of the communists' clutches. In practice it was up to Grant and the Commerical Secretary, who was in fact the resident SIS man in Moscow, but the final responsibility was his and his alone. If they failed . . .

He thought of John and Veronica Lavery who believed Richard was on holiday in Vienna, of Emma Jackson who had forced some of the truth from her father and was no longer speaking to him, of Dmitri Sholatov who had already died, of Richard Lavery himself, and once more of Guy Carey-Ford and what vital information he might or might not have given to his son. If they failed to bring Richard Lavery safely back to London, he would, he decided, resign.

The car drew up in front of the imposing house in Eaton Square, and Bigrel got out. His movements rather stiff, he went up the steps and rang the bell. The door was opened promptly by a manservant in a white jacket. Chris McCann lived well, even for a very senior civil servant, but he had twice married money – and beautiful women. Not that anyone grudged him his luck. His first wife had been tragically killed in a car accident, and Anita was a charmer.

'Charles, how nice to see you!' She meant it and she kissed him on both cheeks with warm affection. 'Come and sit down. Sherry?'

'Thank you, my dear.' Bigrel would have preferred Scotch, but he wouldn't ask for it. 'Where's Chris?'

'Listening to the news. He hates to miss it.' She laughed. 'He's positively manic about it.'

'And sometimes it pays dividends.' Chris McCann came striding into the room. 'Charles, how are you? Have you heard? Guy Carey-Ford's dead. Died peacefully in his sleep, according to *Tass*.'

'When?'

'Last night, supposedly. But the Russians don't usually announce things like that until weeks after the event, so it looks as if our fears are justified. They do intend to make a big production of the funeral.'

'Possibly. After all, Carey-Ford was one of their biggest catches of the last decade, if not the biggest.' Bigrel kept his voice level. He knew there was nothing he could do, that he had to be patient, but it wasn't easy at this critical period.

'His death's bound to revive old memories – not happy ones on our side.'

'It's his family I'm sorry for,' Anita said, sipping her sherry. 'Especially the son.'

'The son? Carey-Ford's son? Jesus Christ! Anita, how the hell did you know he had a son?'

Anita McCann uncrossed her long legs and regarded her husband coolly. She wasn't used to being spoken to in that tone of voice. She resented it, especially in the circumstances, in front of Charles Bigrel. Charles had said nothing. But he was staring at her as if she had uttered some obscenity. She took a deep breath.

Before she could speak McCann was on his knees beside her. 'I'm sorry, my darling. I didn't mean to bite you like that, but it was the surprise.' He looked at Bigrel as if for support.

'My dear, whoever was it that told you Carey-Ford had a family?' Bigrel asked mildly, disbelievingly.

Anita McCann was an intelligent woman. Neither man had deceived her. She knew she was treading on delicate ground. She took her husband's hand but she addressed herself to Charles Bigrel, smiling at him.

'I wouldn't have mentioned it in front of anyone else,' she said firmly. 'I really am discreet. But with you two I relax. It was Poppy Penryn who told me. She didn't say, but I assumed Thomas had told her.'

'Penryn? Damn that man!' McCann got to his feet and went to pour himself more sherry. He didn't offer to refill Bigrel's glass. He was too angry. 'Just wait till I see Thomas tomorrow. He gets hold of some extraordinary story and then gossips about it to that stupid wife of his. My God, but he should know better.'

'Chris, please. I feel this is all my fault.'

'No. It's mine,' McCann said decisively. 'I'm responsible for Thomas. He answers to me.'

'Perhaps – ' Bigrel hesitated. What he wanted was to ask McCann if he could be present when Penryn was faced with his breach of security, but it wasn't practicable. McCann might refuse, which was his right, and that would be extremely embarrassing. 'Chris, I hope you'll let me know Thomas's explanation, what makes him think Carey-Ford ever had a family.'

'Of course, my dear chap. Of course.' McCann had recovered his composure. 'It is odd, isn't it?'

'Very odd,' Bigrel agreed, but he was remembering what Maurice Jackson had said about Penryn's curiosity concerning Richard Lavery, and the connection Penryn seemed to have made between Lavery and Carey-Ford. He was glad when the manservant announced that luncheon was served.

Sunday moved on. For David Grant it moved fast but was full of frustration. By early evening he was up-tight, his nerves jumping. He had an appointment to keep and he was late.

The tram had scarcely stopped before he leapt off. Seeming not to hurry, he made the best possible speed along the underground passage to the other side of the avenue, and just managed to catch a bus going in the direction from which he had come. He dropped his five-kopek piece in the box, tore off a ticket and took a seat by the window. He watched the traffic following and overtaking the bus and studied the passengers who got on. When he saw nothing to alert his suspicions he allowed himself to relax a little.

Reasonably sure that he had shaken his tails, he got off the bus after six stops and began to walk. He was almost opposite the café which was the agreed rendezvous when he spotted the police-car tucked into a narrow side-street. His first thought was that he had been betrayed and led into some sort of trap. Then, as he drew abreast of the café, the door opened and he saw an old man being hustled out between two stone-faced characters. It was his contact, the chess-player he had met that morning in Gorky Park. Grant walked on.

Five minutes later he was stopped and asked for his papers, but everything was correct and it proved to be a formality. Nevertheless, as he continued, he noticed something strange. While there seemed to be an increase in traffic – boxy Zhigulis, so dear to the KGB, were teeming around the streets like small black beetles – pedestrians were becoming fewer and fewer. Involuntarily Grant's pace increased.

He was stopped twice before he reached his destination, the hotel where Richard Lavery was staying. He had decided on a bold approach. There was nothing to lose. He went up to the desk and asked for Mr Richard Lavery. Without appearing to, he was watching the receptionist carefully and didn't miss her reaction. The sallow face remained impassive, but her hand balled into a fist.

'Mr Lavery is no longer here,' she said, speaking English as Grant had done. 'He has left the hotel.'

'Really? When?'

'Last – This morning.'

'You were going to say "last night". Which do you mean?'

'This morning. He has gone, and his baggage. I don't know where. He didn't say. So I can't tell you.'

'Was he alone, or did he leave with – friends?'

'I – I don't know. I wasn't on duty.' The quick, sharp questions had rattled her and her cheeks grew stained with an unbecoming purplish blush. 'He's gone! He's not here!' she hissed.

'Can I help you, Mr Grant?'

Grant turned slowly, unsurprised by the voice behind him. He had been fully aware of the man sitting nearby and pretending to read a copy of *Pravda*. The use of his name, however, was a blow. He smiled at the man, who didn't return the compliment.

'Yes,' Grant said. 'You could get me a taxi, Comrade.'

The man's lips thinned but he nodded at the receptionist, who reached for the telephone. 'Where do you wish to go, Mr Grant?'

'The British Embassy, please,' David Grant said meekly.

At the Embassy Grant drafted a telegram for Charles Bigrel and took it to the cypher room. In clear, it read: 'Believe Carey-Ford died during night. Lavery disappeared soon after. No trace. Much police activity and only hopeful contact with Sholatov link arrested. My cover blown, probably from arrival Moscow. Complete failure. Sorry. Grant.'

Half an hour later the teletype chattered out in reply. It contained three words: 'Return London. Bigrel.' It told him nothing of the bitter despair with which his telegram had been received.

FOURTEEN

'There,' said the Russian girl in triumph. 'Now you may look at yourself.'

Richard obediently opened his eyes. 'Christ!' he said, gazing in amazement at his reflection in the bathroom mirror. He took off the steel-framed spectacles that slightly distorted his vision but did nothing to improve his image. 'Christ!' he said again.

The change was startling. His naturally fair hair was as dark as his brows, and matted down as if shoe-polish had been applied to it. His skin was a yellowish colour, shading to a deeper tan where the dye was uneven. And on his upper lip, tickling his nostrils, was a luxuriant moustache which Stalin might have envied.

Richard tried to stifle his laughter. 'Does it wash off or do I have to wait till it wears off?'

'It's not funny,' Tamara said severely. 'Tomorrow or the next day, when Misha had made arrangements, you'll have to go on the street, among people. You can't stay in Pavel's apartment for ever. Do you want the first KGB man who sees you to recognize you?'

Grinning in spite of himself, Richard said, 'Not even my nearest and dearest would recognize me at the moment.'

'Do you realize what will happen to you if the KGB catch you?' the girl persisted. 'They won't take your word for it – as we did – that Carey-Ford died without telling you anything of importance.'

'No – o,' Richard said, remembering with some cynicism how the three Russians had questioned him until the small hours of the morning and how Pavel, not possessing a Bible, had finally made him swear on an ikon that he was telling the truth. But they had believed him in the end. Whereas the KGB . . . 'I know, Tamara. I'm not a fool.'

'They'll make you wish you were dead, Richard,' she continued earnestly, 'but they won't let you die. When they've stripped you of all humanity they'll still torture you, and if by some chance you ever do get out of the Lubyanka . . .'

'I know, Tamara. I told you, I'm not a fool.' Richard repeated. He put out a hand and gently stroked her cheek. 'Believe me, I'm grateful to you – and to Misha and Pavel – for helping me like this. I only wish I could help you in return.' He smiled at her. 'At least it will be one in the eye for Goransky if I do get safely back to England.'

'One in the eye?' Tamara frowned; she didn't understand the expression.

And Richard didn't have time to explain. There was the sound of hurried steps on the stairs and a quick triple rat-tat on the door. Richard would have leapt for the bathroom but Tamara stopped him.

'It'll be Pavel. He must have forgotten his key.'

She opened the door. It was Misha Kemenev. Clean-shaven, his hair short and streaked with grey, a workman's tool-bag slung over his shoulder, Richard took a second to recognize him.

Kemenev dumped his bag on the polar-bear rug and began to search inside it. 'You must leave at once,' he said, 'both of you. They've taken Pavel.'

'Pavel! When? Why?' Tamara demanded.

'A short while ago, when he came out of the hospital,' Kemenev said. 'I was waiting for him. I intended to pass him a message because I thought it wasn't good for me to be seen around here too often. The KGB were also waiting for him. As to why, I don't know. They've been very active today, checking papers, rounding up suspect Jews.' He shook his head sadly. 'I suppose it's because of Baucher and Meriosova. They must have discovered the bodies.'

'Jews, yes. They always blame us,' Tamara said. 'But why Pavel?'

Kemenev gave an expressive shrug. 'They questioned him after Sholatov died. That was something of a formality as far as he was concerned, and this could be the same. But if they come here and the concierge talks about a fair young man falling into the hall – who knows how much she saw yesterday? – it will be a lot more than formality. We must be somewhere safe before that, somewhere Pavel's never heard of.'

Kemenev, who had at last found what he had been searching for in the tool-bag, sat back on his heels. In his hand was a cheap plastic wallet. He held it out to Richard.

'Here are some papers for you. They are genuine. I borrowed them from a friend who's ill in bed and doesn't need them for the moment. If necessary he'll say they were lost or stolen. They don't fit you like a glove exactly, but they're all I could get. Study them while Tamara and I tidy up the apartment.'

Shocked at the news Kemenev had brought, Richard took the wallet and began to go through its contents. They did nothing to encourage him. The photograph on the identity card bore scant resemblance to the appearance Tamara had given him, and the information concerning its rightful owner – a biologist from the Ukraine – presented insuperable problems. Richard was sure that the first time he was stopped and asked for his papers he would inevitably give himself away. But there was no alternative.

'Where are we going?' he asked. 'Is it far?'

'Far enough. We'll have to go by Metro. Listen.' Kemenev explained what he wanted them to do. 'Are you ready?'

Tamara glanced quickly around the apartment. 'Yes.' She tossed Baucher's jacket to Richard. 'I've mended it. The bullet-hole hardly shows at all.'

'Thanks.' He put it on.

'And your spectacles,' Kemenev prompted.

Obediently Richard stretched out his hand to pick up the spectacles, and at once Tamara said, 'Your ring. No Russian would ever wear a little ring like that. Take it off, Richard.'

'No!' It was an explosive negative, and Richard grinned to soften its impact. 'I'm sorry. I can't. I've worn it so long, it won't come off.' He made a show of tugging at the ring.

Kemenev grunted. 'We're wasting time. Let's go.'

They went. Kemenev led the way, making sure the concierge was busy preparing her evening meal before he signalled to Richard and Tamara to follow him into the street. Stooping as he walked, his tool-bag over one shoulder, he looked like an elderly workman going on night shift. There was no reason to connect him with the young couple walking lovingly arm in arm behind him, no reason to look at any of them twice.

But as they approached the Metro station, Richard suddenly felt Tamara's elbow dig into his ribs. 'Police,' she whispered.

Richard tensed. The policeman, short, broad, po-faced, was standing to one side of the entrance. Clearly the Metro was out. But Kemenev was already too close to turn back without attracting attention. The three of them would have to walk by, directly under the gaze of a man who must surely be on the lookout for them. Richard felt himself begin to sweat.

He tried to free his arm from the girl's, but she clung to him. 'Let go, Tamara,' he said between his teeth. 'Run for it if he stops us.'

She didn't answer him directly. 'Watch Misha,' she said.

Misha Kemenev had reached the Metro entrance. To Richard's horror he didn't attempt to walk past. He stopped. Nonchalantly shifting his tool-bag from one shoulder to the other, he deposited his five-kopek piece in the turnstile and strode through. The policeman barely glanced at him.

'Come on,' Tamara muttered. She changed to Russian. 'We must go to GUM tomorrow, my love,' she chattered brightly. 'I hear they're to have some fantastic new curtains and we've got to buy . . . '

With a minor shock Richard realized they were at the turnstile. Hampered by the spectacles he was wearing, he fumbled with the two coins Kemenev had provided and, silently cursing his clumsiness, nearly dropped one. He could feel, literally feel, the policeman's gaze moving over him like a pinpoint of white heat. Yet when he looked up he saw it was Tamara who was the object of interest, not himself. The man's eyes were running over her, stripping her, enjoying her.

Richard thrust the girl ahead of him and pushed his way through the turnstile. Tamara was still chattering about the joys of shopping at the big department store. The policeman had turned to watch her. Any second, Richard was sure, something would jog his memory and he would recollect what he was meant to be doing and why he was standing where he was. And his attention would shift from the girl to the young man with her. In his mind Richard anticipated the shout to stop, to wait.

It never came. Other people were passing through the turnstile behind them, and they joined a small procession moving through a great vaulted hall whose alcoves were adorned with over-life size sculptures. Tamara was still talking, though not so animatedly. Richard envied her her composure. But as they stepped on the descending escalator she suddenly stopped in mid-sentence and pressed herself hard against him. He realized she was not as free from nerves as he had supposed.

The escalator bore them down and down, speeding them past the heroic mosaics on the walls, into what seemed to Richard to be the bowels of the earth. Then, beyond all expectation, he heard an American voice. 'Is this ever different to our little old New York subway!' it said with wry amusement, and he caught a glimpse of two elderly blue-haired matrons and their Intourist guide as they whisked past on the ascending journey.

Filled with unbelievable anguish, Richard found that he was holding Tamara very close. She broke away as they reached the bottom of the escalator. Kemenev was waiting for them. He appeared to be absorbed in the huge wall-map of the Metro system, but as soon as they drew level he strode off.

Following him they had no problems. A train drew in a minute or two after they reached the platform. Kemenev had elected to go to the far end and, it being a Sunday evening, they got into a half-empty carriage. The doors whispered shut. The train accelerated.

Stretches of dark tunnel alternated with pauses at brilliantly lit stations. Richard sat back, feigning boredom as if, like the other passengers who travelled daily on this line, he was used to seeing the cartoon-style frescoes of great Russian achievements that adorned the walls, so different from the white lavatory tiles and the publicity hoardings of the London Underground. Gradually he relaxed a little. No one paid him any attention, and in the anonymity of the journey he began to feel a spurious sense of security.

Perhaps it was this that made him careless. The moustache that Tamara had fixed so adroitly to his upper lip bothered him. The hair tickled his nostrils and caused the inside of his nose to prick so that he had a continual sniff. He felt in his right trouser pocket where he always kept his handkerchief, but it wasn't there. He tried the pocket of Baucher's jacket. His hand closed on some material and, without thinking, he pulled out the pale blue scarf that Natalya Meriosova had given him on the way to the ballet.

Bright with scarlet splashes, it lay accusingly on his lap, and he stared at it, mesmerized. It was only yesterday, he recalled, that he had used it to wipe the blood and broken flesh from around the bullet-hole before he reluctantly put on the jacket. The blood was still sticky. It was getting on his hands . . .

The quick intake of Tamara's breath brought Richard back to the present. At once he was aware of the three people sitting opposite him. Gazing at the scarf, their faces blank with horror, the two women were slowly getting up and edging away from him to seek comparative safety at the far end of the carriage. They got off at the next stop. The man remained, unmoving, except for his eyes which travelled from the toes of Richard's shoes to his cap, itemizing every detail. No one else showed any interest.

Tamara's grip fastened on Richard's wrist. The train was drawing into Arbatskaya station. Kemenev was already by the doors, waiting to get off. Richard thrust the scarf deep into his pocket and, urged by the girl, made for the exit. The man followed them on to the platform and along the underground passage.

'He's suspicious,' Tamara whispered. 'He'll report us as soon as he gets a chance.'

'What can we do?'

'I don't know. Trust Misha. He'll think of something.'

But Kemenev couldn't work miracles, and as if from nowhere a KGB man had materialized at the foot of the escalator and was checking papers. Kemenev had no option. He had to join the queue. To have turned would have been to draw attention to himself. Without a glance behind he lined up behind a couple of startled tourists and two or three resigned Muscovites.

Almost unconsciously Richard and Tamara slowed their pace, then came to a stop. Richard bent down and pretended to tie his shoelace. But the man behind them didn't hesitate. He started to run, pushing past Tamara, gesticulating wildly and leaving no doubt of his intentions. He was bursting to report what he had seen on the train.

'Leave me!' Richard said urgently. 'Disappear, Tamara. You've a better chance on your own.'

The girl hesitated. She didn't want to leave him, but . . . At the bottom of the escalator the KGB man had waved Kemenev on without bothering about papers. He was listening to the informer, who was pointed down the tunnel and talking fast. She had about twenty seconds.

'Go to Kalinin Avenue. The bookshop. Anyone will direct you. It's not far. We'll find you there.'

Then she was gone, joining a couple of young girls who had come from another train, asking them some question so that as they talked she seemed to be one with them. Richard turned and hurried in the opposite direction. There was a shout behind him, running footsteps. He rounded a corner, found a long, empty tunnel, stretching into the distance. Thirty yards on a boy appeared zipping up his fly, and Richard saw the sign. Men's lavatories. He took to his heels.

It was only as he pushed through the swing-doors that he realized he might be confronted by an attendant. But there was no one on duty. The place was deserted. He went into a cubicle, locked the door, sat on the seat and waited. He knew how vulnerable he was, but if he were to be caught he preferred to be caught here rather than hunted like an animal through the underground system. And at least he had allowed Tamara and Kemenev to get away.

Richard caught his breath. The doors had creaked open. Someone had come in. Richard strained to listen. But there were just the sounds of urination, someone splashing in a basin, the thud of a new section of roller-towel being jerked down. The doors creaked again. Richard thought the man had gone, but his hope was immediately dashed.

'Is there anyone in here apart from you?' an authoritative voice demanded.

'N – no. I don't think so.'

'On the john?'

'I – I don't know.'

There was a crash as a cubicle door was kicked back on its hinges, another crash, and another – down the line. Richard winced. Hurriedly he shuffled his feet and rustled some lavatory paper. Silence outside. Then a fist thundered on the door.

'Come out! At once.'

'Coming. Coming, Comrade. Can't a man even . . . ' Richard mumbled, hoping to disguise his accented Russian. He didn't hurry. He made a noise with more paper, flushed the pan and released the bolt. 'Here I am.' He shambled out, attending to his trousers.

But one glance at the KGB man was enough. Grimly Richard accepted that his play-acting had been a waste of effort. The man exuded triumph. He knew what a prize he had captured. There was no hope of deceiving him.

In a different place at a different time, Richard would have gritted his teeth and admitted defeat. He wasn't by nature aggressive, and until recently everything had come easily to him. But he had learnt a lot in the last few days, not least about himself. If it were humanly possible he intended to get back to London with the signet ring that Carey-Ford had given him.

The swing-doors creaked as the man who had come in merely to urinate sneaked off, wanting no part in what was going on. To Richard the sound was by now familiar, but momentarily it distracted the KGB man and Richard seized his chance. With all his strength he punched the man in the stomach and, as he doubled forwards, hooked him under the chin to send him crashing backwards on to the stone floor.

It wasn't a scientific attack but it had the element of surprise, and Richard was lucky. In falling the KGB man had hit the back of his skull on the edge of a urinal. He lay still, breathing stertorously through his open mouth. It would be some while before he regained consciousness. The danger, however, was that someone else would come in to relieve himself and sound the alarm.

Holding him under the shoulders, Richard hauled the KGB

man across the floor to the furthest cubicle and with a super effort – he was a thick-set heavy character – lifted him on to the seat. His body promptly slumped, and Richard swore. It took him a full minute to prop the man against the back wall, pull down his trousers and arrange his legs so that he looked comparatively natural to anyone glancing in – a ruse to buy time, since it was impossible to lock the door from the outside. Richard prayed it would work.

The next thing was to alter his own appearance. Working fast, Richard pulled off Baucher's leather jacket, thrust his cap and spectacles into one of its pockets and stuffed the whole bundle behind a bucket in what seemed to be a sort of broom cupboard. Then he turned his attention to his face. Staring in the mirror he tore off the thick moustache, leaving small spots of blood along his upper lip, and with his fingers combed his hair straight back off his brow. Superficially he was a new man.

With an assumed air of casualness Richard walked out of the cloakroom and set off along the tunnel to the escalators. He had been half afraid that the man who had informed against him might be waiting to see what happened, but he was nowhere about. Richard passed through the station and came out into the darkening street. He might have been any ordinary Muscovite – except that he had no idea where he was going.

Tamara had said, 'Kalinin Avenue. The bookshop. Anyone will direct you.' But to ask the way was to ask for interest to be taken in him. Richard decided against it. He would try his luck first. The general flow of pedestrians was to the right, and he went with it, half attaching himself to a straggling group of young people who were obviously starting on an evening out. However, when one of the girls laughingly suggested that he should join them, he grinned and shook his head and hurried on. After that he was careful not to get involved with anyone.

He found Kalinin Avenue without difficulty – and the bookshop. It was then that his problems began.

Kalinin Avenue is a long, wide boulevard with rows of rectangles – twenty- to twenty-five-storey apartment and office blocks – perched upon a two-storey shopping and entertainment centre. By day it's full of life and bustle and seemingly aimless pedestrians. But on a Sunday evening, grown dark and damp and cold, people walked with purpose. Window-shoppers were few. And, as time passed, Richard began to feel more and more conspicuous.

An hour later, huddled in the doorway of the bookshop, he resolutely considered his position. It could scarcely have been worse. There had been no sign of Kemenev or Tamara and the chance that he would ever see either of them again seemed remote. He was on his own, in a strange city, without funds, implicated in a double murder, wanted by the KGB – and he knew with total certainty that once the KGB got their hands on him again he would never leave the Soviet Union alive. But he wasn't done yet.

A plain black van drove past. It was going very slowly and its lights were bright. Richard cowered in the shadows of the doorway. The van stopped. The possibility of capture had become immediate. Unexpectedly, instead of reversing in order to get a better view of the huddled figure he had spotted, the driver got out of the van and started to walk back towards the bookshop. Richard, who had been poised to make a run for it, hesitated. The driver had passed under a street lamp and Richard saw that he was an old man, small and lop-sided, with one shoulder higher than the other. He didn't look like KGB.

He stopped just short of the doorway and, looking in the bookshop window, said, 'Richard?'

Richard drew in his breath with a sharp hiss. 'Yes. Who are you?'

'A friend. Kemenev sent me. Come.'

Turning abruptly he trotted back to the van. Richard let him reach it, then hurried after him. The door was open, the engine running. Richard jumped in. Almost before he was seated they were moving off.

The first thing Richard noticed was the smell. It was all-pervasive, but particularly strong around the old man. Instinctively Richard wrinkled up his nose. Yet what did a smell matter? The van was dry and warm – a sanctuary, however temporary. And, most important, he was no longer alone, without hope. He felt a rush of gratitude to Kemenev

139

and Tamara for not having abandoned him, followed by shame that he hadn't asked about them.

'Tamara and Misha, they're safe?'

'Yes. They had no trouble, but we decided it was wiser for them not to be on the streets, which was why I came for you.'

'I'm terribly grateful.'

The old man inclined his head. 'Incidentally, my name is Leonid Vasilev. I do what I can to help but, as you'll appreciate, an opportunity like the present doesn't occur very often.'

Richard frowned. He had understood the Russian, but sensed that the true meaning of what Vasilev had said had eluded him. He made a non-committal reply. Then, without warning, a fit of shivering seized him. His teeth began to chatter.

'Are you all right?'

'J – just cold.'

'There's a blanket behind your seat.'

Richard turned. 'Ch – Christ!'

'Could be. I don't ask awkward questions.' The old man chortled at his own joke. 'Actual fact, the coffin's empty. I brought it along as an excuse in case I was stopped.'

Richard wrapped himself in the blanket, thankful for its warmth in spite of its strong smell – the same smell that permeated the whole van. He recognized it now. It was formaldehyde.

'You're an undertaker,' he said.

'An embalmer,' Vasilev corrected him. 'I've got a business in the old district behind Arbat Square – not far from Arbatskaya station, where you got off the train. We're almost there.'

Richard peered out of the van window. They had left Kalinin Avenue some minutes ago, and were scurrying through dark crooked streets where nineteenth-century houses crowded together with small shops. A sharp right-angled turn brought them into a cul-de-sac and, as Vasilev braked fiercely, the van came to a halt in front of a pair of big wooden gates.

'Wait!' Vasilev ordered.

Richard waited while the old man opened the heavy gates, drove the van into a courtyard and shut the gates again. He felt exhausted. It had been a hell of a day, full of unpleasant shocks. He hoped there were no more to come.

'All right,' Vasilev called. 'Will you help me, please.'

Richard unwound himself from the blanket and jumped down into the courtyard. Vasilev had already unlocked the van's rear doors and was pulling out the coffin. Richard took one end. The long black box was ornately decorated and heavier than he had expected.

'It's lucky the poor man was tall,' Vasilev said, breathing heavily as he shouldered his half of the burden. 'This casket would never fit you otherwise.'

'Fit me?' Richard nearly dropped his end of the coffin. He couldn't believe what he had heard. 'Fit me? What on earth do you mean?'

It was Vasilev's turn to be surprised. 'Didn't Kemenev tell you?' he said. 'That's how you're getting out of Russia, in place of a dead man.'

FIFTEEN

They sat around the table in Vasilev's living quarters above the embalming business – the three Russian Jews and Richard Lavery.

'Nothing can go wrong,' Kemenev said firmly. 'Nothing.'

'Why should it?' Vasilev asked. 'It worked perfectly last time.'

'Last time! You mean you've done this before?'

'Yes. Once.'

'The only chance we've had.'

Richard looked dubiously from one Russian to the other. He kept his voice level. 'What happened?'

'Vasilev just told you. It worked perfectly.' Tamara slid her hand into Richard's. 'You must have faith in us, Richard.'

'I have, complete faith,' he lied. 'But the thought of being shut up in that long box appalls me. Is there any alternative? Supposing I say it's not feasible, I can't do it?'

'Then we'll take you to the British Embassy,' Kemenev said without hesitation, 'but Goransky's bound to know you're there and if he insists you're wanted on a murder charge they'll probably give you up. After all, you don't have diplomatic immunity, and your people won't want to make an international incident out of it.'

Richard thought briefly of Charles Bigrel – and of Carey-Ford's admonition to trust no one. 'No,' he said, reluctantly. 'I don't imagine they would. Okay. Tell me about the coffin plan.'

'It's really quite simple,' Vasilev said. 'The dead man was about your height. You put on his clothes. I attend to your face and hands – the parts that show – and before we leave for the airport I give you an injection so that while you sleep your breathing will be very, very shallow. In short, you'll appear to be a corpse.'

Richard frowned. 'Is anyone going to look at me?'

'Most certainly. The coffin will be inspected before it leaves Moscow, and when it arrives in Vienna. Which is why the lid's not securely fastened until much later.' The old man chuckled. 'Ah, that makes you feel better, doesn't it? Richard, I assure you there's no danger of being suffocated – airholes apart – or being buried alive. You can always give a big heave and free yourself.'

'Thank God for that,' Richard said simply. 'But what if the widow wants a last look at her husband and finds me instead?'

'She'll have no opportunity before leaving Moscow. The coffin goes from here straight to the plane, where it's put aboard – most circumspectly. No one likes to think he's flying with the dead.' Vasilev grinned his amusement; he was used to death. 'Once it gets to Vienna and has been inspected, it's left in a room at the airport overnight. That's when you'll be released. Our friend there is absolutely dependable so you have no cause to worry. Of course, if the widow should prove importunate and forestall you, which is most unlikely, you'll have to shout for your ambassador. But you'll be in Austria so you'll be all right.'

Richard nodded. Once he was in Vienna nothing would matter. He would be safe. The first thing would be to contact Peter Denville. His spirits rose at the thought, and he had to bite his bottom lip to stop sheer joy from spreading across his face. He would be all right, yes. But what of Tamara and Kemenev and old Vasilev?

'What about you?'

Vasilev shrugged. 'If for any reason the widow makes a fuss, there'll be an investigation. Too bad. They'll find her husband under my cellar floor. Misha will put him there tonight, beside the bones of the Austrian diplomat who also served our cause unknowingly. However, it's not a great risk and I'm more than willing to take it.'

'Okay. With luck none of this will affect you, but what about Tamara and Misha?' Richard persisted.

Kemenev answered for both of them. 'Ever since I knew I must kill Franz Baucher I've planned to "disappear" – become someone else. It's possible, even in Moscow. As for Tamara, if Pavel's questioning was a formality, she can continue as usual – like Vasilev. If not, we'll have to think again.'

143

'One day I shall go to Israel,' Tamara said, 'but not yet, not while my mother lives.'

Vasilev got up from the table. 'We must drink to that. And to Richard's safe journey home.' He cocked his head enquiringly. 'You've made up your mind, Richard? You've decided to travel by my escape route?'

'Thank you, yes,' Richard said, suppressing his doubts. 'It wouldn't be right to waste such a chance, would it? Obviously it doesn't occur very often.'

'Not often,' Vasilev agreed. 'In fact so rarely we would never waste it. If you'd refused there'd have been some poor Jew happy to take your place.'

'But don't let that deter you,' Kemenev said promptly. 'It's true you couldn't help us over Carey-Ford but we involved you in Baucher's assassination and, if it hadn't been for you, Natalya Meriosova would have shot me. You saved my life, Richard, and in return I and my friends want to do everything we can for you.'

'Then let us drink,' Vasilev said. With Tamara's assistance he had brought glasses and a bottle of vodka and some square dry biscuits. 'I give you first – Mother Russia and all who fight to free her from oppression and tyranny.'

They stood. They drank the toast Vasilev had proposed. But as the vodka exploded in his belly Richard found himself thinking unwillingly of Guy Carey-Ford, who had betrayed his own country to side with the tyrants and the oppressors. He felt sick.

It was cold in the loft and even here the smell of formaldehyde had penetrated. Richard couldn't sleep. The straw mattress on the floor made an uncomfortable bed, and the single blanket was inadequate. Dark thoughts, like rats, scuttled through his mind.

In the cellar Kemenev was digging a grave for the Austrian businessman who had died of a heart attack while on holiday with his wife. The earth would be hard and not easy to dig, but Kemenev had refused help. Richard strained his ears to listen. Everything was quiet. No noise came from the cellar. All he could hear was the creaking of the old house and a gentle snore from Vasilev, asleep in the room below.

Suddenly there was a new sound. At first Richard couldn't place it. Then he realized what it was. Someone had climbed up the stairs and was clambering through the trap door at the far end of the loft.

'Who's that?'

'It's me – Tamara.'

'Is something wrong?'

'No. I thought you might be cold. I've brought you some more covers.'

Momentarily a torch shone on Richard's face. Careful foot-steps approached. He saw the girl's outline, a black shadow against the general darkness, and felt the weight of the blanket as she tossed it down. He wasn't in the least surprised when she slid in beside him. He put his arms around her and held her close.

'Richard, you won't regret this?'

'No!' He was positive. 'Will you?'

'It's what I want.'

'Good!'

They made love fiercely and aggressively. It was a release for both of them, a physical if not an emotional surrender. Later, after a short sleep, they made love again, this time more gently. And she woke him when she had to go.

'Richard, I have to leave now.'

'Will you be coming back?'

'Only if I have bad news of Pavel.'

'Can I get in touch with you – once I'm home, in London?'

Tamara hesitated. 'Better not, Richard. It's not that I don't trust you. I do. But – you could be deceived.'

Words to remember, Richard thought grimly, as he kissed the Russian girl goodbye – for his own sake as well as others. He didn't question her decision.

Vasilev allowed Richard to sponge himself down and to dress himself in the underwear, socks and trousers that the Austrian's widow had provided. They were an indifferent fit, but adequate.

'The rest I will do,' Vasilev said firmly, 'manicure, shave, make-up. You leave it all to me. First, your hands.'

Obediently Richard held out his hands. Without asking,

145

Vasilev slipped the thin gold watch over his wrist and tried to ease off the signet ring. At once Richard crooked his little finger.

'Not the ring,' he said. 'It's my favourite thing. I couldn't part with it.'

Vasilev didn't argue. 'It's not important, fortunately. But the watch you must leave behind. I'm sorry, but no one buries a corpse with a watch.'

'Perhaps you – or Misha . . . ' Richard said tentatively. He regretted not having given it to Tamara, but it was a man's watch. 'And there's money in my wallet, roubles that Igor Goransky gave me so that I could entertain Natalya Meriosova in suitable style.'

Vasilev chuckled. 'Thank you. We'll gladly accept.'

The old man finished cutting Richard's nails, and made him soak his hands in a solution to give the skin a waxen appearance. Meanwhile he prepared shaving materials. There was a lot to be done, but he worked hard and skilfully, talking much of the time so as to distract Richard from what was to come.

The interruption occurred as Richard, flat on his back, a towel tucked under his chin, was having his lips carefully coloured. There was a shout, running footsteps, and a bang on the door. For one ghastly moment Richard visualized Baucher, followed by the KGB, bursting into the room. He had to remind himself that the shaggy-haired boot-buttoned-eyed East German was dead.

'Comrade! Comrade, there's a man outside. He says – '

'All right, Boris, all right,' Vasilev called testily. 'I'm coming.' And to Richard he whispered. 'It's my assistant. He's been washing the van.' He raised his voice again. 'Is that van clean yet? I don't want a fine because you've not done the job properly.'

The door closed and Richard was alone, his heart pumping, his breathing fast. He lay still. There were voices, first in the courtyard below and then coming nearer. Through slitted eyes Richard watched the door open. Vasilev came in. With him was Misha Kemenev. Richard relaxed.

'Good morning, Richard. You slept well, I hope?'

There was a twinkle in the Russian's eye which left Richard

in no doubt that Kemenev knew how he and Tamara had spent the night. Richard started to smile in response, but the tightness of the skin around his mouth prevented him.

'Careful! Careful!' Vasilev said quickly. 'You'll spoil my handiwork.'

Kemenev gave a roar of laughter. He seemed to be in excellent humour. 'The news is good,' he said, 'as good as we could expect. Pavel is free again. The KGB questioned him about his car and what he had been doing over the weekend, but he was able to satisfy them. And when they showed him a big photograph of Richard here, he managed to look blank. So all is well. Pavel's at the hospital and Tamara has gone to the laboratory as usual. We are ready to fight another day.'

His broad grin faded. 'Others of our friends haven't been as fortunate. Some of the questioning has been savage, brutal – worse than ever, they say. That swine Goransky has given orders that the Englishman be found and the killers of Franz Baucher and Natalya Meriosova taken at whatever cost. The implication is that you've been kidnapped, Richard, which I don't understand, but . . . '

While Kemenev talked Vasilev continued to work on the corpse-like appearance he was creating, and Richard brooded. He hated to think of the people, most of them wholly innocent, who were being bullied and maltreated because of the deaths of Baucher and Natalya. He felt responsible, horribly responsible. If it hadn't been for him – and Carey-Ford . . . Ultimately everything came back to Carey-Ford.

'Are you ready, Richard?'

'Ready?'

Richard forced himself to return to the present. On one side of him stood Vasilev holding a hypodermic syringe. On the other was Kemenev. He had rolled up Richard's shirt sleeve and exposed the inside of the elbow. Now, with great care, he swabbed the skin with alcohol.

'The injection won't hurt,' Vasilev said. 'You'll grow drowsy almost at once. Then you'll fall into a deep, dreamless sleep. When you wake up, you'll be safe in Austria. So it's time for us to say goodbye and God be with you, Richard.'

'Goodbye, Richard. Good luck.' Kemenev punched him

gently on the shoulder. 'Think of us sometimes when you're home with your family and Emma.'

'I will.' Richard was surprised at the strength of his own emotions. He had known these Russians for less than a handful of days but he felt inextricably bound up with them. 'Goodbye and thank you, for everything. I hope things go well for you.'

Richard scarcely noticed the prick in his vein and, as Vasilev had promised, the injection itself was painless. Soon he was conscious of becoming drowsy. Slowly he put on the dead Austrian's jacket and, with Kemenev's help, climbed laboriously into the coffin. He shut his eyes, prepared to sleep. He felt no fear.

SIXTEEN

The next hours were blank. Richard Lavery knew nothing of
the drive to the airport in Vasilev's van, or the coffin's inspection by the Soviet emigration officials, or the flight to Vienna, or the coffin's reception by the Austrian authorities and
its second inspection. He was cocooned in a deep sleep.

When at last he woke it was very slowly and with some
reluctance. He was warm and comfortable and his eyelids
were heavy, too heavy. He couldn't open his eyes. His lashes
seemed to be stuck together. Instinctively he brought up his
hand to wipe his face and his hand struck against something
soft and yielding. Pillow, he thought lazily, and nearly
drowned in sleep again. But his fingers had found his cheeks,
his nose, his eyes. He was touching them but he couldn't feel
them, not satisfactorily. The sensation was wrong.

He swallowed. He tried to open his mouth and wet his lips
with his tongue. That didn't work properly either. With a
great effort he forced open his eyes. He could see nothing. The
darkness was almost total. And there was a strange yet familiar smell – formaldehyde. Suddenly Richard was fully
awake. He knew where he was.

Tentatively he put out his hands and touched the padded
sides of the coffin. As he did, his fingertips brushed across the
underside of the lid. Terrified, he pressed against it, but it
didn't move and he desisted. His heart was pounding. A pulse
started to throb in his neck and he couldn't breathe. Fear
flowed over him in waves.

His instinct was to flail about, to shout and kick and bang
with his fists – anything to draw attention to himself. But he
was so restricted physically that he could scarcely move, and
somehow he controlled his rising panic. Somehow he managed to fight down his fears. Somehow he compelled himself
to breathe slowly and evenly. Somehow he made his mind
work.

The Russians had assured him that nothing could go wrong, but something had. At best the effects of the injection that Vasilev had given him had worn off too quickly. At worst the dependable friend at Schwechat airport was off-duty, or stricken by a sudden illness, or forgetfully swilling pints in his favourite beer-cellar. Everything depended on what part of its journey the coffin had reached.

Straining his ears, Richard listened in the hope of picking up some clue. There was nothing to be heard. After a few seconds, however, he sensed a susurration of sound and became conscious of movement around the box in which he was incarcerated. For a moment he thought he could smell incense. Then there was a great swell of organ music.

Shocked, Richard put his hand to his mouth and bit the outside edge of his little finger. The taste was revolting, like a. mixture of candle grease and carbolic soap. Involuntarily he snatched his hand away – and knocked Carey-Ford's signet ring against his teeth. His spirits leapt. At least he still had the damned ring.

He spat, deliberately, to rid himself of the waxy taste, and once more forced himself to consider his position. Organ music surely meant that he was in some kind of church. Therefore he was no longer in Moscow or on the plane. He was in Vienna, presumably safe, at least from Igor Goransky and the KGB. Nevertheless, he didn't know what to do.

It was essential that he shouldn't cause a scene by breaking out of the coffin at the wrong moment. It would be an embarrassment to himself and everyone around. Far more important, when the authorities started making enquiries it would probably mean disaster for old Vasilev. But what had happened to the bloody man who was supposed to help him? What had gone wrong? How long could he let his own funeral service continue? And, the unaskable question – was the coffin lid already firmly fastened down?

Fear clawed at Richard again, turning to near-panic as the coffin was suddenly jolted from side to side and swung into the air. For one shattering moment he imagined it being slid into the furnace of a crematorium and consumed in a blast of fire. Then reason reasserted itself. And, as he realized what was really happening – that he was being carried down the aisle on the shoulders of friends of an Austrian businessman who was buried in Vasilev's cellar and whose name he didn't even know – Richard had to restrain a wild, unseemly desire to laugh.

He told himself to hold on, just a little longer. From the angle of the coffin and the dangerous swaying motion, it was apparent that the pall-bearers and their burden were now outside the church and descending the steps. He guessed that the next thing would be to load the coffin into a motor-hearse for the drive to the cemetery. He waited for the jolts, the sense of motion that would tell him he was right, and when they came he was over-whelmed with relief. At last it was time to act.

Lying on his back in the close confines of the coffin it was difficult for Richard to get much leverage. He did his best. He pushed and heaved, but the lid didn't budge. He told himself to stay calm. Vasilev's promise that he would be able to get free whenever he wished was no longer valid. It had ceased to have any meaning once the coffin was removed from Schwechat airport, probably earlier. But if he made enough noise someone would hear him.

Systematically Richard began to pound with his fists and drum with his feet. It was exhausting and the padded sides of the box served to deaden the sound, but he persevered for as long as he could. Eventually – in fact it was after only a small parcel of seconds – he took a rest. He waited anxiously, his breathing heavy within his chest, his heart labouring. Nothing happened.

He started again. This time, in addition to kicking and thumping, he shouted. The effort seemed to sap his strength even more quickly than before. Sweat poured off him. His breath grew shorter and shorter. Excruciating pains shot up his legs. His arms were leaden. He couldn't go on. But he did.

At last he had to stop. And almost immediately there were three distinct knocks on the coffin lid. Full of gratitude, Richard returned the signal.

'Let me out! Let me out!'

'Yes, as soon as we can. But you'll have to wait. Are you all right?'

'Yes, but hurry.'

Richard had had the presence of mind to speak in German and he was thankful when the man answered in the same language. Weak from the reaction he waited, trying to compose himself. Time dragged. He could feel the motion of the hearse and thought he detected movement and odd noises outside the coffin. But he wasn't sure. He fought the impulse to call out again.

Suddenly there was a loud creak and without warning the lid was pushed back. Richard stared up into a pale young face with wide-set frightened eyes and a dropped jaw.

'Mein Gott!' the undertaker said and quickly crossed himself. 'What has happened? W – who are you? You're not Herr Braun.'

Richard didn't answer. He was taking great gulps of air, air that seemed to him incredibly fresh, though in fact it was thick with the smell of incense and hot-house flowers. He lifted his head and looked around him.

As he had guessed, he was in a motor-hearse. The coffin in which he was lying was on a low catafalque, surrounded by a brass rail. Wreaths which had lain on the lid were scattered on the floor. The young undertaker was actually kneeling on a cross made of white and purple lilies. But, careless of the wreaths though he might have been, Richard noticed that he had had enough sense to draw the curtains at the sides and rear of the hearse so that no one could look in.

'Who are you?' he repeated. 'What are you doing here?'

Richard struggled to sit up. 'Help me out of this bloody box,' he said.

'No. Not yet.' Quickly the undertaker put the palm of his hand on Richard's chest and pushed him back into the coffin. 'You can't – not here. You'll have to wait. We're almost at the cemetery.'

Knocking off his top hat in his agitation the young man clambered over the battered wreaths to the front of the hearse. Richard swore at him, but he paid no attention. Presumably he needed the advice, the moral support of his colleague. Richard made a gigantic effort and finally managed to push himself into a sitting position. Now he could see the two funereal figures conferring together – and he could see where they were taking him.

As he watched they swung between a pair of tall, wrought iron gates into a cemetery and accelerated at an indecent speed up the driveway. On either side were neat grass edges, neat trees and neat graves, many with elaborate tombstones. Ahead was a small chapel of rest. The hearse didn't stop. Skidding on the gravel, it drove around to the back of the building and into what appeared to be a large garage.

The two undertakers practically fell out of their seats and ran around to the rear of their vehicle. With some difficulty, because of the cramped space and because they were small and slight, they hauled Richard out of the coffin and propped him against the nearest wall. They were far from gentle. They had recovered from their first shock, and were prepared to hide their fear behind a show of aggression.

'Who the hell are you?' the older man, who had driven the hearse, demanded.

Richard said nothing. His limbs felt stiff and uncoordinated, but if he was to get away from the cemetery quickly and without making banner headlines he had to be mobile. He also had to cajole, threaten, somehow square the two undertakers. He wished he didn't feel so weak and dizzy.

'Who are you? And where is he – Herr Braun?'

'That's what you're going to have to explain to his widow and the rest of his family,' Richard said, sounding far more authoritative than he felt. 'You collected him from the airport. He was in your care. What have you done with him? No one's going to believe some cover-up story about a live man getting out of the coffin on the way to his own burial.'

While he was speaking Richard had been flexing his arms and legs. Now he took a step forward. Instantly the two men backed away from him. Having no idea what a fearsome sight he presented Richard was surprised. But he pressed home his advantage, moving closer to them.

They were a funny-looking pair, he thought, lugubrious little men, as befitted their trade. Obviously they were father and son, in business together, and not doing well. Father needed a new suit – his present one had a greenish sheen – and the cuffs of the son's shirt were frayed. Richard thought of old Vasilev.

He forced himself to sound menacing. 'This could ruin you

and your firm,' he said, 'and I promise you it will. I'll see to it personally. Unless . . . '

'What?' Father and son exchanged glances. It hadn't been difficult to intimidate them. 'What can we do? The mourners will be arriving any minute. Some of them are already in the chapel. And the pall-bearers will be collecting outside to take in the coffin. What can we do except – '

'I'll tell you. Listen!'

The undertakers were quick to grasp the idea. They worked hard and fast. With Richard's help they packed the coffin with anything that came to hand, a small pile of bricks that was lying in a corner of the garage, some prayer books from a cupboard, a cassock hanging behind the door of a washroom. It only remained to screw down the lid again, rearrange the flowers and tidy the hearse. The funeral could proceed. And the widow Braun need have no cause to complain that her husband's body hadn't been treated with the greatest respect.

'I'll be gone when you get back,' Richard said, 'and you've never seen me. Do you understand? Forget this ever happened. If you don't – ' He left the threat to their imagination.

There was a crunch of heavy footsteps on the gravel, someone coming to enquire why the hearse hadn't appeared. The undertaker pushed his son out to meet the newcomer and whispered to Richard.

'You'll hear nothing more of it from us.' He gestured towards the washroom. 'Better clean yourself up before you go.' He leapt into the driver's seat, adjusted his top-hat and composed his features, and moved the hearse sedately from the garage.

Richard didn't loiter. He dashed into the lavatory, relieved himself, and was about to have a quick wash when he caught sight of his reflection in the cracked mirror above the basin. He stared at it, horrified. His face was a mass of waxen wrinkles, his eyes sunk in deep pits, his skin yellow except for the rouged cheekbones, his mouth a round red hole and his hair, which Tamara had so disastrously boot-blacked, a matted grey cap. He looked grotesque.

And there was little he could do about it. The water in the tap was cold. There was no soap, no towel, and time was precious. He could hear the recorded music from the chapel.

154

Soon the mourners would be moving to the graveside. At any moment someone might interrupt him – a verger, a grave-digger, one of the gardeners. Hurriedly Richard splashed water over his face and tried to scrub it clean with his hands. It was useless. Vasilev had done his work too well.

Abandoning his efforts, Richard dried himself as best he could on the flap of his shirt, and inspected the rest of his appearance. The suit that Herr Braun had taken on holiday to Moscow was too short for him in the leg and too wide in the shoulders. That was scarcely important. What was important was that the Austrian's shoes were too small. Already Richard's feet hurt. He wasn't going to be able to walk far.

A swift search through the suit pockets brought him no comfort. Vasilev, determined on realism, had made sure they were completely empty, which meant that Richard hadn't a penny. Indeed, apart from the clothes he stood up in and Carey-Ford's signet ring, which luckily Vasilev seemed to have glued to his finger, he had nothing, not even a handker-chief. But he was in Vienna and he would get to Peter's flat somehow, if he had to crawl there.

Half a mile from the cemetery Richard began to think this was a real possibility. Every step had become an agony and, when he discovered he had been limping around the sleepy surburban streets only to return to a place he had left some while ago, he could have wept. Instead he cursed Herr Braun for the smallness of his feet, and resolutely sat down in the gutter and took off his shoes. When he stood up he nearly fainted. He had to wait for a minute until the world steadied again.

And he wondered how much longer he could go on. There were few people about. Those who were either crossed the road to avoid Richard, or hurried by. No one stopped, though several times he began to ask the way. Considering his pecul-iar appearance Richard didn't blame them, but it was de-pressing. Despite his efforts he was getting nowhere and he was beginning to feel really ill. When a taxi he tried to hail nearly ran him down it was the last straw.

Richard reached a decision. Remembering a church he had just passed, he retraced his steps. He came to the presbytery and pressed his thumb on the bell. He kept it there until the door opened.

'What is it?' She was a short, fat woman in a large starched apron – the priest's housekeeper – and one look at Richard was enough. 'The Father can't see you now. He's busy.'

She made to shut the door but Richard was too quick for her. He thrust his foot into the decreasing gap and shouldered his way into the hall. He was determined not to be repulsed and spoke savagely.

'Where's the priest?'

'I'm here, my son.' A little old man had appeared in a doorway. 'Come along and tell me how I can help you.'

'Thank you. You're very kind.'

'Father – ' The housekeeper began to protest.

'It's all right, Frau Schmidt. Perhaps you'd bring another cup.' He smiled at Richard. 'You'd like some tea, young man?'

'Tea?' Richard was vaguely surprised. He had been sure it was morning. 'What time is it?'

'Five o'clock.'

'Five o'clock – in the afternoon! And the day? It's – Tuesday?'

'Yes, that's right,' the priest said reassuringly. 'Come along now.'

Tuesday afternoon! Richard allowed himself to be led into a room with a lot of dark, heavy furniture. He was stunned. He had been in that coffin far longer than he had supposed. No wonder he felt so weak and muzzy-headed – and hungry. His mouth watered as he saw the priest's pathetic tea – two sardines on a piece of toast.

'Would you like something to eat?' The old man had followed his gaze. 'Here, why don't you have this?' He put the plate in front of Richard. 'I haven't started yet. And Frau Schmidt will bring me some more.'

'Thank you. Thank you very much, but – I don't have any money.'

The huge brown eyes in the scrawny face were sympathetic, the voice gentle. 'No, my son. I didn't suppose you would. Very few of my unexpected visitors do.'

Richard began to eat. He was ravenous. He stuffed the food into his mouth. Then suddenly he didn't want it anymore. It was difficult to swallow and tasted horrible.

'You don't understand,' he said firmly, unaware that to the priest he sounded drunk. 'You don't understand at all. I don't want your money – anyone's money. What I want is to use your telephone. That's why I came here . . . Use telephone. Important. Essential. Must phone – phone Peter – '

'Peter? Which Peter is that?'

The question was softly spoken and it seemed to come from a great distance. Moreover something odd was happening to the little priest. He might be paper thin, but he ought not to be floating around the room.

'Please stand still,' Richard said, or thought he said.

The priest ignored the request. 'Peter who?' he persisted.

'Denville. Peter Denville.' The words were slurred; no one could have understood them. Richard made a big effort. 'British Embassy,' he said, and slid sideways out of his chair on to the floor.

SEVENTEEN

It was a week before news of Richard Lavery percolated either to London or to Moscow. Charles Bigrel was among the first to hear it. But Igor Goransky learned not long afterwards.

Richard had been very ill. The doctor whom the old priest had summoned was baffled. The young man was well cared-for and nourished and obviously he had taken an excess of drugs, but what drugs and in what circumstances were mysteries. The doctor would have liked to transfer him to hospital, and to call in the police. The priest refused.

Father Schreiber spent long hours sitting at Richard's bedside, watching and praying. For most of the time Richard lay in a deep sleep, on the edge of coma, but sometimes he became very agitated, threw himself about and talked – in English or Russian. When this happened the priest sponged him down, rearranged his bedclothes and tried to calm him. Father Schreiber knew no Russian, but he had a smattering of English and he was an astute man. It didn't take him long to realize that if he wanted to help Richard the best thing he could do was restore him to his friends. But who were his friends?

Father Schreiber had no intention of making a mistake. He waited patiently, comforting Richard through patches of semi-consciousness and generally tending to him until, on the Monday after his impromptu arrival, the patient at last emerged into a state of complete clarity. Delighted, the priest propped another pillow behind Richard's back and called to Frau Schmidt to bring a bowl of her best gruel. He didn't ask any questions.

He said, 'Good morning. I'm glad you've woken up properly. It means you're getting **better.**'

'I've been ill?'

'Yes, quite ill.' The priest smiled brightly. 'I'm Father

Schreiber. You came to see me last Tuesday, and collapsed. Frau Schmidt and I have been taking care of you.'

'That's very kind of you.'

'Not at all. You're welcome to stay as long as is necessary. You're quite safe here. No one will bother you, I promise.'

'Thank you.'

The next time Richard awoke he was alone. His mind was unclouded and he set himself to think. He could remember everything, up to the moment he started to eat the priest's tea. After that came a succession of horrendous nightmares, the product of various drugs he had been given. But they seemed to have ceased. He was feeling much better, though appallingly weak, and he still had the ring. Thoughts of Carey-Ford were interrupted by the priest.

'Father, I owe you an explanation, but – '

'There's no need, my son. Just tell me if there's anyone you'd like me to contact on your behalf, relations, friends. Or is there anything I can do for you myself?'

'If you would telephone the British Embassy . . . '

Peter Denville arrived at the presbytery within the hour. Horrified by Richard's appearance, he managed to stem the spate of questions he yearned to ask. He listened to what Richard had to say, which wasn't a great deal. He promised to bring him clothes, to arrange to recompense the priest, to buy Frau Schmidt a present and to move Richard to his flat the next day. He also persuaded Richard to let him get in touch with Charles Bigrel.

And, as soon as Peter reached home, he telephoned the London number that Bigrel had given him. A half-hour later Bigrel, having been located by Lorna Day, returned the call.

'That's good news,' he said. 'Very good indeed.' He had never spoken more sincerely.

'Sir, Richard told me to tell you that he saw his – er – father twice. He was with him when he died. But he stressed the fact that he had nothing interesting to say about it.'

Bigrel frowned. It couldn't be true. He refused to believe it was true. If Carey-Ford had actually been allowed to talk to Lavery and yet had failed to give him the information which supposedly he had been so anxious to pass to the British, it made a nonsense of everything. Questions raced through Bigrel's mind but he suppressed them. The questions – and the answers – would have to wait.

'Really. Well, no matter,' Bigrel said evenly. 'The thing to do is to get him home, isn't it? I think perhaps it would be a good idea if I sent David Grant to Vienna. He can cope with passport and other difficulties and make sure Lavery has a safe journey. Grant'll be with you tomorrow.'

'Right. Thank you, sir.' Peter was relieved.

The following day, at the same time as Richard was saying goodbye to Father Schreiber and David Grant was boarding a plane at Heathrow, Igor Goransky sat at his desk in KGB headquarters and considered what action he could take. It was three hours since he had received a Telex message from the Soviet Embassy in London saying that Lavery was in Vienna, but he still had no plan. For once in his life he felt completely indecisive.

When his assistant asked if he would see Dr Mirov on a matter of vital urgency he nearly refused. Then he changed his mind. Mirov wasn't in the habit of coming unbidden to Dzerzhinsky Square. What he had to say might be of interest.

'Well, Mirov, what is it?' Goransky didn't bother with greetings.

'It's to do with Carey-Ford, Comrade.' For a moment Mirov seemed unable to continue. 'I'm sorry, Comrade, most terribly sorry.'

'What the hell are you talking about?' Goransky allowed himself a flash of temper. He disliked Mirov, though the man had his uses. 'Carey-Ford's dead and buried, and with all due honour.' He gave a sardonic smile. 'I attended the funeral myself.'

The doctor cringed. 'Comrade, his ring is missing! It was a gold ring. He always wore it, on the little finger of his left hand. It's disappeared.'

'Disappeared?' Goransky tugged gently at his beard. He had to control his sudden rising excitement. Some sixth sense told him this was important. 'Are you sure? It's not somewhere in the clinic?'

'I'm positive, Comrade. I instituted a search immediately I

heard. And I've questioned every one of the staff myself. As you know, Comrade, they're all hand-picked, and – '

'Yes. Yes, of course.' Goransky cloaked his impatience. 'Have you any idea when the ring might have been – lost?'

'Yes. The stupid bitch of a nurse didn't think fit to mention it at the time. She assumed I'd removed it. But she noticed it was missing when she was washing down the body. So it can't have been buried with him by accident. And, Comrade, I have wondered if – '

'Don't wonder, Mirov. Forget about it. Forget the whole thing.' Goransky was no longer indecisive. He knew what had happened to Carey-Ford's signet ring. He was prepared to bet his life on it. Indeed, he thought grimly, he might well be doing just that. 'Tell the staff Comrade Baucher took it for safe-keeping and that I have it now. Do you understand?'

'But Comrade Baucher couldn't – '

'Do you understand?' Each word was separate, distinct, ice-covered.

'Yes, Comrade.'

'Good.'

Goransky waved a hand in dismissal. He had a lot to consider, a lot to arrange if he were to do something about Richard Lavery and the ring that Carey-Ford had so obviously given him. And something had to be done. He was sure of that, though what he didn't yet know, or even why.

EIGHTEEN

There was no arguing with Grant. Peter Denville had tried. He thought Richard should stay in Vienna for at least the rest of the week; Richard wasn't well enough to travel. Grant overruled him. He was determined they should return to London on the first possible flight. Although he didn't say so, he had his doubts about Richard's safety. And while Peter helped Richard to bath and wash the dye from his hair and generally restore his appearance, Grant got busy organizing the journey.

He left for London with Richard the following morning. An embassy car collected them from the flat and took them to Schwechat airport. Here, escorted from a VIP lounge – Richard in a wheelchair – they were boarded last. At Heathrow the procedure was reversed. An ambulance came out to the aircraft to collect them. All formalities were waived. Without even entering the Terminal building they were driven straight to London.

Now that he was back in England Richard wasn't ungrateful to Grant. He hadn't welcomed Grant's arrival in Vienna. He hadn't felt ready to be interrogated. But, in fact, Grant had confined himself to making arrangements for the journey, and hadn't attempted to discuss Guy Carey-Ford or the Russians' treatment of Carey-Ford's son. That, evidently, was to be left to Charles Bigrel. When Grant wasn't seeing to Richard's welfare, he read – a paperback of *War and Peace*.

It had given Richard a chance to assemble his thoughts and decide exactly what he was going to say to Bigrel, a task which hadn't been easy. If only he knew whether Carey-Ford had said 'Bigrel suspects' or 'Bigrel suspect'. It was the difference between friend and enemy. At least there was no doubt of Carey-Ford's warning not to trust anyone, 'especially not high-up bastards in the UK', which would include Charles Bigrel – and a lot of other people. For the umpteenth time

Richard wished he could have had five minutes private and honest conversation with Carey-Ford. He wasn't even sure that he understood about the ring.

'We're going to a nursing home in Upper Wimpole Street,' Grant said conversationally as the ambulance headed across Baker Street.

'A nursing home! Why?' Richard was startled, angry, instantly on guard. 'I thought Bigrel wanted to see me.'

'He does. This evening, I expect. But after all the drugs I gather you've had pumped into you, you could do with a good check-up first.'

'If that's all it'll be – '

'That's all.' Grant grinned. Taking off his spectacles he began to polish the lenses with a handkerchief. 'If you'd prefer to go straight to your flat, just say.'

Richard hesitated. The casualness of the offer, the very ordinary gesture with the spectacles, both were reassuring. Besides, the flat would be miserable, dusty, deserted, no food – no Emma. He couldn't face it at the moment. He hadn't got the energy to cope.

'Okay,' he said resignedly. 'But I'll want to go home tomorrow.'

'Fine. I'll fix it.'

It wasn't the only thing Grant had in mind to fix. But there was no point in telling Lavery. He was suspicious enough already.

The nursing home, however, did much to allay Richard's doubts. It was bright, cheerful, efficient and had little resemblance to the clinic where Carey-Ford had died. Here Richard had what the doctor – again, completely unlike Mirov – described as 'a thorough going-over'. Thorough it certainly was, so thorough that Richard even had to account for the layers of sticking-plaster from Peter Denville's medicine cupboard on the little finger of his left hand. He passed them off as covering a small cut of no consequence.

Grant appeared again as Richard was having tea. 'I bring good news,' he said. 'According to the medicos you're as strong as a horse and your recent excesses have done you no harm. I also bring this.' Like a conjurer he produced from his briefcase a bottle of malt whisky.

'A present?'

'Not exactly. Charles Bigrel proposes to call on you at six, and he likes his Glenlivet.'

At twenty minutes to six Bigrel told Lorna Day that he was leaving the office and would not be back. The phone rang as he was speaking.

'I've gone,' he said quickly. 'I'm not here.'

Lorna put her hand over the receiver. 'It's Mr McCann.'

'Damn! All right, I'll take it.' He perched himself on the edge of Lorna's desk. 'Hello, Chris. Charles here. What can I do for you?'

'Just wanted to tell you, Charles. I've straightened out that story Poppy Penryn was supposed to have told Anita.'

'You mean about Carey-Ford having had children?'

'Yes. Nothing to it, of course. And I'm afraid I went for old Thomas quite unfairly. It was really Anita's fault. She seems to have misunderstood. Poppy must have said something like, "Wouldn't it be awful to be his son", and Anita jumped to the wrong conclusion. You know what women are, Charles.'

'Yes, of course. Thanks for letting me know.'

'Sorry to have been so long over it. And my apologies, on Anita's behalf, for having given you an unnecessary shock.'

'Forget it, Chris.'

Bigrel put down the receiver thoughtfully. He wished he could take the advice he had given McCann. The incident at the McCanns' luncheon party had been nagging him for the last ten days – McCann had certainly taken his time producing an explanation – and he couldn't dismiss it from his mind so easily. He couldn't understand why the two women should have been discussing Carey-Ford at all. Until news of his death hit the headlines and caused a spate of stories there had been no mention of Carey-Ford in any of the media for months. So, what had suddenly caused Poppy Penryn to start gossiping about him?

Bigrel didn't allow himself to brood on the problem. There were other more pressing matters to consider, not least his coming visit to Richard Lavery. He was looking forward to it with an eagerness that would have surprised many people who believed him to be an unemotional man. Indeed, it surprised Bigrel himself. He couldn't manage his customary snooze in the car. He didn't wait for Tyler to open the door for him. He strode into the nursing home as if he owned the place, and was polite but abrupt to the doctor and nurses who greeted him. He had to take a grip on himself before he went in to Richard.

'Hello. I'm Charles Bigrel. I'm very glad to see you safely back in London.'

'Hello, sir.'

For some reason it reminded Richard of his first meeting with Carey-Ford, though Bigrel wasn't amused at being called sir. He expected it. They shook hands awkwardly, Richard caught by surprise.

'I suppose it was because of Emma Jackson that you decided to go to Moscow in the end?'

'Yes. Igor Goransky gave me no choice – unlike you, sir.'

Bigrel ignored the sarcastic comment. He had noticed the bottle of Glenlivet, and blessed David Grant. 'Shall I pour us both a whisky while you tell me about it?'

'If you would. Thank you.'

Richard waited until Bigrel had got the drinks and pulled up a chair beside the bed. He told his story calmly, dispassionately, giving as much factual detail as he could, but glossing over his personal reactions. It wasn't easy under Bigrel's unwavering gaze, and he was thankful he had decided to stick as closely to the truth as possible.

' . . . and that's all,' he said. 'At any rate as far as Carey-Ford's concerned. The rest is something else again.' He hadn't mentioned the signet ring.

'Yes,' Bigrel said.

Richard waited. He expected some response, some curiosity, but Bigrel seemed lost in a dream. There was a long, disconcerting silence.

Then Bigrel said, 'What did you think of him – as a man? Did you hate him?'

'No. How could I? He was dying. I – In other circumstances – ' Richard found himself stammering. 'I don't understand how he could have – gone to Russia like that.'

'It is difficult.'

Bigrel sounded unmoved but, in fact, he was jubilant.

Lavery had answered the question he had not been asked. He and Carey-Ford had been in sympathy with each other. And that, Bigrel was convinced, meant that Carey-Ford would have seized what he knew to be his only chance. There was something more, something that Lavery hadn't told him yet.

'And you say that's all,' he said, 'as far as Carey-Ford's concerned?'

'Yes. He didn't give me any sort of secret information.' Richard was definite. 'Perhaps he might have done if our conversation hadn't been so closely monitored. I know that's what you hoped for. That's why you were prepared to take, in my opinion, sir, the bloody measures you did. You and Goransky and Sholatov's people – '

'Sholatov's people?'

'Oh yes.' At last, Richard thought, he had managed to shake this imperturbable man. 'A group of Russian Jews. They were eager to learn this "secret" too – eager enough to murder a couple of KGB in order to get hold of me. But at least they got me out of the Soviet Union – once I'd convinced them I had nothing for them.'

'I see. Well, that's fascinating ' Bigrel pushed back his chair and stood up. Sholatov's people, the contacts he had failed to make since Dmitri Sholatov's death. They could still be useful, extremely useful. 'Let me get you another drink and you can tell me what happened next.'

To Charles Bigrel's surprise Lavery was in some ways less forthcoming about the Russian Jews than he had been about Guy Carey-Ford. He described and discussed Misha Kemenev, but he was vague about the flat to which he had been taken and even more vague about the girl. He refused point-blank to explain how he had got out of Russia.

'I'm sorry, sir, but it was an escape route that had been used before – and might be used again. I gave them my word.'

'Quite. I understand.'

Bigrel didn't press. The flat refusal to cooperate had convinced him of something he had already begun to suspect. For some reason – and Bigrel didn't believe it was because of the pressures originally put on him by Grant – Richard Lavery distrusted him. It didn't make sense.

Temporarily pigeon-holing the problem, Bigrel looked at

his watch. He didn't have an appointment, but he didn't think he could get any more out of Lavery for the moment. He gave him a thin smile.

'I must be off. Perhaps we could have another chat. Later this week or early next week?'

'Of course, sir – if you consider it would be any use. I expect to be away for a long weekend. Otherwise whenever you like.'

'Where are you going?'

'Not out of the country,' Richard said sharply, responding to the abruptness of the question. 'My passport's still in Moscow. Just to visit my parents.'

Bigrel nodded. 'Good.' The young man would have to be followed and it helped if one knew the destination. 'David Grant will pick you up about eleven tomorrow and take you to your flat. Save you a taxi. Is that all right?'

'Yes. Thank you.' Richard hesitated. 'Incidentally, I'd like to telephone my mother. Would you mind if I asked for a phone?'

'Not a bit,' Bigrel said at once. 'I'll arrange it on my way out. And phone anyone you wish. I know I can rely on your discretion. Good night.'

'Good night, sir.'

Richard, left with the impression that the remark about discretion had been two-edged, smiled dubiously to himself. Suddenly he felt exhausted. He was glad to be alone. He hadn't enjoyed the meeting with Charles Bigrel.

The telephone arrived, closely followed by dinner. Turtle soup, grilled trout, strawberries and cream, a nice piece of Stilton, half a bottle of white wine – a very pleasant meal. Lifting the various covers, Richard decided to leave his calls until he had eaten.

The phone rang as he finished the soup. Frowning, Richard reached for the receiver. No one knew he was in the nursing home – except for Bigrel and Grant, and it was unlikely that either of them would be phoning him at this time. His hello was interrogative.

'Is that Richard Lavery?' It was a woman's voice, low, husky, unknown to Richard.

'Yes. Who are you?'

'Who I am is unimportant. Do you still have the ring your father gave you?'

Richard hesitated. 'Yes.'

'Good.' There was a sigh of relief. 'Then listen to what I have to say. I shan't repeat myself. Tomorrow make a small brown paper packet of the ring. Go to Brompton Oratory. Sit at the back of the church, at the centre aisle end of the right-hand pew. At precisely half past one leave the packet in the corner of the pew and get up and leave. Tell no one. Forget the whole thing. Don't try to be clever or you'll regret it.'

The line went dead, not giving Richard time either to agree or refuse. He pushed away the trout. He no longer felt hungry. This was a situation he had not expected.

NINETEEN

'Here we are.' Grant slotted the car into a parking place in the quiet square and turned to grin at Richard. 'And here are the keys to the kingdom.'

'What?'

'The new keys to your flat.' Grant tossed them into Richard's lap. 'I've had a proper lock put on the door – a Chubb. And for good measure I added a Judas spy-hole. It's nice to know who's standing on the mat before you open up.'

He had expected objections but they didn't come.

'Thanks,' Richard said.

Grant gave him a sharp glance. 'Is something wrong?'

'At the moment – no. But you seem to imply there may be.'

'Not really. You're back in London. You've talked to Bigrel. Presumably you've told him everything there is to tell. Why should Goransky bother about you any more? He's a professional. He doesn't fight battles already lost.'

Grant took Richard's briefcase and together they strolled across the road to the flats. To Richard everything was both familiar and strange. It was difficult to believe it was less than three weeks since he had left here to go and stay with Peter in Vienna. His old life – London, the law practice, weekends in the country, parties, concerts, walks in the park, friends and Emma – it was a world away now.

'Mind you,' Grant said, continuing the conversation, 'if I were you, I wouldn't go asking for trouble. No loitering in dark alleys. No midnight swims in the Serpentine. No invitations to the Russian Embassy. I'd avoid that sort of thing. Better be careful than sorry, as the saying goes.'

Richard laughed, but there wasn't much warmth in his laughter. He opened the front door and led the way into the flat. There was a vase of roses in the hall, more roses in the living-room, a bowl of fruit on the table. Everything was clean and fresh and sweet-smelling. He turned to Grant.

'You?'

'Not with my own fair hands, no. But I kept busy yesterday organizing it. Bigrel's orders. He feels we owe you something. Incidentally, if you'll make a list of things you lost on the expedition, funds will be available. All right?'

'Terrific. I scarcely deserve such generosity,' Richard said, and thought, 'Beware the Greeks bearing gifts'. He wished that Grant would go.

As if mind-reading, Grant said, 'Well, I must be off. There's food in the fridge. Your car's okay. I've had it checked. And I've left a number by the phone. In the unlikely event you need me, you know what to do.' He smiled hopefully.

'Sure. Many thanks.'

Rid of Grant, Richard went at once into the bedroom. It was as he had left it, except cleaner and tidier. He flung open the wardrobe doors, wanting but dreading to see the empty hangers where Emma had kept her clothes. He found himself staring at some bright orange slacks. The other hangers, too, were full. Emma hadn't removed her belongings. She was still using the flat. Grant, damn him, must have known, but he hadn't bothered to mention the fact.

Swearing under his breath, Richard went into the hall and put up the chain on the door. If Grant had told Emma he was to be home this morning she might decide to come back for lunch, and he had no desire to be interrupted – not at this moment, not without warning. He went in search of a box, a small box that might once have held a ring.

In a drawer, amongst a jumble of bits and pieces – including an old watch he was glad to see – he found exactly what he wanted. Even the bed of cotton wool remained. All that was needed was something of the approximate size and weight to be a substitute ring. This wasn't so easy, but eventually he thought of a coin and, raiding the change purse that Emma always kept in the kitchen, he chose a fifty-pence piece. Brown-papered and taped, the packet now looked and felt authentic. He slipped it into his jacket pocket.

He was just in time. The doorbell gave a loud, imperious ring. He didn't bother with the new spy-hole. He slid off the chain and opened the door. As he had expected, it was Emma.

To Richard she looked radiant. He didn't notice the bruised

170

marks under her eyes or the false gaiety of her smile. She seemed to him as she always was, happy, carefree, full of vitality. She put her arms around his neck and kissed him on the mouth.

'Darling, I'm so glad you're home again. I've missed you terribly.'

Richard didn't respond, though he alone knew what it cost him. 'Emma, I wrote you a letter. Did you – ?'

'Yes. I read it.' Dropping her shoulder-bag on one chair and her jacket on another Emma went through into the kitchen. 'I'm in a ghastly hurry. Business is booming. It seems no self-respecting tourist can go back to the States these days without buying a toy or a game. So it'll have to be a quickie lunch. I wouldn't have come until this evening – I've been staying with Betty while you've been away – but David said you'd been ill and – '

'David? You mean Grant?'

'Yes. I call him David. He's a nice, kind man, Richard. You mayn't like him, but he likes you. He said I'd be the world's worst idiot not to marry you, and I agree. Carey-Ford doesn't matter a damn.'

'He told you?' The words were surprised out of Richard. 'About Carey-Ford and – '

'No. Maurice told me, my bloody father. And I haven't spoken to him since. I was appalled by what he'd done to you. Darling, *please* . . .'

As she talked Emma was picking things out of the refrigerator and passing them to Richard. Bread, butter, ham, pâté, lettuce, tomatoes, celery, cheese. Automatically he took them from her. Automatically, while she washed the lettuce and made the dressing, he found plates and knives and forks. They might, Richard thought, bitterly, have been married for ten years.

Suddenly it was all too much for him. He couldn't argue with Emma, not now. Yet it was more important than ever that she shouldn't be involved with him. She had already been put at risk once because of Carey-Ford. He couldn't allow it to happen again. If he loved her – and, dear God, he did . . .

Abruptly banging down the glasses he had taken from the

171

cupboard, Richard walked out of the kitchen. His head ached and he felt slightly sick. He slammed the front door behind him and ran down the stairs. It was better in the open air.

He stopped at the first pub he came to. Too early for the lunch-time trade, it was half-empty. He perched himself on a stool at the end of the bar and asked for a double whisky. Putting his hand in his inside pocket to get his wallet, he remembered.

'Sorry. I've forgotten my money.'

The barmaid who had already poured the drink gave him a disbelieving look. There was a sudden silence in the pub. Then someone said, 'You should've drunk it before you told her, mate', and the laughter exploded. Richard walked out, hating the lot of them.

The branch where he banked wasn't far, but it was in the opposite direction from the Oratory, which was irritating. When he got there several of the wickets were closed and there were queues in front of the others. The cashier was a new girl, determined not to make mistakes, and slow. She insisted on checking Richard's account to make sure he was entitled to draw out fifty pounds.

By the time she had counted the notes twice and grudgingly handed them over it was one o'clock, too late for the drink and sandwiches he would have liked. Richard set his watch by the clock in the bank and started off for the Oratory. Firmly keeping his mind away from Emma, he thought of the box in his pocket and the person who was coming to collect it. He hadn't made any plans. There were too many imponderables. But his sense of anticipation was growing.

He didn't allow himself to hurry. It was a quarter past one when he pushed open the door of the Oratory and went inside; the timing was perfect. He stood at the back of the church and waited for his eyes to adjust to the dim light of the interior. The smell of incense was very strong. A mass had been said at twelve-thirty. The tail-end of the congregation still remained, perhaps as many as a dozen, their heads bowed in prayer.

Richard watched from the seat the anonymous voice had instructed him to take. Two women and a man got up and left. Another woman went to light a candle and knelt again

172

in front of the statue of the saint she had favoured. A verger was tidying hymn books. Some choirboys came down the aisle, giggling and pushing each other, free now of the priest's vigilant eye. More people were leaving.

Richard glanced at his watch. Unless the old thing was gaining or losing, it was exactly one thirty. As ordered, he took the packet from his pocket and wedged it into the corner of the pew. But he didn't leave the church. Instead, making sure that no one was paying him any attention, he moved across to the deeper shadow thrown by the angle of a confessional and leant against the wall. Here, with luck, he could stay unobserved until someone picked up the little box. And when that happened he would have to decide what to do, whether to accost whoever it was or merely follow him – or her.

Almost at once the door opened. A young girl with a rucksack came in. She ignored the holy-water stoup and didn't genuflect. Richard's heart leapt. But it was a false alarm. The girl trudged up the aisle, threw her rucksack into a pew and slumped down beside it. If her intention wasn't to show reverence to her Maker, it wasn't to collect the ring either.

The girl was followed by a couple of tourists who walked around curiously. The man was taking photographs. Richard regarded them with suspicion. He was also keeping an eye on the verger who, in his zeal for tidiness, could come inadvertently on the packet.

Then an elderly woman – one of the last of the worshippers – got up slowly and painfully from her seat. Leaning heavily on her stick she began to walk down the aisle. A belated choirboy, perhaps kept behind as a punishment, knocked heavily against her as he scurried past. She staggered and almost fell. The verger hurried forward, calling to the boy to stop.

Momentarily Richard's attention was distracted. When his gaze returned to the pew where he had put the packet, he saw the photographer sitting there, his camera directed upwards to the roof. Without thinking, Richard stepped from the shadow of the confessional and made towards him. He had forgotten the man's wife. Startled by Richard's sudden appearance she let out a frightened cry. The husband at once

173

abandoned his photography and, glaring at Richard as if to defy him to assault them, the couple backed out of the church.

Richard reached the pew and glanced quickly into the corner. The packet was still there. The photographic fiend was clearly innocent; his reaction had merely been that of one who expected to be told that photography was forbidden. But had Richard's inspection of the pew attracted attention? He moved hurriedly to the side aisle and looked around once more. No one seemed to have noticed.

But wasn't anyone going to collect the damned thing? Richard waited impatiently while the verger and the arthritic woman finished lecturing the choirboy. The woman turned and made her way down the aisle, genuflecting painfully by the back row of pews. The verger opened the door for her. The girl with the rucksack was leaving too. But another woman had come in, middle-aged, bustling, with a large shopping basket stuffed with groceries. Richard watched her carefully – it would be easy to slip a packet in among the purchases – but, after a brief indecision, she trotted up the aisle and knelt at the altar rail.

The time was now ten minutes to two. The church was virtually empty and the verger inclined to be curious. It was pointless to stay. Angry and frustrated, Richard decided to take the packet and go.

But the little box was no longer there. Richard stared in disbelief at the place where he had left it. Somehow he had been tricked.

The verger was coming towards him with a question on his lips. Richard ignored him. He swung out of the church and set off back to the flat. He wanted to get home. But he was forced to wait for what seemed interminable minutes at the kerb before he could cross the Brompton Road. Cars, taxis, buses, vans, even a bicycle swept past. It needed courage or foolhardiness to step on to the pedestrian crossing and assume that the double-decker bus or the coach full of German tourists or the girl in the open sports-car would stop for you. A knot of people was gathering. Soon one of them would lose patience and they would all cross.

Meanwhile a man standing beside Richard spotted an

empty taxi. He signalled commandingly. The driver disregarded the signal. The man, irritated at being ignored, started to run along the pavement in pursuit. Cynically Richard watched him dodging pedestrians, nearly falling over a pram, knocking against a lamp-post. He hadn't a hope. Suddenly Richard's interest quickened.

Someone else wanted that taxi, and she was going to get it – the elderly, crippled woman who had been in the Oratory. Even at a distance Richard recognized her, the white hair, the long beige-coloured coat, the stick she was brandishing at the taxi driver. But this was a different woman. Purposefully thrusting between two strolling shoppers, she had sprinted out into the road, swung open the door of the taxi and jumped in before it had come to a halt.

Richard cursed his own stupidity. An enveloping coat, a wig, a bit of play-acting, and he had been taken in. He remembered the woman's deep, painful genuflection as she came to the end of the aisle. Embarrassed by her suffering, he had averted his eyes. But she had been supporting herself on the last pew. She must have slid her hand over the side, found the packet and secreted it in a pocket of her coat. And he hadn't wanted to witness her pain! Dear God, what a sot, what a bumbling innocent he was. Even after Goransky and Baucher and the Russian Jews, he had learned nothing.

Momentarily the traffic had backed up and Richard, jostled by those around him, threaded a path through cars and taxis and buses to the centre island, and thence to the far pavement. Within ten minutes he had reached his flat. He felt tired and dispirited – disgusted with himself. He had achieved nothing. It would have been better, much better, not to have gone near the Oratory.

Praying that Emma would have returned to the shop, he let himself into the hall. He saw the note at once. It was on the table where they always left messages for each other. It read: 'I shall be back this evening about six-thirty. Please be here, darling. We must talk. I love you. Emma'.

Richard crushed the note in his fist and swore. It was all Maurice Jackson's fault. If the sod hadn't interfered in the beginning . . . And then to tell Emma. Now she would be determined to stay with him, to show that Carey-Ford didn't

175

matter. He would have to do something about it, preferably before tonight.

But first he needed a drink and some food, in that order. He went into the living-room. He couldn't remember if he had any whisky in the flat. He opened the cupboard where the liquor was kept. There stood three bottles of gin and three of whisky. The gin was Gordons, the whisky Glenlivet. David Grant! Richard's mouth stretched into a wry grin.

The telephone rang. Still thinking of Grant, Richard picked up the receiver and said hello. There was a pause. He could hear breathing.

'Is that Richard Lavery?'

He recognized the voice immediately. It was the woman who had phoned him at the clinic yesterday evening, the woman who had given him his instructions about the ring. The same woman who had been in the Oratory?

'Speaking,' he said.

'Richard Lavery, you're a very foolish young man. We want that ring. We mean to get it. The next time I give you orders about delivering it you are to obey them to the letter. Do you understand?'

'Yes, lady – with the white wig?'

Richard had no idea why he said it. To irritate perhaps. To get a small revenge for having been duped. Whatever the intention, the response was immediate. There was a sharp intake of breath and then silence. But she hadn't put down the receiver. The line was still open.

'Goodbye,' Richard said.

'No. Wait!' It was a terse order. 'What – what makes you think I was wearing a wig?'

'It slipped when you were running for the taxi,' Richard said with calculated malice.

She laughed scornfully. 'Rubbish! You're a fool, Richard Lavery. A stupid fool! And I warn you, if you don't do exactly as you're told in future, you'll be sorry.' She paused as if aware of the weakness of her threat, and added venomously, 'And it won't just be you who'll suffer. That bitch of a girl you live with, she'll be sorry – for the rest of her life.'

It was a full minute before Richard realized that he was still gripping the receiver, his knuckles white, his hand shaking. The direct threat to Emma had been unexpectedly shocking. His imagination worked overtime. He clenched his teeth. Whatever happened she had to be kept safe. But how? To cut himself off from her as he had intended might not be enough. What else could he do? His gaze fell on the piece of paper Grant had left beside the telephone. If only he could trust David Grant.

Five minutes later Richard made up his mind. He needed help. Emma had to be protected. And that meant he had to trust someone. Grant, who was Bigrel's man, might seem a funny choice, but there was really no one else. He would tell Grant the Russians were threatening to kill Emma if he didn't tell them Carey-Ford's 'secret'. It was close enough to the truth. Purposefully Richard dialled David Grant's number.

TWENTY

Charles Bigrel stroked his alabaster egg and studied its veining that he knew by heart. He had a sense of impending disaster. Ever since he had learnt of the relationship between Carey-Ford and young Lavery and had tried to exploit it, the Russians had been a step behind him. Now, when to be rational – and Igor Goransky was essentially rational – they should have given up, he suspected they were a step ahead.

Thinking aloud, he said, 'Carey-Ford wanted to get some vital information to me. He had his chance, thanks to Goransky. Lavery says he didn't take it. I don't believe Lavery. Yet why should he lie?'

'Perhaps he's not sure the info was meant for you,' David Grant suggested. 'Carey-Ford may not have been too explicit.'

'Then who the hell does he think it's meant for?'

'I don't know,' said Grant, 'and there's something else that puzzles me. Why haven't the Russians assumed he's already told us all?'

'The question had occurred to me,' Bigrel said dryly. 'They always seem remarkably well-informed about Richard Lavery.'

There was a silence while the two men considered their thoughts. Grant was thinking of Emma Jackson. She had been exasperatingly obstinate yesterday. But he had convinced her finally, by a mix of fact and fiction, and she had agreed to leave Lavery to himself for a week or two. Later he had helped her to move some of her belongings to the flat above the toy-shop, and he had been thankful to see that Betty Acheson was extremely burglar-conscious; the place was more secure than most. He had also, unknown to Emma, arranged for police surveillance. It was the best he could do. But he couldn't pretend that it was a hundred per cent satisfactory.

Bigrel's thoughts were even grimmer. He was thinking

about a traitor, a man who was giving – possibly selling – his country's secrets to the enemy, a man who was one of his own colleagues. His mind screamed 'Why?', but he knew that the 'why' was unimportant at the moment. What was important was proof. You couldn't accuse someone without offering evidence. The 'why' could come later, with a lot of other things such as how much had been betrayed, who else had been corrupted, what was compromised. Proof, that was what was needed. But how to get proof, how to produce incontrovertible evidence when he himself could still doubt the man was guilty? Suddenly he caught his breath.

'Are you all right, sir?' Grant asked sharply.

'Yes. Yes. I'm sorry. Stupid of me.'

Bigrel spoke absently and Grant gave him a puzzled look as he got up and rescued the egg that Bigrel had bowled off his desk. Bigrel smiled his thanks. He couldn't explain that he had just been hit by an extraordinary idea. Because he wasn't the kind of man to waste time on idle speculation he hadn't previously given much thought to the form that Carey-Ford's precious 'information' might take. Now he wondered if it were conceivable that Carey-Ford had known about the traitor.

'You say Lavery's already gone off to the country?'

'To visit his parents. Yes, sir. He changed his mind. He hadn't intended to go until today, but he went yesterday afternoon to save argument with Emma.'

'And he'll be back when?'

'He said Sunday evening.'

'Right.' Bigrel flipped over his desk calendar. 'I want to see him on Monday morning. Ten o'clock. Arrange it, please, David.'

'Yes, sir. Ten o'clock, Monday morning, it shall be. And let's hope he comes clean this time.'

The remark was met by a cold stare. 'I propose to see that he does,' Charles Bigrel said. 'But it's up to you to ensure that he's here, David – sound of mind and body.'

'Naturally, sir.' Grant grinned, his eyes owl-like behind spectacles. 'Assistance is a bit thin on the ground, but – '

He broke off as there was a soft thud in the adjoining office and glanced swiftly at Bigrel. Bigrel had heard it too. He made

179

an impatient gesture and began to talk equably while Grant took silent strides across the floor and flung open the door.

'Lorna!'

'Hello, David.' She took in his surprise and relief. 'Did I disturb you? I dropped a book.'

'Lorna, my dear, come in,' Bigrel called. 'How are you? We weren't expecting you this morning.'

'We thought we'd caught a spy,' Grant said, 'ear to the keyhole.'

Lorna Day smiled wanly. 'Sorry to disappoint you.' She turned to Bigrel. 'Good morning, sir. I'm feeling a lot better today. Having the abscess lanced was a great relief, but I'm afraid the tooth's going to have to come out next week.'

'That's a shame.' Bigrel was sympathetic. He hesitated. He didn't want to press her. 'I've got some work I'd like you to do for me, Lorna, but if you don't feel up to it you're to say so at once and go home. Understood?'

'I'm fine, thank you, sir.' Lorna tried not to sound irritable. She disliked causing a fuss. She said firmly, 'You won't forget you have a meeting at the FCO at eleven-thirty, will you, sir? And you're lunching with the Prime Minister afterwards. You should be leaving in about twenty minutes. The traffic's heavy today.'

'I've not forgotten.'

Bigrel suppressed a sigh. The meeting he could deal with. It was the luncheon he wasn't looking forward to. He knew exactly what would happen, what would be expected of him.

The Permanent Under-Secretary at the FCO was about to retire. His replacement would cause a general shuffle in the higher reaches of the diplomatic service. Almost certainly the PM's decision had already been made, but it was a courtesy to Charles Bigrel to ask for his comments on the short list of recommendations. In the past this had presented little difficulty. Today it would be different. Yet he was determined not to voice his suspicions. To act precipitately might be as bad as not to act at all.

'These days one always gets a good luncheon at Number Ten,' he said, his words a good deal less serious than his thoughts.

John Lavery drew the curtains of his wife's bedroom so that the sunlight shouldn't disturb her afternoon rest. He bent and kissed her on the brow. How frail she looked, he thought, and tired and ill and worried. Indeed, she was all those things.

Inevitably the last week or two, with the media's renewed interest in Guy Carey-Ford because of his death, had put a strain on her limited resources. His own edginess, which try as he might he'd not been able to hide, hadn't helped either. He didn't for one moment believe the story of the boy having picked up some bug in Vienna. Sighing heavily, John Lavery went downstairs.

The telephone rang as he reached the hall. He picked up the receiver and gave his number. From where he stood he could see through the drawing-room door and the French windows into the garden. Richard was walking aimlessly about the lawn.

'Richard Lavery?' he said. 'Yes, of course. Hang on. I'll get him.'

Richard, recalled from unhappy thoughts of Emma, came running. 'Who is it, dad?'

'A woman. She didn't give her name.'

Richard nodded his thanks. He could guess. He didn't need to hear the low, husky voice that had become so unpleasantly familiar to him. At first he had believed the woman might be Russian, but he had a good ear and he was sure now that the voice was English.

'What do you want?' he said.

He nearly added, 'You bloody traitor!' because, English or not, she was certainly working for the Russians.

Only the man for whom Carey-Ford had intended the ring should have known it was in Richard's possession, and it was implicit in what Carey-Ford had said that he would claim it in person. That left Goransky. There had always been the possibility that someone at the clinic would have noticed the ring was missing and that it would be reported to the KGB. Why Goransky should want it was a mystery – it was a perfectly ordinary gold signet ring; Richard had examined it with the utmost care – but it seemed he did. Remembering the threat to Emma, Richard gritted his teeth.

'Do you have the ring with you?' the woman asked.

'Why do you want to know?'

'Because if you do, I'll give you an address. Post the ring tomorrow morning and we'll receive it on Monday. Have you paper and pencil?'

'Yes.'

It was, rather surprisingly, the same approach as before. The only difference was that instead of a pew in the Brompton Oratory a tobacconist's shop in Paddington was to be used as a *poste restante*. Richard could imagine the place, outwardly run-down and sleazy, its windows plastered with cards offering dubious services, but nevertheless doing a brisk business, customers coming and going constantly. It would be a waste of effort for him to watch the entrance and try to identify whoever picked up the packet. He didn't bother to take down the address. He had no intention of posting the ring.

'We shall expect it on Monday morning then,' the woman continued. 'And, Richard, I hope you realize how kind we're being to you, giving you another chance. It is the last chance. Have no doubt of that. So don't play any more stupid tricks. Think of Emma Jackson.'

Richard swallowed the anger that rose like bile in his throat. 'No, I won't,' he said, 'but you must give me till Tuesday. You know how unreliable the post can be, especially in the country. In fact, wouldn't it be better if I sent it from London? I'll be back Sunday night.'

'No. Do as you've been told.'

'As you say.'

Thoughtfully Richard put down the receiver. They would take no action now before Monday, with luck even Tuesday. He had bought a little more time, time for whoever was to claim the ring to come to him. And then, according to Carey-Ford, he would know. Know what? Supposing no one **ever** came?

In his frustration Richard drove his fist into the drawing-room door, sending it crashing back against the wall. Instantly he was ashamed of himself. He thought of his mother resting upstairs, and listened. There was no sound from her. But John Lavery, startled by the noise, had stopped cutting the dead heads off the roses and was hurrying back into the house. Richard went to the French window and called to reassure him. The telephone rang again.

'Yes.' It was an aggressive monosyllable.

'Richard Lavery? David Grant here. Everything okay with you?'

'Yes, why shouldn't it be?'

'You sounded somewhat fraught.'

'The phone goes too damn often.'

Grant was quick. 'Even in the country? Another threat, if you don't come clean?'

Richard hesitated. By admitting the continued threats he was admitting he had something to hide. Goransky was too astute to chase shadows and Grant knew it. But what the hell, when Emma was at risk?

'Yes,' he said. 'And don't you forget, Grant. I hold you responsible. If anything happens to Emma I'll have your skin for it.'

'It won't,' Grant said soothingly, making a mental decision to stay in London and keep a check on Emma Jackson rather than drive down to the Laverys as he had intended. 'That's one reason I phoned, to tell you the precautions we've taken. The other was to say Charles Bigrel would like to see you at ten o'clock on Monday morning. All right?'

'Why not?' Richard said, and laughed.

Grant was instantly alert. 'Have I said something funny?'

'Not in the least. I was just thinking of Monday,' Richard said. 'What with one thing and another next week should prove interesting.'

But first there was a peaceful weekend and, if he couldn't enjoy it himself, he could make it reasonably enjoyable for his parents. He didn't have to gloom, or even worry about Emma – not until Monday. Saying goodbye to Grant, Richard went resolutely into the garden to join John Lavery.

It was after nine when Richard set off on Sunday. He had intended to leave before but his mother had pressed him to stay for supper. Anyway, there had been no real reason to go earlier. The traffic would be no heavier now, and he could still make London in comfortable time. He didn't want a late night.

Comparatively cheerful, Richard turned on the radio. He liked driving. He found it relaxing, and on the whole it had been a pleasant, restful weekend. He felt considerably better for having been cossetted. Almost without thinking he headed the car through the lanes he knew so well. Tomorrow – but tomorrow was another day.

He was a short distance from the minor road that would take him to the motorway when he saw there had been an accident. A girl had been knocked off her bicycle by a light van. She lay on the grass verge, apparently unconscious. A man was kneeling beside her. As he heard the car's approach he scrambled to his feet and ran into the middle of the lane, waving his arms helplessly in the direction of the girl, the van, the crumpled bicycle. It was self-evident what had happened, but Richard didn't blame him for being upset. The girl was very still. She looked as if she was badly hurt. She could be dead.

Drawing up a few yards short of where she was lying, Richard got out of his car. His knowledge of first aid was fairly elementary. Keep the patient warm. Don't move her. Fetch help. He reached into the back of his car and pulled a rug off the seat. As he turned and hurried towards the girl he heard someone running very fast down the lane.

His mind had time to register that he had passed no one, there were no houses near, the runner had sprung from nowhere. Then the driver of the van punched him in the stomach.

He was a big man, ginger-haired, red-faced, powerful, and the punch was delivered like the kick of a mule. Richard doubled up, clutching his middle and gagging – but not for long. He was lifted by the front of his shirt in one ham-fisted hand and punched again, this time on the jaw. As he crashed to the ground on his back, someone kicked him on the side of the head, just missing his eye.

For a few seconds Richard blacked out. When he came to, he found two men bending over him, the one he instantly nicknamed Ginger, and a thin foxy-looking character, still breathing hard from his run down the lane. They seemed to be searching him. They already had his wallet and were tearing out his cuff-links. He prayed they wouldn't be curious about the layers of sticking plaster on his little finger.

But Ginger had felt the hardness of the ring as he pulled off Richard's watch. He started to tug at the plaster. The other man had torn open Richard's shirt and was feeling for any kind of necklet he might be wearing. They were both so intent on what they were doing that they didn't hear the approaching motorbike.

It was the girl, a tall, leggy brunette, who warned them. Abandoning her pretence of accident victim she had scrambled to her feet and was dusting herself down, picking bits of grass from her skirt. She had shown no interest in Richard.

'Someone comin',' she said laconically.

'Don't just stand there, then,' the foxy man said. 'Chuck the bike over the 'edge. We don't need it no more. And let's get this codger into the van.'

'The bike's too 'eavy for 'er to throw,' Ginger objected.

It was Richard's opportunity. They were at odds with each other, for the moment distracted. And someone was coming, someone who might help him. He drew in his knees and, with all the strength he had, jack-knifed his body upwards.

Ginger, who was standing astride Richard, didn't have a chance. He caught the full force of the blow between his legs. Whimpering with pain, tears coursing down his cheeks, the big man clutched himself and hopped around in agony.

His accomplice was no hero. Startled by Richard's violence, he leapt backwards and, as the motor-bike roared to a standstill beside them, he ran for the van. He flung open the back doors and climbed in. The girl was already in the driver's seat, starting the engine. Ginger staggered after them.

'Are you all right, Mr Lavery?'

Richard looked up into a pale face framed by a neat brown beard. The new arrival helped him to stand. On his feet Richard became conscious of his aching stomach muscles and the throbbing in his head. He felt his jaw tenderly. It was already beginning to swell. By tomorrow he would look as if he had been in a drunken brawl.

'I'll live – just about,' he said, 'but I'm glad you turned up when you did. It was you that scared them off.'

'Sorry I didn't get here before.'

'You could hardly have known – ' Richard began, and

stopped. The man had called him by name, 'Who are you? How did you know I was Richard Lavery?'

'My name's Wilson. Under Mr Grant's orders at the moment. My job's to see you don't get into trouble, but I guess I made a balls-up of it.' He grinned ruefully. 'Grant was coming down himself, then he decided to stay in London and keep an eye on your Miss Jackson. That left me on my own. Which should have been okay, except the buggers let the air out of my car tyres. Of course, it was a dead give-away. I knew at once they'd set an ambush for you. But lucky for me I always keep the bike in the boot of my Ford, so I managed to arrive before they did you too much damage.'

'Lucky for me, too,' Richard said as he climbed painfully into his car. Why, he was asking himself, had he been attacked this evening? There was no way they could know until tomorrow that he hadn't posted the ring. It didn't make sense. 'Why?' he said, unaware that he spoke aloud.

Wilson shrugged. 'To punish you for something you've done or failed to do. To stop you doing something. To steal something from you. To distract you from something quite different. It's your choice, Mr Lavery.'

'Thanks,' Richard said. 'But you try guessing. It could be for all four reasons.' He was nearer the truth than he knew.

TWENTY-ONE

It seemed to Richard that he had no sooner gone to sleep than he was awake again. He glanced at the clock on the bedside table. The time was eight twenty. It was Monday morning. The shrilling of the telephone had woken him.

He pulled himself gently into a sitting position and was immediately aware of the tenderness of his stomach muscles. He felt as if he had been trodden on by a horse. And his head was splitting. He touched the swollen jaw and his temple. Thank God they had missed his eye. Cursing Ginger and his companions, he swung his legs carefully over the side of the bed and stood up.

The telephone had stopped ringing. Grant must have answered it. Grant had spent the night on the sofa in the living-room. Summoned by Wilson after Wilson had driven Richard back to London, he had insisted on staying. It had been quite unnecessary. But perhaps he could be of some use now.

Richard poked his head out of the bedroom door and called, 'Hi! I could do with some coffee and a couple of pain-killers.'

Grant appeared, fully dressed but grey-faced and unshaven. Richard wondered if he had slept in his clothes, or not slept at all. He looked grim.

He said bluntly, 'That was Wilson on the phone. There's been an explosion and a small fire in the toyshop. The girls have been hurt. I don't know how badly. They've been taken to hospital. If you'll get yourself dressed I'll make some coffee and we'll go.'

'Stuff the coffee!' Richard said thickly. 'Why couldn't you – '

He turned away and went back into the bedroom. He flung on some clothes. His face was too sore for shaving and it didn't matter what he looked like. He was ready in three minutes flat. Grant was waiting.

They drove to the hospital in Grant's car and in almost

total silence. It was the morning rush-hour. Richard stared out of the window at the dense traffic and the hurrying pedestrians without comprehending what he saw. Everything was unreal to him. His mind was totally concentrated on Emma.

And Grant was busy driving, seizing every opportunity to cut in, to make an extra yard or two, to beat the lights. Though he wasn't as personally involved as Richard he was almost as apprehensive. Cold anger filled him and it was with a fierce anticipation that he saw Wilson waiting for them at the top of the hospital steps.

'There's no news yet,' Wilson said immediately, forestalling questions. He hurried on. 'They're still in the casualty department. But I've arranged for beds in the private wing for later, and there's a room that we can use. It belongs to one of the doctors who's on leave. I'll show you.'

The consulting room was small but relatively comfortable, and it was private. They could talk. Grant didn't mince words. As soon as the door closed behind them he turned on Wilson and let his anger rip.

'What the hell happened?' he asked savagely. 'It was your show, Wilson. You were responsible and you've really ballsed things up. God help you when Bigrel hears about it.'

'Shut up, Grant,' Richard said tersely. 'Let him speak.'

Wilson threw Richard a grateful glance. 'It was a letter bomb, sent through the post, delivered in the usual way. I was having breakfast in a café across the road when the thing went off. I didn't hear the bang but it started a fire and there was a fair amount of smoke. I went in through the shop front. The fire was almost out by the time I got upstairs, but the place was a shambles.'

'What sort of shambles?' Richard asked sharply.

'Blood, bits of – ' Wilson began.

Grant caught him up. 'It was my fault. I should have ordered a postal check. Sorry, Wil. Forget what I said before. What about the girls? Have you any idea how badly they were hurt?'

Wilson shook his head. 'Not, not really. They were burned and shocked and cut about. To what extent I don't know.'

There was a tap at the door and a nurse brought in a tray of tea and some biscuits. 'I thought you could do with this,' she said. 'It may be a longish wait. Miss Jackson and Miss Acheson have just gone into surgery.'

Grant sent Wilson off to the toy-shop and went himself to telephone Charles Bigrel. There was no question of Richard Lavery keeping his ten o'clock appointment and Bigrel had to be informed. Afterwards, Grant tried to get some more exact information about Emma and Betty, but with little success. When he returned to the consulting room it was empty.

He had several anxious minutes. But eventually he located Richard in a telephone booth at the end of a corridor. Tapping on the glass door, Grant mimed enquiry, but Richard waved him irritably away and he had to content himself with leaning against the wall and watching. He wasn't going to let Richard out of his sight again. It had been a nasty shock to find him gone.

Richard turned his back on Grant and concentrated on what was being said. When the nurse had told him he was wanted on the phone he had been surprised. Then he had thought of the woman with her threats if he didn't send the signet ring and he had shaken with helpless anger. The nurse had asked if he were ill.

But it was a stranger, a man, who said in a pleasant authoritative voice, 'Mr Lavery, you won't know me, though it's quite possible you may have heard of me. My name is Thomas Penryn. I'm Head of the East European and Soviet Department at the Foreign and Commonwealth Office. Mr Lavery, I've just been informed of what has happened to Miss Jackson and her friend and I want to say how very, very sorry I am. Is there any news of their condition?'

'No, not yet. They both need operations, though how serious no one seems to know.'

'How dreadful! Has Maurice Jackson been told? Is he there?'

'I've no idea.'

'Poor Maurice. He dotes on that girl.'

'Yes.'

If Richard sounded short he didn't care. He was in no mood to receive sympathy from some unknown Whitehall mandarin, especially when the sympathy was mainly for Maurice

Jackson. He cleared his throat.

The response was immediate. 'Mr Lavery, I realize you have a great deal on your mind at the moment, but please bear with me. What I have to say is extremely important. I'll try to be brief. First, you must appreciate that I'm fully aware of the situation that has led to today's tragic events. Most unfortunately I've been out of the country – at a United Nations meeting in New York – or I would have contacted you immediately you returned from your own visit abroad. Secondly, I think we should meet as soon as possible. I believe you may have been given something for me and I have information that you should have. Do I make myself clear?'

Richard swallowed hard. At last someone – and someone in authority – was about to claim the ring. He was ashamed, after what had happened to Emma and Betty, that he could still feel excited at the prospect.

'Quite clear,' he said.

'Good. Then perhaps we could lunch together. I keep a small flat in London. I prefer it to a club. Do you know Claversham Mansions?'

'Near Victoria Station, yes.'

'Could you meet me there at twelve-thirty, Flat 81? We can have a drink and then go down to the restaurant.'

Thinking of Emma, Richard hesitated. But outside the telephone booth David Grant was talking to a nurse. As he caught Richard's eye he gave him a thumbs-up sign. Richard's heart leapt. It had to be good news.

'Yes. Yes, I think so.'

'Splendid. I'll expect you then, Mr Lavery. There's just one other thing. May I suggest you don't mention this conversation or our prospective meeting to anyone. It might be wiser, for security reasons. You understand?'

'Yes, of course.' Richard was scarcely listening. Without waiting to say goodbye he replaced the receiver and pushed open the door. 'What's happened?'

The nurse turned round and smiled at him. 'Mr Lavery, you'll be glad to hear Miss Jackson's out of surgery now. The operation was completely satisfactory. The surgeon was able to remove the splinter from her eye and it's done no damage. She'll be fine again in a few days.'

'Thank God for that.'

Relief overwhelmed Richard. He could have kissed the nurse. He found himself grinning inanely at David Grant until something about Grant's expression, sympathetic though it was, suddenly chilled him.

'Miss Acheson hasn't been so fortunate,' the nurse continued. 'She's lost her right hand. It was impossible to save it. And there's some fear for her sight. They're still operating.'

'It was Betty who opened the packet,' Grant explained. 'She got the full force of the blast and her clothes caught fire. Emma was standing some distance away. Apart from the splinter in her eye, she wasn't actually hurt by the bomb. The burns she received were from putting out the flames on Betty. Incidentally, they'll let you see her in a few minutes.'

Richard nodded his thanks. He couldn't trust himself to speak. His joy at Emma's escape was blunted. He didn't need Grant to tell him that the packet had been adressed to Emma, the bomb meant for her. If Betty hadn't assumed it was part of the toy-shop's mail, it would have been Emma . . .

'What?'

'I asked who you were phoning,' Grant said.

'No one,' Richard said, and quickly collecting his thoughts added, 'It was the woman who threatened me before.'

At once Grant was interested. 'She knew you were here, at the hospital?'

'Apparently. She was pointing out how – how vulnerable I was,' he lied.

David Grant gave him a speculative glance. 'She took her time about it,' he said.

'Yes,' Richard agreed, wondering what story he might invent to satisfy Grant.

A nurse, come to say that Miss Jackson would like to see him now, saved him the effort. In fact Emma, heavily sedated, was on the edge of sleep. But when Richard bent over her and kissed her on the lips she opened her undamaged eye and smiled at him. Her hands and arms were bandaged. Richard could have wept.

'Hello, darling.'

'Richard.' Her expression changed. 'What have you done to your face?'

He had forgotten his appearance, forgotten the damage that had been done to himself. 'I – ' He paused. 'I was mugged,' he said, 'but I'm okay. It was nothing. Forget it. You're the one that's important. Oh, darling, I'm so sorry you've been hurt. Thank God you're going to be all right.'

'And Betty? How's Betty?'

It was a question Richard had been dreading. 'She'll be fine. You mustn't worry.' He put out a hand and stroked Emma's cheek.

'What about the shop?'

'Everything's being looked after. Darling, David Grant's outside. Could you bear to talk to him for a minute or two?'

'I'd rather talk to you.'

'Please. I'll be back later, I promise. After you've had a sleep.'

Emma regarded him with her one good eye. 'This is all something to do with what David was saying about the Russians putting pressure on you because of your father, isn't it?'

'Yes. But it'll be over soon, I hope.'

'Richard, you mustn't give in to them because of me, because of that bomb.'

'I won't.' He kissed her. 'Emma, you're wonderful. I love you. Goodbye, darling.'

'Goodbye. Take care, my love.'

Richard went to the door. 'Grant,' he called. 'She'd like to see you for a minute.'

'She would? Thanks.' Mildly surprised, Grant was also pleased.

He wasn't so pleased when, moments later, he turned from Emma's bedside to say something to Richard and found he was no longer there. He ran into the corridor. There was no sign of Richard. And Grant knew he had been tricked.

Claversham Mansions was a sprawling edifice built to noble proportions at the turn of the century. It had seen many vicissitudes. Gutted by fire bombs in 1942, its interior had been refashioned after the war into small and expensive service flats. The service had ceased to exist, but costs continued to soar. The flats changed hands frequently. Many were sub-let. By the Eighties it had become a drab, anonymous place full of faceless tenants.

Richard arrived punctually at twenty-five past twelve. He had spent the intervening time in getting to the bank, buying himself a new watch, having coffee and sitting in Westminster Cathedral. There was no porter, but he found Flat 81 without difficulty.

'Mr Penryn?'

'Yes. And you're Richard Lavery. Come along in.'

They shook hands. Richard was reassured by the warmth of the greeting and by the sight of a black briefcase with a gold crown embossed on it thrown casually on to a divan. He had had second thoughts about his telephone conversation with Penryn, but there had been no satisfactory way of checking on it. He was glad now he had done nothing. At first impression he liked the man.

'Whisky or gin?' Penryn was groping in the bottom of a cupboard. 'Or some dregs of sherry? I apologize for my meagre hospitality but, as I told you, I've been away and Poppy – my wife – and I only use this place as a *pied-à-terre*.'

'Whisky, please,' Richard said, looking around the small, characterless room.

'Good. Though I'm afraid it's not Charles Bigrel's favourite Glenlivet.'

The drinks poured, Penryn waved Richard to a chair and sat himself opposite. He asked for the latest news from the hospital. He winced when Richard told him about Betty and took a deep swallow from his glass. There was silence. Suddenly it occurred to Richard that Penryn was nervous, or at least on edge. Then Thomas Penryn began to talk and Richard could think of nothing except what he was saying.

'Mr Lavery, I understand from Charles Bigrel that you've been somewhat reticent about your enforced visit to Moscow, so what I'm about to tell you may or may not be a surprise.' Penryn paused to weigh his words. 'Your father, Guy Carey-Ford, was never a traitor.'

'What?'

'Ah, I see it is a surprise. I thought perhaps he might have told you himself, or at least hinted at it when he was dying.'

'No. No, he didn't.' Richard stammered his disbelief. 'I don't understand.'

'I assure you it's the truth,' Penryn said gently, 'though less than a handful of people have known it; myself, Charles Bigrel, a Russian Jew called Dmitri Sholatov who had come over to us and was Carey-Ford's conduit – and latterly Igor Goransky. To be precise, Goransky didn't know – and doesn't know. But he has the strongest of suspicions, suspicions he'd hate to admit. If it became known that he'd been duped all these years by Carey-Ford he'd be disgraced. He'd lose his job, his privileges, possibly even his life.'

'You mean Carey-Ford was really a British agent?' Richard was stunned. He couldn't believe it. Because he wanted so very much that it should be the truth he didn't dare believe it. 'But what about his defection, the secret information he took to Russia?'

'It was grossly exaggerated. It wasn't nearly as valuable as was made out, and anyway it was bread upon the water. It's been returned a hundredfold.' Penryn leant forward in his chair as if to emphasize what he was about to say. 'Mr Lavery, the whole thing was a giant deception conceived by British Intelligence, and until a few months ago it worked splendidly.'

'Then what happened?'

'One of the Jewish dissidents implicated Sholatov, and Sholatov's relationship with Carey-Ford came under suspicion. Carey-Ford was already ill, dying in fact, and Goransky couldn't take any action against him. It was too dangerous. If he so much as implied that Carey-Ford might be betraying the Soviet Union he was admitting his own incompetence. But, ostensibly because of Carey-Ford's health, he could keep him *incommunicado*, and this produced a big problem, because we knew that Carey-Ford had a piece of vital information to pass to us. Which, of course, is where you came in.'

Penryn stood up and stretched out a hand for Richard's glass. Richard shook his head. He had scarcely touched his drink. He was still trying to absorb what he had been told. For some absurd reason he wasn't as elated as he felt he should be. Penryn's edginess seemed to have communicated itself to him.

'Mr Lavery, some while ago Carey-Ford obtained evidence to suggest that he had an opposite number in London,' Penryn continued, reseating himself. 'The parallel isn't exact, but there was reason to suppose that a very senior civil servant in the FCO – one of my colleagues – had been working for Igor Goransky over a period of years. Of course Carey-Ford warned me at once. Unfortunately we didn't know who the traitor was. And you can imagine what that meant.'

'I can guess.'

'A ghastly time not knowing who to trust and who not to trust. Setting little traps that misfired. Then, gradually, suspicion seemed to harden around one man. That was almost worse, since he was someone above reproach and I could take no action, not until I was sure I wasn't about to make a dreadful mistake. The situation was dynamite.'

Penryn paused. This time Richard said nothing. Penryn took a long drink and resumed.

'Only Carey-Ford and I had any ideas of the possible identity of the traitor, and for obvious reasons we wanted it kept that way. So we agreed that, if Carey-Ford discovered our suspicions were correct, he would send me a signet ring via the usual channels. But Sholatov was killed and we lost contact. Mr Lavery, you understand how important this is. Did your father give you his signet ring?'

'Yes, he did.'

'Thank God for that! You have it with you?'

'Yes.'

Penryn finished his drink and banged his glass down on the table beside him. He was clearly excited. 'Give it to me, please.' He held out his hand.

Slowly Richard inserted his thumb nail under the edge of the sticking plaster on his little finger. His instinctive reluctance to part with the ring puzzled him. Carey-Ford had said, 'He'll come for the ring and then you'll know.' Well, Thomas Penryn had come for it and Richard did know – that Carey-Ford was not and never had been a traitor. What more could he expect?

Richard ripped off the sticking plaster and eased the ring from his finger. 'Here you are, Mr Penryn.'

Penryn had been watching. His eyes were very bright and there was a thin film of perspiration on his upper lip. 'You had it there all the time,' he said. 'How terribly clever of you.' He took a silk handkerchief from his top pocket and began to polish the ring. He seemed to be inspecting it. 'Did Carey-Ford give you any kind of message?'

'A message? For you? No.' Richard shook his head. 'It would have been difficult. He was ill, dying, and the KGB were listening to everything that was said.'

'Yes, of course.'

But he sounded vaguely disappointed and Richard said, 'The ring's sufficient, isn't it? You're sure who the traitor is now.'

'Yes, indeed, and I'm extremely grateful to you, Mr Lavery, extremely grateful.' Penryn took out his wallet and carefully put the ring in one of its inner pockets. He picked up his own and Richard's glasses. 'Let me get you another whisky. I insist. We can drink to poor Carey-Ford while you tell me how the Jews succeeded in spiriting you out of the Soviet Union.'

As Penryn went to pour the drinks Richard glanced at his watch. It was twenty past one. He had had no breakfast. He was hungry. He didn't want another whisky. He wished he could suggest that they went to have lunch.

'How did they manage it, the Jews?' Penryn asked 'Do they have a regular escape route to Vienna?'

'Not exactly.' Richard frowned. There were surely more immediate things to consider than how he had got out of Moscow. Penryn, he thought, was a strange man. 'Mr Penryn, what happens next? I appreciate you don't want to tell me who this traitor is. From what you said earlier, that Bigrel knew the truth about Carey-Ford, I can assume it's not Charles Bigrel and, except for yourself, I've had no contact with any other senior official. But what about this woman –'

'What woman?'

'The English woman who's working for the Russians, the one who keeps telephoning and – '

'. . . threatening you if you don't let her have the ring. Yes, of course. Stupid of me. My mind was elsewhere for the moment.'

'What can be done about her?'

Richard heard his voice as if from a great distance. Suddenly he felt icy cold. His heart was banging against his ribs.

His brain was racing. He had told no one that the woman had demanded the ring; he had never mentioned the ring. Why should Thomas Penryn have assumed . . .

'She carries out her threats,' he said, his throat dry. 'Look at Emma and poor Betty – and the way I was mugged yesterday evening. What's to prevent her continuing these attacks?'

There was no answer.

Richard had been quick to notice Penryn's slip. He hadn't been quick enough to cover his own confusion. The silence had been loud. And now the sudden stillness behind him was a warning, though barely audible.

As he sensed Penryn's closeness and anticipated the blow, Richard flung himself sideways. The whisky bottle that had been intended to crack his skull missed its mark. But it landed on his shoulder with sickening force. Pain shot up his neck and he grunted in agony. Instinctively he let himself roll on to the floor where he crouched, breathing hard.

Penryn, still clutching the bottle, began to circle the chair so as to put himself between Richard and the door. Richard got carefully to his feet. The whisky bottle sang past his ear. It threw him off balance. At the same time Penryn jumped, bringing Richard crashing to the ground.

Penryn had been lucky. The bottle had been a wild throw and, as Richard stumbled away from it, he had caught a foot in the flex of a table lamp. He was already falling as Penryn brought him down.

Now, half winded, he lay on his back, Penryn's weight on top of him. At close quarters the older but bigger and heavier man had the advantage. Richard fought to free himself. Penryn's thumbs were pressing on his windpipe. He couldn't breathe. Above him Penryn's face – red, sweaty, teeth bared – was growing black. Richard felt his strength ebbing. But one groping hand had found the whisky bottle that had rolled under the chair.

With a short vicious swing Richard slashed it across Penryn's face. He heard the bone crunch. Penryn screamed. Blood from Penryn's nose was falling in Richard's eyes, but the pressure on his throat was gone. He took great gulps of air and started to push at Penryn's weight. He had misjudged his opponent.

Richard was almost free when Penryn launched another attack, kicking, biting, gouging with the violence of a madman. For perhaps thirty seconds they struggled desperately. Then Richard, who hadn't lost his grip on the bottle, brought it down on Penryn's temple with a crushing blow – and again and again, till Penryn lay still.

Slowly and cautiously, like an old man afraid that he might fall, Richard stood up. He didn't look at Penryn. He knew the man was dead, that he had killed him. But it meant nothing to him. He might have been in a trance, his senses dormant.

Taking his time, he found his way to the bathroom. He washed his face and hands in cold water, combed his hair and did the best he could to tidy up his clothes. In the living-room again, he removed Penryn's wallet and took from it Carey-Ford's signet ring. He slipped it back on his little finger. Then he went to the telephone and dialled the number that David Grant had given him. He hoped it wouldn't be a long wait.

TWENTY-TWO

Grant burst into Charles Bigrel's office with a lack of formality that for him was extraordinary. He had managed to shave in the course of the morning, but his clothes were dishevelled and he looked unkempt. His eyes behind the big hornrims were dark with disbelief.

'More bad news?' Bigrel glanced up from the sandwich lunch he was eating at his desk. His voice was level. 'You've found Richard Lavery and . . . '

'He found me, sir.' Grant steadied himself. 'He's just telephoned to say he's at Flat 81, Claversham Mansions, Victoria and would I like to come because he's – he's killed Thomas Penryn.'

Bigrel drew a deep breath and expelled it slowly. 'That is not possible,' he said.

'It's what he told me and he sounded in his right mind.'

'Then you had better go. We had both better go.' Bigrel swallowed the last bite of his sandwich and washed it down with coffee. He pressed the intercom switch. 'Lorna, the car, at once, please, and cancel my appointments for the rest of the day.' A frown creased his forehead. 'Lorna, are you there?'

'Yes. I – I'm sorry, sir. Of course I'll do that. But – '

'But what, my dear?' Bigrel had walked into the outer office. 'Lorna, are you not well?'

She was pale, Grant thought, but she always had that dead white skin complementing her red hair. Poor old Lorna. She wasn't at her best today – nor was he for that matter – and Bigrel was obviously in no mood to make allowances.

'I'm sorry, sir,' she repeated. 'It's this tooth of mine. It's been giving me hell. I've had hardly any sleep over the weekend. And I was wondering – Would you mind if I went home now?'

Bigrel grunted. 'That would be very inconvenient. Very inconvenient.' He showed no sympathy. 'I'm afraid I'll have

199

to ask you to stay – at least for a couple of hours, until I telephone. All right?' He didn't wait for Lorna to answer but swept out of the office.

Grant made a helpless gesture and followed. It was one of those days. Everything was going wrong. He was relieved when, after what seemed a long wait outside Flat 81 Claversham Mansions, Richard Lavery at last opened the door. He stood back and let Bigrel precede him into the hall.

'Where is he?' Bigrel didn't waste time with a greeting.

Richard gestured. 'In there. Behind the chair.'

'Wait.' It was an order.

Minutes later Bigrel called to them to come. He motioned to Richard to sit down. Grant lounged against the wall, wishing he could see more of the dead man than an expensive pair of calf shoes. Bigrel, his face set in grim lines, had placed himself so that this was impossible.

'Mr Lavery, can you tell me what happened?' Bigrel said. 'Briefly, please. We can fill in details later.'

'I'll try.' Deliberately Richard shook the paralysis from his mind and arranged his thoughts. 'Carey-Ford knew that among the most high-ranking government servants in the UK there was a traitor, a communist agent, but he didn't know who it was. He set a trap. He gave me his signet ring. He counted on someone at the clinic noticing it was missing and reporting the fact to Goransky. He hoped Goransky would believe the ring was connected with the "secret information" that everyone thought Carey-Ford had – in which case, of course, he'd have to get hold of it.'

'Go on,' Bigrel said as Richard stopped. 'You're doing very well, being very clear.'

'Carey-Ford told me not to mention the ring to anyone, so that whoever asked for it could only have been acting on Goransky's orders. The demand for the ring would in fact condemn him as the traitor. And when I knew, I think I was to tell you.'

Richard passed a hand over his face. He was still unsteady from the trauma of having killed, bruised mentally as well as physically from his experience. He made another effort.

'In the event it wasn't as simple as that. Carey-Ford was desperately ill. The Russians monitored everything. And I wasn't very bright. It wasn't until – until this business today that I really understood what Carey-Ford had intended. In fact I nearly blew the whole thing. The threats, the demands for the ring, the attack on me, that bloody letter bomb, they all led me to think in one direction. I suppose that's what they were meant to do. When Penryn phoned me at the hospital,' – Richard glanced apologetically at Grant – 'I was distraught about Emma and Betty, and from what he said I thought he was the answer to all my problems, the one man I could trust. If I'd not noticed him make a stupid mistake and he'd not panicked and attacked me with that whisky bottle . . . '

'It's extremely unlikely you would be alive now,' Bigrel said.

'I know. I think he was going to poison me and leave me here to rot. He was absolutely insistent I should drink with him. Or perhaps dope me and throw me out of the window,' Richard said. 'Either way, I doubt if any connection would have been made between my death and Thomas Penryn.'

'I most sincerely hope not.' Bigrel gave a bleak smile. 'Because, Mr Lavery, Penryn is no traitor. He may have his faults, but he's an honourable man.'

'No! To hell with that!' Richard started from his chair. 'That's not true. He tried to kill me. You said yourself – '

Grant was quicker. 'Not Penryn? Then who? Who's that?'

Grant pointed to what he could see of the body lying on the carpet, and Bigrel moved aside. Grant came forward slowly, almost fearfully, as if he dreaded whom he might find. And for long seconds he stared at the broken, bloody face of a man whom he had liked and respected, even admired.

'It's Christopher McCann,' he said at last. He turned to Bigrel. 'Chris McCann – a traitor! It's incredible. For Christ's sake, Penryn would have been bad enough, but McCann . . . '

Charles Bigrel sat in the back of the car with Richard Lavery. His eyes were shut. He wasn't asleep but by pretending to doze he made conversation impossible, and he gave himself a chance to review what he had done and consider what he proposed to do.

It had been an accident. He had decided that the moment he saw McCann. McCann had been too battered for a natural death to be plausible. But a shooting accident, a momentary carelessness with a gun, would cover his injuries. It could be arranged. He had already given David Grant instructions, set things *en train*, but there was still a lot to be done – the body to be removed, the flat to be searched and rendered negative, the 'accident' staged, people to be primed with the right stories. Fortunately the other intelligence services would give all the support that was needed.

Individuals were apt to be less cooperative. Bigrel thought of Anita McCann. He believed her innocent. But she was McCann's wife and she had lied at that luncheon, pretending that Poppy Penryn had told her Carey-Ford had a son when in fact McCann must have let it drop inadvertently. And, of course, McCann had leapt on her admission; he had always been ready to divert suspicion to Penryn. Yes, Bigrel decided, he hoped it wouldn't be necessary but, if it were, he could put pressure on Anita to accept her husband's death without question.

As Tyler weaved the car in and out of the traffic, Bigrel continued to review the situation. Nothing must be missed, no vital aspect neglected, every weakness probed. Whatever happened there must be no breath of scandal. McCann's new appointment hadn't been officially announced yet, though it was common gossip and everyone knew where in a year or two's time it would almost certainly lead – to Permanent Under-Secretary of State and Head of Her Majesty's Diplomatic Service. If it were as much as hinted that such a man could be a communist agent the entire Western world would lose faith in Britain's security and the Western alliance would be correspondingly weakened. That must not be allowed.

Sighing, Charles Bigrel opened his eyes. The car had drawn to a halt. Tyler was opening the door. Richard stumbled out on to the pavement.

'Where are we?'

'This is where I live,' Bigrel said. 'We need to talk, you and I, but there are a couple of things that must come first. You've not had lunch, have you?'

'No, but – '

'Then you shall have tea and hot buttered toast.'

Richard didn't argue. He sat in Bigrel's study and ate and drank what was put in front of him. He thought about Emma and Betty Acheson and hoped that this was the end of the affair, that there would be no more threats, no more violence.

And he thought of Tamara, the Jewish girl, in Moscow.

Bigrel was on the telephone. He seemed to be making a succession of calls. Richard paid no attention. But suddenly Bigrel was waving the receiver at him.

Hand over the mouthpiece, Bigrel said, 'Say nothing. Just listen.'

Bewildered and irritated, Richard did as he was told. Someone was reading a list of engagements for the following week. Meetings at the Ministry of Defence, the FCO, Cabinet Office. Reception at Lancaster House. Dinner at Number Ten. These were Bigrel's engagements. And the woman who was reading them . . .

'Is it or isn't it?' Bigrel was curt.

'Yes.' Richard assented without hesitation. He would have recognized that low, husky voice anywhere. 'Who –

Bigrel gestured to him to be quiet and took back the receiver. 'Thank you, Lorna. That's all I want,' he said. 'But there are two things you should know. Richard Lavery has just identified you – and Christopher McCann has been killed.' There was a pause while he listened to what the woman had to say. Then he murmured a goodbye.

'Who is she?' Richard asked again.

'Lorna Day. She's been my Personal Assistant for more than eleven years.'

'Is that why you warned her?'

Bigrel shook his head. 'You don't understand. There's no reason why you should.' He sighed. 'She wasn't a real traitor. There's no certainty she was even a communist. She probably votes Conservative. But she was in love with Chris McCann and he used her. She's been making herself sick over what's been happening the last few days.'

'That will be a great consolation to Betty Acheson.' Richard was bitter.

'I doubt if Lorna knew in advance about the letter bomb or that attack on you. McCann would have had contacts with access to petty criminals and – '

Bigrel was interrupted by the telephone. He listened for some time, saying 'yes' and 'no' and finally 'very many thanks'. He didn't explain the call to Richard, but it was obvious that things were going the way he wanted.

Returning to his chair he said, 'There are always a lot of

loose ends in this sort of business, so much that can never be fully understood. One knows the sum, but not the particular items that make it up – the weakness and strength of an individual, the odds against chance, the suspicion, the loyalty to a cause or a person, the seemingly irrelevant remark, the coincidence. So many loose ends, so much surmise. However, one has to try.' He smiled. 'Mr Lavery, are you prepared to tell me now all the things you didn't tell me the first evening we met?'

'Yes, of course, sir, but – there's something I have to know first.'

'What?'

'That man – McCann – said that Carey-Ford was never a traitor, that he was always working for the British. Is that true?'

'Yes. It's quite true.'

Charles Bigrel's response was immediate and Richard drew in a long, lingering breath of relief. He felt the sting of tears in his eyes. His emotions were chaotic.

'Thank you.'

'You deserved to know. And so, I think, do those close to you – Emma, the Jacksons, your own parents, your friend Peter Denville, but the general public can't be told, not yet.'

'Why not?'

'Because,' Bigrel said earnestly, 'if we claimed that Carey-Ford had been a British agent, Igor Goransky would be ruined, and probably a few other heads would roll in Moscow. But – the Russian set-up being what it is – that's all. And in return they'd claim, and substantiate, that McCann was a communist, which would do this country and the West immeasurable harm. You see . . . ' He went on to explain.

Richard listened. He wasn't altogether convinced, but he wasn't prepared to make an issue of it. If Carey-Ford had trusted this man Bigrel, so could he. With his thumb he felt the hardness of the signet ring on his little finger; he was unaware that this was becoming a habit. He wondered if he would ever understand what motivated men like McCann, or why people like Guy Carey-Ford, his own father, and Charles Bigrel and David Grant should choose to lead such strange and hidden lives. Somehow he doubted it.

TWENTY-THREE

The wedding of Richard Lavery and Emma Jackson took place the following September. They were married in the village church – to please their parents, or so they said. It was a small wedding, just family and a few close friends. Peter Denville was best man.

The ceremony had been postponed until Betty Acheson was well enough to attend. She had made a good recovery. Her sight had only been slightly impaired and she hoped to have an artificial hand fitted later in the year.

David Grant, unfortunately, couldn't be present. He was in Rome, enquiring into the disappearance of a British diplomat. But Charles Bigrel was there, stealing a few hours from his work. His new PA was efficient but he still missed Lorna Day, who had died in her sleep from an overdose of sleeping pills and liquor.

Charles Bigrel, as befitted Emma's godfather, had given her a pleasantly large cheque, and there were a lot of other wedding presents – loot, Emma called them. The most surprising was delivered from the Russian Embassy, a rather fine ikon. It came with thanks and best wishes from Igor Goransky.

Richard's first reaction had been to sell it and give the money to charity, preferably a Jewish charity, but Emma dissuaded him. She was already pregnant – she had decided it would be a boy and his name would be Guy – and she thought that one day Carey-Ford's grandson might like to have that ikon.